CRAVING ROSE

THE ACES' SONS

BY NICOLE JACQUELYN

Craving Rose
Copyright © 2019 by Nicole Jacquelyn
Print Edition
All Rights Reserved

No part of this book may be reproduced or transmitted in any form or by any means, electronic or mechanical, including photocopying, recording, or by any information storage and retrieval system without the written permission of the author, except for the use of brief quotations in a book review.

This is a work of fiction. Names, characters, businesses, places, events, and incidents are either the products of the author's imagination or used in a fictitious manner. Any resemblance to actual persons, living or dead, or actual events is purely coincidental. The author acknowledges the trademarked status and trademark owners of various products referenced in this work of fiction, which have been used without permission. The publication/use of these trademarks is not authorized, associated with, or sponsored by the trademark owners.

DEDICATION

To Raider,

Thanks for protecting my kids from the monsters under the bed,

comforting them when they were sad,

and giving us all so much joy.

No one has ever had a companion that was loved as much as you were.

Rest easy, girl.

Prologue
Rose

I DIDN'T LET my eyes stray from the men across the room, as if somehow, by refusing to look away, I could take some of his pain and pull it into me. I wanted to yell that I was right here, that I was more important than they knew, that it was *my turn*. Jesus, wasn't it my turn yet? What were they waiting for? Dropping my head back against the wall, I grit my teeth against the scream building in my throat. That's when he looked up and met my eyes as they used a pair of pliers to rip another nail off his right hand. I opened my mouth to say something, anything.

Don't do it. I could read the warning in his eyes louder and clearer than I'd ever heard his voice. The message was both firm and pleading, a mixture that I'd never thought I'd see. His blue eyes were dry as they held mine. I'd cried enough for both of us, but he'd barely made a sound all day, no matter what they did.

I gave the slightest nod, my lips trembling. I'd follow his silent order. I'd stay still and quiet in my corner. It was the only thing I could do for him.

My gaze roamed his face, taking in the fine lines around his eyes that I'd seen crinkle every time he smiled. The thick eyebrows and suntanned forehead that had the slightest line from where his helmet rested. His hollow cheeks that never rounded no matter how much gas station food he snuck for lunch, and the strong jaw that was so tense it had to ache. My gaze lingered on his lips, the ones I'd seen kiss his daughter tenderly and open wide in laughter on more occasions than I could count.

When our eyes met again, I could barely see him through my tears. I choked back a sob and he blinked slowly, his nostrils flaring.

I lost sight of him as the man who I'd see in my nightmares casually stood between us. "Don't think anyone's comin' for ya," our captor said in disgust, tilting his head to the side.

My stomach sunk, even though I knew he was wrong.

"We don't hear somethin' soon..." the other asshole shrugged.

Tossing the bloody pliers onto the dusty pool table, they strode through the basement and up the stairs. They didn't bother shutting the door behind them. Where would we go? Both of us were tied up and hadn't moved in what seemed like forever.

"He call yet?" one of the men said, his voice drifting from upstairs. "We don't get our money soon, I'm outta here."

I closed my eyes and swallowed back a sob as the voices drifted away.

"It's okay, Rosie," he rasped. His neck strained as he leaned toward me as far as he could. "It's going to be okay, baby. This is nothin'."

"Your hand," I sobbed. "Your poor fingers."

"They'll be fine," he said, his shoulders bunching as he jerked at his restraints. "God, baby, you gotta stop crying like that. You're gonna make yourself sick."

"I'm sorry," I whispered, hiccupping. I could barely catch my breath.

We'd been there for days. In the beginning, I'd been so confident I was almost cocky. They'd knocked us around and tied us up, and the entire time I'd been thinking, *just wait until my dad gets ahold of you.* When they'd separated us, I'd panicked for a second, but assumed that it would be over soon enough. But as time went by and the men who'd kidnapped us grew angrier and angrier, I started to worry. It wasn't until the torture began that I lost hope that I'd ever see the outside of that basement again.

"You don't have to be sorry," he said painfully, jerking at the duct tape binding his forearms to the arms of the chair. "I fuckin' hate that I can't hold you."

"Do you think they're coming?" I whispered, searching his eyes. "Why aren't they here yet?"

"I don't know," he said with a sigh, wincing as he shifted in the chair. His hand looked like raw hamburger and the front of his shirt was stiff with dried blood. I hadn't been able to see where they'd cut him, but it had to be bad if he'd bled that much. I bit the inside of my cheek as I felt hysteria rise within me. "Casper and Hulk are down south," he said, so low I had to read his lips. "Maybe they're waitin' on reinforcements."

"That doesn't make sense," I breathed in confusion. "They're only two men down. That's nothing."

His eyes grew soft as he watched me. "We don't know what this is, Rose," he murmured. "These freaks could be part of somethin' much bigger than we can see from this fuckin' basement."

"I can't just sit here anymore," I said, my misery turning to frustration. "I can't watch them hurt you."

"You will," he said firmly.

"No." I shook my head frantically. "I can't."

"You will."

"I'll tell them who I—"

"I swear to God," he hissed, cutting me off as he strained so hard at his bindings his wrists and hands turned purple. "Don't you say one fuckin' word. Not one fuckin' word, Rose."

"But maybe—"

"I'd rather die than let them put one fuckin' finger on you." He said, his face losing all expression. "Do you understand me? Is that what you want?"

"Don't say that."

"I will do whatever it fuckin' takes to keep you safe," he ground out. "Anything."

"You'd leave me alone with them?" I asked, my heart beating loud in my ears.

"I'd take the fuckers with me," he replied flatly. "One of us has to get out of here, and if I have to choose, it'll be you."

I squeezed my eyes shut and shuddered, everything inside me going still.

"She needs *you*."

"She needs a mother," he argued roughly.

"It's only a matter of time," I whispered, finally saying out loud what we'd both been thinking for days. "You know it's coming." I opened my eyes and stared into his. "It doesn't matter if I keep my mouth shut."

His head fell back as he slumped against the chair in defeat. We both knew that eventually, they'd get tired of trying to get information from him and they'd realize that I was a much better target.

Staring at his throat, I remembered all the times I'd peppered kisses there. I wasn't a super affectionate person, I never had been, but I couldn't seem to help it with him. I wanted to touch him all the time. I'd spent hours drawing patterns on any piece of his skin I could reach. I'd run my fingertips across his eyelashes when he was sleeping, and rubbed my nose against the soft skin of his ear when we were lying together in bed.

"Get up," he said suddenly, glancing at the doorway.

"What?" I whispered dumbly.

"Up, baby. Quiet, yeah?"

I stared at him in confusion, but I still awkwardly pushed myself to my feet, using the hands taped behind my back as leverage against the wall.

"How much give you have around your ankles?" he asked quietly, watching as I shuffled my feet a little.

"Not much," I whispered. I moved toward him, but froze when he shook his head.

"Pool table," he said, tilting his head toward it. "Quiet as you can, baby."

I glanced over and my stomach rolled as I realized what he wanted me to do. At the edge of the table was the bloody pair of garden shears that our captor had tossed as he left. They weren't pliers. I swallowed against the vomit rising in the back of my throat. They were heavy duty, curved scissors.

Holding my breath, I pressed one foot forward an inch, then the other, trying not to lose my balance. As I got more confident, I moved a little faster and that's when I tripped, landing hard on my knees. I held back a groan as I panted through the pain.

I rocked back and forth a couple of times, trying to generate enough momentum that I could stand again, but it was no use. Refusing to give up, I shuffled forward on my knees. I was thankful that he was silent as I huffed and struggled. One small word of encouragement and I would've completely lost it.

It took forever to get to the table, and when I reached it, I dropped my head against the wide leg. Then I turned onto my hip and used every ounce of energy I had left to grip the table as I pushed myself to standing.

I stared in horror at the skin and blood coating the shears.

How was I supposed to pick them up?

Something thumped upstairs and I jerked.

"Turn around and lean your ass against the table," came the quiet words from behind me. "Then reach back and grab 'em."

I nodded and straightened my shoulders, looking away from the gore as I turned and did what he said. The shears were slick and I almost dropped them as I stepped away from the table.

"Now what?" I asked, my heart racing.

"Come to me."

I sagged in relief. I hadn't touched him in so long, and the ten feet between his chair and my place against the wall had seemed further and further away the longer we were separated. I hated him a little, for making me stay where they'd shoved me—but I loved him for it, too. He was so determined to keep me safe that he hadn't let me take the chance of being caught where I wasn't supposed to be, even though both of us had suffered for it.

Careful not to trip, I made my way toward him, everything inside me growing warmer and warmer as I got close to him. I refused to let the moment be ruined by how much worse his wounds looked up close, not when I'd begun to think that I would die in that basement without ever feeling him again.

"My love," I whispered tearfully as I leaned down, the words falling softly between us. I'd only ever used them in them in the darkest, quietest parts of the night, the sentiment too private and fragile to throw around recklessly. His gaze grew tender, the way it always did.

"All tangled up," he replied, tilting his head up so our lips could meet.

Everything around us disappeared for that short moment, and I felt a burst of hope fill my chest. Maybe we could get out of this. Maybe, just maybe, we could leave this nightmare behind.

"We have to hurry, baby," he said as he pulled away, shattering the fragile moment like glass. I sniffled and rested my forehead against his for just a second before straightening up again.

"Turn around and hand me those shears," he said, his jaw firming. "In my right hand, alright?"

"Your fingers," I rasped, shaking my head.

"Nothin' for it," he replied. "My left hand is shit. It's gotta be my right."

I searched his face for any sign that he'd change his mind, then turned slowly until my back was to him. I closed my eyes and pictured the shears, gingerly turning them in my hands until the handle pointed toward his fingers. I groaned silently as my fingertips brushed against the gore covering the blade.

"That's it," he whispered, "lean back just a little."

When the tool was safely in his grip, I inhaled deeply with relief.

"I need you to lean down," he ordered. "I'm gonna cut the tape right between your wrists."

Doing as he asked, I waited silently as I felt the duct tape pull. I didn't make a sound as the sharp end of the blade dug into my skin and I felt blood drip down my hand.

"I'm sorry, I can't get a good grip," he choked out. "Fuck."

"Keep going," I whispered back. "Don't stop."

"I won't."

It felt like it took forever before my hands were free, but as soon as I felt the pressure ease I tugged hard. The pain in my previously numb arms was excruciating as I swung them a little. Twisting, I gently gripped the shears and pulled them from his mangled fingers.

"No," he said as I reached for the tape holding his arm to the chair. "Get the tape on your ankles before you fall over."

I didn't think anything of his order as I bent over to release my ankles. Adrenaline was racing through my veins as I listened for any type of disturbance upstairs. This was the first time they'd left us alone for any length of time, and I knew that we probably didn't have long before they came back.

"Done," I murmured as I straightened and reached for him again.

"No, baby," he said firmly, his eyes meeting mine. "Just you."

"What?" I asked in confusion. "No. What are you talking about?

No."

"You gotta go."

"I'm not leaving you here," I snapped, reaching for his arm again.

"Goddammit, Rose," he replied sharply. "Stop."

I froze.

"I'm not going without you," I said.

"You have to."

"No," I replied stubbornly around the lump in my throat. "No."

"There ain't no way you can carry me up those stairs," he whispered roughly. "And I won't be able to make it."

"Why?" I looked down his body, and that's when I saw the deep wound in his left thigh. My mind raced as I tried to remember when it had happened, but I couldn't. He'd never made a sound. "Oh, God," I breathed.

"You have to go, baby."

"I can't." My body jerked as I held back a sob.

"The only way I'm gettin' out of here is if you go get the cavalry," he said, his eyes growing glassy as he stared at me. "But, baby, if that don't happen—"

"Don't," I choked out, shaking my head.

"If that don't happen," he repeated, ignoring my denial, "it's enough to know that you're safe. Alright? If you love me, you'll get the hell out of here as fast as you can."

I couldn't even nod as I stared into his eyes, my heart breaking into a million pieces.

"Don't look back, Rose," he said through gritted teeth. "Don't stop until you're behind the gates."

"I love you," I whispered.

"I know you do," he replied. "That's why you're gonna get out of here. Now, Rosie. Before they come back."

A sense of calm fell over me. I knew with absolute certainty that if I didn't leave right then, I wouldn't. I'd stay with him and let the chips fall where they may.

"I'll be back with the cavalry," I whispered, as I kissed him gently. "You just hold out until we get here."

"I love you," he replied. "Now, go."

I stumbled back a few steps, my eyes still on his. Then, before I could change my mind, I spun around and headed for the stairs. I didn't look back. I couldn't.

The wooden stairway was sturdy and didn't make any noise as I quietly made my way to the first floor of the house. When I got to the top, I gripped the shears in my hand and peeked around the corner into the empty kitchen. That's when I spotted a door to the outside, just feet away from where I was standing.

A bead of sweat rolled down my back as I tiptoed toward the door. There was a lacy curtain covering the top half of the window, and I could just barely see the outline of a blue car in the driveway. I opened the door gingerly, turning the knob so slowly that I felt a little click when the latch disengaged.

As soon as I'd stepped out onto the porch, everything inside me froze. It felt like everything happened in slow motion as the guy who'd been sitting on the edge of the steps smoking a cigarette reached for my leg and I brought up the pruning shears and buried them in his right eye.

It was the most revolting thing I'd ever seen or felt in my life, and I almost screamed as he reached for it, trying to pry it out of his face. Instead, I jumped off the porch and ran to the car.

The doors were unlocked and I climbed inside as the guy fell over and hit the porch with a loud thud. I had seconds, maybe less before the other guy came outside. I hit the automatic door locks and got to work.

Muscle memory is a funny thing. When you think you need it, you can't remember what the hell you're doing. But when you don't think about what you're doing, your body just goes through the motions it's done a thousand times. That's what happened as I rested my foot on the gas pedal, tore at the plastic beneath the steering wheel and yanked out wires beneath. As soon as I'd found the group I needed, I frantically used my teeth to strip the ignition and battery wires, then twisted them together.

I glanced up in fear as I heard the other man come outside and start yelling, but my hands didn't pause. Sparking the battery wires against the starter wire, I pushed down on the gas pedal and started the car. Throwing it into reverse, I screamed as the man reached for my door handle.

I shoved my foot against the gas pedal just as his hand came up and I saw the gun he pointed at my face. Ducking down as far as I could, I shoved the gear shift into drive. Gravel flew as I peeled out, flying down the long gravel driveway, and I kept my head down as I raced toward the main road.

I sobbed in relief when I realized that I recognized the strip of deserted highway. If I turned right, I was only a couple miles from the swimming hole we'd gone to since we were kids. Left would take me straight back to the clubhouse.

I knew these roads. I'd learned to drive on them. I pressed the gas pedal against the floorboard and barely let up as I hit the first corner. Tires squealed as I straightened the car out, but I didn't slow down.

My hands slipped over the steering wheel, slick from the blood dripping down my arm. Blinking against the sweat and tears that burned my eyes, I leaned forward and took the next curve too fast, but I refused to hit the brakes. Steering out of the skid, I kept going. I looked both ways and blew through a stop sign, and then another.

"Oh, God," I whispered, praying that I could make the car go faster. "Please. *Please.*"

Every second it took to get to the compound was agony, and when I saw the familiar turn and the large gate that blocked the driveway, I sobbed in relief. I was almost there.

I slid into the gravel and barely glanced at the prospects guarding the gate before I plowed right through it, the large latch shattering the windshield as the entire gate flew up against the car, catching for a moment before it flew off behind me.

Within seconds I was in the forecourt, slamming the gearshift into park as I tumbled out of the car.

"What the fuck?" someone yelled as a wave of men ran toward me.

"Rose?" my dad thundered, sprinting toward me. "Thank Christ!"

"Daddy," I called, stumbling forward.

"I got you," he said as he reached me, pulling me tight against his chest. "You're okay, I got you."

"I left him there," I sobbed, the weight of that truth so heavy I didn't know if I could bear it. "We have to go back. We have to go *now*."

Chapter 1

Rose

I stood at the counter and watched as the man I loved slid a backpack full of clothes onto his shoulder.

"You said you loved me," I choked out, staring at Copper in confusion. "What are you doing?"

"I do love you."

"No, you don't."

"I do."

My stomach twisted painfully. "You don't do this to people you love. You don't just *end* things."

"It's just not working out," he replied, leaning against the doorframe.

"I know we haven't been getting along, I—"

"We're not compatible," he said flatly, cutting me off.

"That's bullshit," I replied, anxiety making my voice falter. "That's not a real thing. When you make a commitment, you figure it out. You find a way to move past the hard parts."

"I don't want the hard parts," he said flatly. "Life's too fucking short."

"Then we'll talk it out," I stuttered. "We'll make it so it's not hard."

"You're condescending," he said, in frustration. "You think you're better than everyone. You talk to me like I'm less than you."

"I don't think you're less than me," I said in horror, my eyes starting to water.

"You give me the cold shoulder when you're pissed. And if I say anything about it, you won't touch me for a week." He scoffed. "I told you not to use sex as a weapon, and sure as shit, you cut me off when you're pissed about something."

"That's not even a thing," I ground out, my cheeks growing hot. "That's a myth perpetuated by men. Women like to be taken care of outside of bed and if that doesn't happen, they're not interested in climbing into bed."

"Spin it however you want," he said derisively. "I told you not to do that shit and you did it, anyway. I'm done."

"That's not even how it was," I argued, frustration making my voice quiver.

"You're mean," he said flatly. "You're a mean person."

"Please," I said, hating myself for the pleading tone of my voice. I wasn't mean, was I? Sarcastic, yes. But mean? I swallowed hard. "Please, if you love me, then we can work this out."

"There's nothing to work out," he replied. He stuffed his hands into his pockets.

"I thought we would get married," I whispered pathetically.

"You actually think you deserve a *proposal*?" he asked incredulously, the words so awful and shocking that I took an involuntary step backward.

"Then don't say that you love me. Stop saying it," I said as he turned away, my voice breaking. "Because you don't."

"Don't tell me how I feel," he snapped back, not even bothering to look at me. "And I'll say whatever the fuck I want."

It would've been easier if he'd slammed the door behind him when he left. I could've pretended that he would cool down and come back later. The quiet snick of the door latch was infinitely worse. It said that he was totally calm, and thoroughly finished.

A slightly hysterical laugh shot out of my mouth and I slapped my hand over my lips. What the hell had just happened? What in the actual *fuck*?

Jesus, I'd thought I was going to marry *him.*

I gasped for air as the full reality of the situation hit me. He was gone. He left and I knew, deep in my gut, that he wouldn't be back. Bracing my hands on the counter, I struggled to take a deep breath.

I'd never be able to touch him again. I'd never wake up to find him beside me. I'd never get a secret smile across the room, like an inside joke that only we knew. I'd never cook his favorite meals or hear about his day. He'd never again whisper that he loved me and kiss me goodbye before leaving for work.

I closed my eyes as my entire chest tightened. Oh, God, I'd thought I was going to marry him and he didn't even *like* me.

I let the tears roll down my cheeks and plop against the counter as I called myself every kind of idiot. Once again, I'd believed in a promise from someone that didn't deserve my trust, and once again, I'd been burned.

I'd known it wasn't a good idea to get involved. I'd known that I was going to get my heart broken, again, but I'd jumped in with both feet, anyway. I couldn't seem to give up on the elusive happily ever after. It always felt right out of my reach.

I pushed off the counter and wiped my hands down my face. I wasn't going to fall apart. I wouldn't let myself. At least not in the middle of the kitchen.

Grabbing the clothes I'd left sitting on a chair when Copper dropped his bomb, I headed toward the bathroom for a shower. Leave it to me to get dumped on the day of my only niece's birthday party.

"WHAT DO YOU mean, he dumped you?" my cousin Lily hissed later that day as she helped me fill water balloons.

"He said he was done," I replied, barely glancing at her as I continued what I was doing. "And then he left."

"Oh, my God," she said indignantly. "What an asshole."

"It is what it is," I mumbled, secretly thankful for her support.

"He'll come back with his tail between his legs, just like they all do," she said, handing me another bunch of balloons. Then a few seconds later, "Do you *want* him to come back?"

I'd been running that scene in the kitchen over and over again in my head all day, observing it from different angles and asking myself the same question.

"He doesn't like me," I replied quietly, shrugging as I met her eyes for a moment. "It's not even that he's angry or that he left. Either of those two things would hurt my feelings, but I could forgive him. But he really doesn't like me."

"He's a dick," she snapped.

"That doesn't make him a dick," I replied. "It's just a fact. He doesn't like me. You can't help who you like and who you don't. It just *is*."

"And he couldn't have figured that out five months ago?" she asked. "Before he practically moved into your house?"

"It hurts," I mumbled, almost embarrassed at the admission. "But it also kind of helps."

"How is that?" she asked, jerking back as the water spigot sprayed us a little while I struggled to wrap a water balloon around it.

"When I think about the what ifs, I remind myself that he doesn't like me," I replied. "He genuinely doesn't like me as a person. So there's nothing I could've done differently. I didn't do anything wrong."

"Of course you didn't do anything wrong," she said softly, bumping me with her shoulder. "And I like you."

"I like me, too," I said simply.

"What's taking you so long?" my niece Rebel yelled as she came up behind us. "Dad's team is winning because we're out of ammunition!"

"God forbid," I replied, gasping dramatically as I handed her a couple of full balloons. "You can have those, but only if one of them flies straight toward your Uncle Tommy."

"But Uncle Tommy isn't playing," she replied in confusion, trying to hand one of the balloons back.

"He is now," I said, winking at her.

I grinned as she raised her eyebrows and nodded.

"He's going to kill you," Lily said as Rebel ran away. "You won't escape the water balloon war now."

"Worth it," I muttered. I looked over at her and lifted up the bucket of full balloons. "Man the battle stations," I said seriously.

"Aw, shit," she whined, jumping to her feet. "We're going to need some cover."

A few minutes later, we'd constructed a barricade out of lawn chairs just far enough from the spigot that we could attack anyone trying to reload.

"This was a horrible idea," Lily screeched as a water balloon exploded against her chest. "Do you know how long it took me to iron my hair?"

"Should've never cut it," I shot back, leaning around the edge of the chairs so I could lob a balloon at my oldest brother Will. "Then you could've braided it."

"I thought you liked my hair?" she shot back, handing me another balloon.

"I do like it," I replied, throwing the balloon at the ground in front of the little person running toward our encampment. It exploded when it made contact and Lily's stepson Gray squealed happily. "You're the one bitching about how long it takes to style it."

"I wasn't bitching," she bitched. "Ceasefire!"

I leaned back on my heels as Gray slid behind the barricade.

"Are you coming to help us?" I asked, wiggling my eyebrows.

"No," he replied, a sly grin pulling at his lips. Before I could stop him, he threw balloons at both Lily and I. We were in such close quarters that the balloons bounced right off us and landed on the ground, but Lily still screeched indignantly.

"You little sneak!" she yelled, chasing him as he ran away. "No ice cream for a month!"

Gray giggled as he sprinted across the yard toward his dad. Leo was laughing his ass off and I was pretty sure I knew exactly who'd given Gray those balloons.

"You're about to be overrun," a voice yelled from behind me. I jerked my head back toward the spigot and my eyes widened in horror as I realized that Gray had been all the distraction my brother Tommy had needed to keep me occupied while he connected the hose.

"Oh, shit," I yelped, scrambling out of my spot. I grabbed my rescuer's hand and we sprinted across the yard as the cold water sprayed against our backs. By the time we'd reached my parents, I was laughing and gasping and I could feel water running down the backs of my thighs.

"When did you get here?" I asked Kara as I let go of her hand.

"Right before Tommy won the war," she replied, wrinkling her nose.

"Only the battle, toots," I said with a laugh, throwing my arm over her shoulder. "I'll get him later."

"Hi, Kara!" Rebel yelled excitedly, running toward us. "It's my birthday!"

"I know," Kara replied, grinning as Rebel pulled her into an exuberant hug. "That's why we're here."

"You came for my birthday?" Rebel asked, pulling back to look into Kara's eyes. "You're the best!"

"I brought you a present, too," Kara said conspiratorially as Rebel hugged her again.

"Let's go get it," Rebel said, putting her hand in Kara's.

I smiled as they crossed the yard. Rebel and Kara were only months apart, but their personalities couldn't be more different. My niece had Down syndrome, which meant she was delayed in some ways, and I swore made her more advanced in other areas. As far as I was concerned, who cared if she ever learned algebra? Reb was the most empathetic, loving, and genuinely happy person I'd ever met, and those traits were far more important in the grander scheme of things.

"If you think I'm done, you're sadly mistaken," my brother Tommy said casually as he came up beside me.

Glancing to the side, I burst out laughing. His entire chest was soaked.

"Don't be a whiner," I replied, elbowing him as we walked toward the barbeque.

"Me and Heather have plans after this, ass," he grumbled.

"You'll dry."

"What happened to you two?" Kara's dad Mack asked as we reached him and Will.

"Water balloon war," we both replied at the same time. "Jinx."

"Looks like Tommy won," Will said with a chuckle.

"He used the hose!" I griped.

"Don't pout because I'm smarter than you," Tommy replied.

"*I'm* not a cheater."

"Who's a cheater?" my cousin Cam asked as he joined us. His eyes widened as he took us in. "Oh, shit."

"Should've taken your shirt off first," Will said, pointing to his own bare chest.

"I would've, if your kid had given me some warning before she hit me with a water balloon."

"That's my girl," Will said in satisfaction.

"Glad I missed it," Mack said with a laugh.

"Oh, it's not over," I muttered darkly.

He winked at me and I felt my cheeks heat. Jesus. He was the only guy I'd ever met that could make me blush, and he'd never even made a pass at me.

"I'm going to see if Moll needs help," I said, spinning before my brothers could see my reaction.

"Get me a beer," Will called out.

"Get your own beer," I called back, flipping him off over my shoulder.

"Classy, Rose," my mom called sarcastically.

"I do my best," I yelled back as I pushed in the back door of my brother's house. He and Molly had bought a small, two-story house near my parents' place a few years ago, but it was still a work in progress. With Tommy's help, they'd refinished the wood floors and replaced all the windows, but they were still gradually working on the smaller things. Currently, none of their kitchen cupboards had doors.

"Need any help?" I asked, Heather and Molly turning toward me in surprise.

Cam's wife Trix didn't even bother turning around. "Mack's out there, isn't he?" she said, dryly.

"Shut it," I snapped. Heather laughed.

"I don't know why you avoid him," she said. "He's awesome."

"I never said he wasn't."

"She's got a crush," Trix said, laughter in her voice.

"I'm not fourteen," I replied, moving further into the kitchen.

"Then stop acting like it," she shot back.

"I'm glad they came," Molly said, looking out the window. "Reb is probably giddy."

"She was pretty excited," I replied, reaching for a bowl covered in tin foil. "She and Kara were going to find the present they brought her."

"Kara's a sweetheart," Molly said, smiling. "Reb says she's her best friend."

"Cute," Heather said, grinning.

"Yeah," Molly agreed. "She doesn't have many friends her own age."

"Charlie and the boys," Trix pointed out.

"They're family," Molly said. "It doesn't count."

"Wrong," I replied. "Lily's my best friend."

"You two might as well be twins," Heather said with a guffaw. "She has to love you."

"Hey!" I snapped, throwing a cherry tomato at her.

"Not in my kitchen!" Molly yelled, stepping in between us as she threw her arms up in the air.

"Yes, Mother!" Heather sang. "I'm going out to hang with my husband."

"It's so weird when you say that," I said when she bumped into me as she passed.

"You were at the wedding," she said dryly.

"Yeah, but then you guys did that weird thing where you pretended you weren't married for like, ever."

"We started again," she said dreamily, clasping her hands under her chin. "And kept the magic alive."

"You're losers," I said, throwing another tomato at her.

"Rose Hawthorne!" Molly screeched as Heather hurried out the doorway.

"Happy birthday, dear Rebel," we all sang as the guest of honor bounced in her seat. When she blew out her candles, we cheered.

"I make the first cut," she reminded Molly. "Because it's my birthday."

"I remember," Molly said, handing Reb a long knife. "Cut wherever you want."

"Do it across the cake," Cam and Trix's son Curtis advised, leaning over the table. "Totally crooked."

"But then the pieces won't be the same size," Rebel pointed out, staring at Curtis like he was crazy.

"So?" he said with a shrug.

"Do *you* want a smaller piece?" she asked reasonably.

"I see your point," he replied, deflated.

My lips twitched as Rebel cut a precise line two inches from the edge of the cake.

"I know *I'll* be pissed if my piece is smaller," Mack murmured from behind me, making me laugh quietly.

"Hungry, are you?" I asked, still watching Reb.

"Starving," he murmured, making my cheeks heat again. Dammit.

"Didn't you eat?" I turned to look at him and played it cool, hoping the fading light would hide my red face.

"Yeah," he replied simply.

We stood there and watched the kids diving into their cake, and I struggled to find something to say. I hated that he made me so flustered. I'd known him forever. He was at least ten years older than me, and he treated me like his friend's kid sister—but that didn't seem to matter. The minute Mack joined whatever group I was in, I acted like a complete weirdo.

"Rosie," my dad called. When I turned to see him staring at me grimly, my stomach lurched. Dammit. Someone had spilled the beans.

"What's up, Father dear?" I asked as I headed his way.

"You and Copper are done?" he asked, searching my face.

"I think Copper is more done than I am," I said with a humorless laugh. "But yeah. Who told you?"

"The grapevine," he muttered, pulling me against his side. "You alright, sweetheart?"

"I've been better," I confessed, fighting against the tears burning at the backs of my eyes. There was something about my dad's gruff sympathy that got to me every time. When I was a kid, I'd always been brave as hell until my dad entered the room. His concern always made me act like a big baby.

"Man's a dipshit," he said, kissing the top of my head. "You're too good for him, anyhow."

"You say that now," I replied drolly.

"Now that you're shot of him, I *can* say it," he said with a huff. "He's a good soldier, don't get me wrong. But the kid is stupid as fuck."

I snickered.

"That's why we've never agreed to his transfer up here," he said quietly. "Though you didn't hear that from me."

I tipped my head back and grinned at him.

"I'm real glad you won't be the one perpetuating those genes," he said, his lips twitching.

"You're terrible," I said happily.

"Truth hurts," he said with a shrug.

My laugh was cut off as I felt something thump against my back, followed by the sensation of icy water dripping into the back of my shorts.

"I told you I wasn't finished!" Tommy yelled maniacally.

"Boy," my dad called back as he lifted his arm off my back and shook the water off it. "You better run."

"Oh, shit!" Tommy yelped.

The next few minutes were chaos. Earlier in the day, our water balloon war had been confined to a certain portion of the yard, far away from where all the old timers were congregated. There were no boundaries this time. I ducked and screamed as full water cups, buckets, squirt guns, balloons and the hose were used to full advantage. Even worse than the icy water were the pieces of cake being tossed around. It was a free for all, the entire group, from old Poet to little Gray getting in on the action.

"Got you!" Cam's son Draco yelled, tossing a balloon at me as he ran past where I was trying to hide by the porch steps.

"Where the hell do they keep finding more balloons?" Molly yelled, her eyes wide as she raced toward me. She yelped as Will shot her in the ass with a long spray of water. "William!"

"I have an idea," I gasped, laughing. Grabbing her hand, I dragged her inside.

"You're a little cheat," she said, giggling as I closed and locked the door behind us. Better safe than sorry.

"I think the word you meant was brilliant," I shot back as I rounded the kitchen table.

"Oh, no," she said as I slid open the window over the sink.

"I've never been so glad that you and Will are taking your sweet ass time on this house," I said with a laugh when I verified there was no screen on the window. "Now, *shh*."

Turning the water on as high it would go, I pointed the sprayer toward the yard and waited. It didn't take long before someone stopped beneath the window, just like I'd hoped.

I laughed maniacally as I sprayed the large shadow, assuming it was one of my brothers or cousins. I was obnoxious and loud and feeling very proud of myself until he turned, and blocking the spray with an upraised hand, met my eyes.

"Shit!" I squeaked, my hand automatically letting go of the trigger.

"What?" Molly peeked over my shoulder. "Oh, no," she whispered.

"Payback's a bitch," Mack said calmly, his eyes steady on mine as he slicked his hair back with one hand.

As he headed toward the back door, I yelped and ran toward the front of the house. "Tell Reb I love her!" I called to Molly. "I'll see you guys later."

"Coward," she yelled back, laughing her ass off.

She was right. I was a coward. But I was okay with that.

I quietly opened the door and peeked outside to make sure the coast was clear, then sprinted over the deck and jumped over the stairs. My car was parked at the end of the driveway, and I fished the key out of my pocket with a grin. I would've hotwired it if I had to, but then I'd have to go to the garage Monday morning and ask my dad to fix the dash. I let out a huge breath of relief as I reached for the door handle, then screamed like a banshee as arms wrapped around my waist and lifted me into the air.

"You actually thought you'd get away?" Mack asked, laughing as I started kicking my legs.

"It was an accident," I yelled, twisting and turning. He was soaked, and the few dry patches on my t-shirt were quickly becoming damp from where he pressed against me.

"You sprayed me with the kitchen sink," he replied incredulously.

"I thought you were one of my brothers!" As soon as he set me back on my feet, I twisted and took a few steps back, watching him warily.

"Well, that's insulting," he said, making me laugh.

"See," I said, stepping toward my door. "It was all a misunderstanding."

He stepped forward and I stepped back again. "Misunderstanding or not," he murmured, his lips twitching, "I'm still soakin' wet."

"And I'm *very* sorry for that," I replied, nodding.

"It doesn't *feel* like you're sorry," he said, taking another step toward me.

"I am." I lifted my hands in front of me like I was trying to ward him off. "I really am."

"See," he murmured, tilting his head to the side. "I just don't believe you."

I screeched as he rushed me, and laughed hysterically as he threw me over his shoulder.

"I'm sorry," I yelled through my laughter as he carried me back toward the house. "I'm *really* sorry!"

"Uh huh," he grunted as I twisted and turned, trying to escape.

We rounded the corner of the house and I amped up my squirming. He was bringing me right back into the thick of things. At any moment, my brothers and cousins would catch sight of us and I'd be at their mercy.

"We can talk this out," I said, pushing against his back as I tried to straighten. "We can be allies."

He scoffed and wrapped his arms tighter around my thighs.

Before I could comprehend what was happening, I was being flipped back over and dropped gently into the plastic kiddie pool filled with cold, dirty water. I gasped as the water covered me from breasts to thighs, staring up at him in disbelief.

"I think we're even now," he said, grinning. "Allies?"

Ignoring the way his smile made my stomach explode with butterflies, I scowled at him.

"Oh," Tommy yelled, laughing like a hyena. "Looks like the little cheater met her match!"

"You're supposed to have my back!" I yelled, splashing water ineffectually at him. "Where's the loyalty?"

"This is war, Rose," he said seriously. "Every man for himself."

"I don't think that's how it works," Mack muttered with a chuckle.

I climbed out of the pool, dripping wet and pointed at him. "What did you say to me? *Payback's a bitch?*" I smiled as his eyes widened. "Remember that."

"You think you're gonna get me in that pool?" he asked in amusement.

"I don't have to," I replied smugly. "I'll remember this."

"Ah, man," Will said, coming up behind me with a towel. "You should probably just sit your ass down in the pool and be done with it. She's not kidding. One time, she waited two months before getting payback. You never know when it's going to happen, and then BAM!"

"I'll take my chances," Mack replied, his eyes still holding mine.

"Thanks," I said to my brother as he handed me the towel.

"Molly thought you might need it," he murmured with a chuckle.

After one last glare at Mack, I wrapped the towel around myself and stomped away, my shoes making a squelching noise with every step.

LATER THAT NIGHT, I was curled up on the couch, the reality of my breakup hitting me with the force of a sledgehammer. I was alone. Again.

I wasn't a person that needed people around me all the time, and I liked my space, but coming home to my empty apartment had felt lonely. And I didn't handle *lonely* very well.

I'd gone from living with my parents to sharing a room with Lily in Connecticut while she went to Yale, so when I'd rented my apartment all by myself, the freedom had seemed pretty fucking fantastic at first. I'd stayed up all night and left lights on whenever I felt like it, and stunk up the place with takeout. But it hadn't taken long before I realized that I didn't *like* living alone.

I actually liked cooking for more than one person. I liked letting someone know when I'd be home at night, or if I wouldn't be home at all. I liked having someone to watch a movie with and eat dinner with and bitch about my day to.

Pulling my blanket tighter around my shoulders, I stared blankly at the TV. Maybe I'd jumped in to a relationship with Copper too quickly because I hated living alone. We'd gone from dating to practically living together within a few weeks, and I hadn't listened to anyone when they'd warned me that I was headed for disaster. I'd liked having him to come home to. Sure, he talked over me sometimes, and I could never be mad about anything without him spinning it around until suddenly I was on the defensive side. And maybe he got mad when I wasn't in the mood for sex, which drove me crazy, and he never put my needs before his own. But knowing rationally that he wasn't good for me didn't seem to matter, because now that he was gone, I was heartbroken, anyway.

"I need a cat," I mumbled, using the remote to shut off the movie I was barely paying attention to. A cat would be great. So much less work than a dog, but still someone I could come home to after a long night at work.

I sniffled and closed my eyes, trying not to cry again. I'd done enough of that in the shower earlier. God, why had I been so trusting? Why had I put so much time and energy and love into someone that clearly didn't even like me?

I swallowed back a sob and startled when someone started knocking on my front door. Who the hell would be knocking at ten-thirty at night? My heart started thundering as I walked toward the door, grabbing the baseball bat I kept in the entryway just in case. Maybe it was Copper. I hated that, even after all the things he'd said that morning, I still hoped it was him.

"I had a feeling you could use some company," Lily said as I swung open the door. She strode inside, pushing me gently out of the way.

"You didn't have to come over," I argued, closing and locking the door. I shook my head as I took in her flannel pajamas and the ratty old blanket in her arms. "Leo took one look and kicked you out, didn't he?" I joked drolly.

"Leo doesn't give a shit what I wear," she replied loftily, pointing her nose dramatically toward the ceiling. Then she crossed her eyes and stuck her tongue out at me. "Just kidding. He hates these pajamas."

"I wonder why," I said dryly. "You look like an old lady."

"You always steal the covers," she replied, turning off lights as she led the way to my room. "I wore fuzzy socks, too."

"How can you wear socks to bed?" I mumbled. "Feet should be able to breathe at night."

"Feet should be warm," she argued, climbing onto my bed as I unwrapped the blanket around my shoulders and tossed it toward her.

"You really didn't have to come over," I said, taking off my rings and earrings and putting them on my nightstand. "I'm fine."

"You're not fine," she replied.

"I'm disappointed," I admitted as I climbed in beside her and turned off the lamp. "But I'm fine."

"You said you loved him," she said quietly as we turned to face each other. "That doesn't just go away because he took off."

"No, it doesn't."

We were quiet for a while, and the relief of having her there almost made me cry again. Lily was my best friend. My soul sister. We'd been best friends since the first time our moms had put us in the same crib to sleep.

"He wasn't the one," she whispered, reaching out to brush my hair away from my face. "He didn't treat you like you deserve."

"Maybe that was my fault," I whispered back. "Maybe I pushed him away. I'm just not good at this."

"*Beep*," she said obnoxiously loud before lowering her voice again. "Wrong. There is absolutely nothing wrong with you. Nothing. He was a man-child who made you feel like shit."

I snorted at her apt description.

"There's a guy out there," she said, tucking her hands under her cheek. "And he's going to love all the different parts of you. The surly part that you show the people at work, and the sweet part you show us, and everything in between. He's going to think it's hilarious when you curse, and smack your ass when you're giving him attitude, and he's going to have a comeback for every smartass thing you say."

"Maybe I should've toned it down a little," I murmured. "But I'm just not good at the lovey dovey stuff, you know? I have three brothers who show love by smacking each other on the back and putting me into a headlock."

"Don't do that," she said, shaking her head a little. "No man worth anything will make you believe that you have to make yourself smaller so he can feel bigger."

"He did that," I admitted, my voice nearly inaudible.

"I know he did," she replied, her eyes sad. "I saw it. And I wanted to say something, but you were so dedicated to making things work with him that I didn't want to make it harder for you."

"Why do I keep finding these guys? Why am I such a magnet for men that don't know how to stick it out?"

"None of those guys were right for you," she said. "Maybe you should stop looking."

I scoffed.

"Maybe you should let the next one come to you," she said, ignoring the noise I'd made. "I swear, it always happens when you're not looking for it."

"Oh, what do you know?" I teased huskily. "You've been in love with Leo since you hit puberty."

"Probably before that," she said, rolling her eyes. "But we didn't get together until I'd stopped pursuing him. It had to happen at the right time."

"It feels like I'm never going to meet him, that one perfect guy made just for me," I confessed. "Everyone else has paired off, and I'm always just in the corner standing by myself because whatever loser I'd been dating had dumped me."

"We're twenty-three," she said with a chuckle. "You have so much time to find the right guy. The one who will give you babies and treat you like you're the center of his universe."

"What if I never find him?"

"Then I guess you'll just have to move in with me and Leo and we can be sister-wives." She smiled as I laughed. "But you don't get to bang him. We'll just get you a really good vibrator."

Our laughter shook the bed and I wheezed, trying to catch my breath.

"Oh, my God," she said, still laughing. "I forgot to tell you."

"What?"

"I found a grey pubic hair."

"What?" I practically shouted.

"Yep. Just hanging out down there, like, *what's up, old lady?*"

I choked and laughed harder.

"I'm going to have to wax," she gasped through her giggles. "But I'm afraid I'll have more when the hair grows back in."

"Sixty year old carpet and twenty-three year old drapes," I said, barely able to talk through my chuckles.

"Oh, God," she rasped, slapping the bed. "Why the fuck didn't anyone warn us?"

"Because no one else discusses their pubes with us?"

"Well, they should!"

It took a while for our laughter to die down, but by the time it did, I felt a million times better. There was something to be said about quiet conversations in the dark with your best friend—they had the power to heal even the worst days.

"Thanks for coming," I said as we settled back down.

"Of course."

"Was Leo pissed that you were spending the night here?"

"Nah," she said, shaking her head. "They can get by without me for one night. Gray was already asleep, and Leo said he was going to watch his stupid car shows and eat pickled asparagus in bed."

"Ew." I wrinkled my nose. "That's disgustingly descriptive."

"And he's all mine, ladies and gentlemen," she said, waving her arm toward the ceiling like a game show host.

"I want that," I said with a sigh.

"Don't worry, Rosie," she said, pulling her blanket up around her shoulders. "I promise, you'll have a disgusting man of your own someday."

"Copper was disgusting," I muttered as I closed my eyes.

"Wrong kind of disgusting," she mumbled back.

Chapter 2

Mack

"Kara Louise MacKenzie, if you don't get your ass moving, I'm leaving without you," I called up the stairs as I stuffed my feet into my boots.

Swear to God, that girl couldn't get ready in time no matter how early I woke her. When she was little, watching her move around like a zombie in the morning had been cute, but the older she got, the less cute it was. If she made me late for work again, her ass was grounded for a week.

Okay, she'd probably be grounded for a day. I wasn't real good with the follow through, even though I knew I needed to be. It was hard to punish a kid who got good grades, treated others with respect, and smiled at me like I was a freaking superhero. My baby girl was a good kid, no matter how nuts she drove me.

"Kara!" I yelled again as I shoved my wallet in my back pocket. "Let's go!"

"I'm coming," she yelled, hopping down the stairs as she tried to push her feet into her sneakers. "I'm ready."

"Tie 'em," I reminded her as she stumbled to a stop beside me. "You know the rules."

"Yeah, yeah," she said, leaning over to finish putting on her shoes. "No shorts, no short sleeves, laces tied, no flip flops—"

"We're ridin' the bike," I said, cutting her off as I grabbed our helmets off the couch. "You had all winter to wear whatever shoes you wanted."

"I can't wear flip flops in the winter," she pointed out as she followed me toward the door. "My feet would get wet."

"You got a change of clothes in that backpack?" I asked as I locked up behind us. The sun was already shining, and I inhaled the scent of cut grass, enjoying that first whiff of fresh air.

"Yeah," she said, clearing the front steps in one jump, the backpack thumping hard against her back as she landed.

"Then you can wear shorts and flip flops all day until I pick you up."

"I don't know why I have to go to Trix's," she grumbled as she expertly tucked her hair back and shoved her helmet on. "I'm twelve. I don't need a babysitter."

"We've had this conversation," I replied, checking her chin strap, even though she'd buckled it herself about a thousand times. "If I'm gone for a few hours, you can stay home. Not when I'm gonna be gone all day."

"Everyone in my class stays home while their parents work," she pointed out for the millionth time as I climbed on my bike and waited for her to climb on behind me. She had to practically yell so that I could hear her through the helmet. "I'm old enough to take care of myself."

I chuckled as I fired up the bike and let the pipes drown out her complaining. I laughed harder as she pinched me lightly on the side in annoyance.

Maybe I was overprotective. Hell, I *knew* I was overprotective. I just didn't give a shit. When your wife kills herself in a bathtub full of water, leaving your five year old to fend for herself for God knows how long before you got home from work, it changes your perspective. I knew Kara could fend for herself. She was smart and capable and she didn't get into trouble. That didn't mean that I was comfortable with her being alone all damn day.

As we rode toward the compound, I felt Kara relax behind me. She looked a lot like her mother, she had her eyes and her smile and her dimples, but damn if she didn't get her love of the open road from me. My little girl had always loved riding on the back of my bike, and there had been more than a few rough days when we'd spent hours cruising down back roads with no destination in sight.

As we pulled up to Cam and Trix's house on the property next to the compound, Trix came onto the porch to greet us.

"Be good," I told Kara as she climbed off the bike and pulled her helmet off. "I'll be here around five to get ya."

"Sounds good," she said, kissing the side of my helmet like she'd done since she was a toddler. "Love you."

"Love you back."

"Hey, thanks for letting her hang out," I called as Kara bounded up the front steps.

"She's always welcome," Trix replied, smiling at Kara. Then she looked at me. "The boys are always on their best behavior when she's here, 'cause they're trying to impress her."

I felt nausea pool in my gut and instantly regretted that Kara had already gone inside the house.

"Your face!" Trix laughed, pointing at me. "I'm just fucking with you. The boys treat Kara like she's their triplet. Plus, Charlie's coming to hang out later, so they can ditch the boys."

"That ain't funny," I said, letting out a long breath.

"Yeah, it was," Trix replied. "I wish I would've taken a picture."

I flipped her off as I started the bike again and ignored her laughter as I turned around. Less than five minutes later, I was parked at the clubhouse and walking into the garage. The bays were already wide open, and a few of the guys were working, but most of them wouldn't be in for a few hours yet. I didn't blame them. I'd never been a morning person myself, especially before Kara was born. I'd party all night and start working while I was still buzzed the next day. Things were different now, though.

If it was up to me, I'd start at five and be done by one so I could have the rest of the day to do whatever. Especially in the summer when Kara didn't have a million school things going on. Unfortunately, Kara considered waking up at five complete torture, and if she didn't get enough sleep, she was a monster, so we usually made it out the door a couple hours later.

"Mornin'," Trix's husband Cam called as I pulled on a pair of coveralls. "Kara at our place today?"

"Yep." I nodded as he strode toward me. "Trix said Charlie's goin' over later."

Cam chuckled. "Gonna be a full house."

"Pretty sure you've got the room," I said drily. After a house fire had completely wrecked their place years before, Cam and Trix had rebuilt bigger and nicer than they'd had before. The house was huge and gorgeous.

"They'll probably spend most of the day outside, anyway," he said, sipping his coffee as I checked to make sure all of my tools were where I'd left them the night before. We didn't have a problem with theft, the brothers didn't steal from each other, but we damn sure had a problem with *borrowing*.

"Good," I said. "Thanks for letting her hang at your place. I hate leaving her at home all day."

"No worries," Cam said easily. "Trix likes having a full house. Says it keeps the boys out of her hair."

"Still." I shrugged. "That's one more kid to keep track of."

Cam waved me off and walked away.

I hadn't grown up the way he had, with honorary aunts and uncles pitching in to help with the kids, no questions asked. I was glad that's how Kara was being raised, though. When I was a kid, I'd started looking out for myself by the time I was seven. My parents didn't have the cash for a sitter, and we didn't have any family or friends that would've kept an eye on me for free.

I could still remember the cold metal of the key pressing against my chest under my shirt all day at school. I'd been so afraid that I'd lose it and be locked out of the house that my mom had put it on a string and I'd worn it as a necklace for years.

I didn't want that shit for Kara. I never wanted her to be worried when or if I'd come home. I didn't want her to be afraid every time she heard a car pull up outside because she didn't know if it was me or some stranger. She'd gone through so much already that I was determined to make her life as normal and secure as possible.

It took me a few hours to finish up the minivan I'd been working on, and by the time I'd parked it outside, I was dying for a cup of coffee and something to eat.

"Hey, prospect," I yelled at the scrawny kid picking up cigarette butts along the wall of the building. "Drive the Camry into my bay, yeah? I'll be out in a minute."

I peeled my coveralls to my waist as I went inside the clubhouse, the heat of the day already making me sweat. When I got inside, there were a few brothers peppered throughout the room, and I waved as I moved past them to the bar, where a couple carafes of coffee were lined up.

"Where's that pretty lass of yours?" Old Poet asked as I grabbed myself a mug. "She didn't come with ya today?"

I shook my head. "She's at Cam and Trix's, hanging out with the boys."

"She'll have them trippin' all over themselves," he said, grinning.

"Don't remind me," I grumbled, holding back a groan as I got my first taste of coffee. Poet's wife Amy always made the coffee at the club. I didn't know what she did to it, but it tasted ten times better than the shit I made at home.

"Well, you tell her that I'm still waiting on my cribbage rematch," he said, pointing at me. "I still believe she cheated."

"I think she's just good at it," I replied, my lips twitching.

"She definitely cheated," he argued. "Just not sure how she did it."

"You sure you want a rematch?" I asked.

"Hell, yes. I want to catch her."

I laughed at the disgust in his voice. The old timer was one of the scariest men I'd ever met—and I'd met some scary ones—but he was the biggest softy when it came to women and kids.

"I'll let her know you're waiting on that rematch," I said, lifting my cup in salute.

"Do that," he said with a nod. "You're doin' a good job with that one. Sweet as sugar and wily as a fox."

I agreed and filled up my coffee before walking back outside. There was a door that went straight from the clubhouse to the garage, but unless it was raining, I preferred to walk out the front door and around to the open bays. It gave me a few minutes to get some air before I was stuck inside with the smell of oil and grease clogging up my sinuses. Don't get me wrong, I loved what I did and I was damn good at it—I'd been working on engines since I was tall enough to see under the hood—but the smell was overpowering, especially when the weather was warm and there was no cross breeze.

"Camry's inside," the prospect called as I passed him. "Keys are on the seat."

"Thanks, man," I replied. Some of the guys treated the prospects like shit, but I didn't. A little hazing went a long way, and they were already doing the shittiest jobs imaginable—sometimes literally. I remembered how it felt to be at the bottom of the pecking order all too well, and I wasn't going to make it even more miserable for the poor fucks.

I finished my coffee quickly and rolled under the Camry, and almost instantly, I was covered in black sludge.

"Fuck," I muttered, reaching up to try and find the leak. I was going to be pissed as hell if it got into my eyes, but I didn't want to stop to find some safety glasses and lose my chance to find out where the shit was coming from. By the time I was finished a few hours later, I was covered in grease and oil. It was everywhere. My hair, beard, I could even feel it in my fucking ears.

"Jesus, what happened to you?" Casper asked as I peeled off my coveralls and left them in a pile.

"That fuckin' piece of shit," I mumbled, pointing at the Camry. "I don't even know how they managed to drive it here."

"People are idiots," he replied easily.

"No kidding." I made my way back into the clubhouse and went straight to my room, peeling off my white tank top and unbuckling my belt as I went. I needed a shower, pronto. Thankfully, I always kept a few spare sets of clothes for me and Kara at the club. They'd come in handy more than a few times over the years.

My room didn't have a bathroom connected, so I stripped down to my boxers and grabbed a towel, leaving all my shit on the floor as I left the room. There usually weren't too many people around in the middle of the afternoon, and it wasn't as if I had anything they hadn't seen before.

The hot water was fucking terrific, and I stayed in the shower longer than I usually would have. By the time I was done, my fingers were pruning up and I was pretty sure I was done for the day. I was still a couple hours short, but I didn't mind making it up later.

Walking back to my room in my towel, I could make out women's voices in the main room of the club, but since my hearing was pretty much shot, I couldn't decipher who it was. Hopefully, Kara had come over with Trix if the women were congregating. It would save me a trip over to their place. Maybe my girl would want to grab some suits and head to the swimming hole. It was still early enough to get a couple hours of swimming in before it started to cool off outside.

I wasn't paying attention as I got dressed, because I was too preoccupied with thoughts of the damn river, and I almost ate shit when I slid my foot into my boot and straight into a gooey, wet, mess.

"What the fuck?" I pulled my boot back off and stared uncomprehendingly inside. It was filled with something thick and yellow. I glanced at the door that I'd left open while I'd showered, lifting the boot closer to my face.

There was almost an inch-deep layer of tapioca pudding in my goddamn boot. *Why was there tapioca pudding in my goddamn boot?* Reaching for my other boot, I cursed. It was full of the shit, too.

My blood was boiling as I grabbed both boots and stomped in my socks toward the main room of the club. I kept slipping every time my tapioca sock made contact with the cement floor, which just pissed me off more. I didn't know who thought it would be funny to fuck with my perfectly-worn-in-and-comfortable-as-hell-boots, but there was going to be hell to pay when I figured it out.

Poet barely even looked at me when I passed, him, but pointed toward the front door while he tried to hold back laughter. Yeah, I was pretty sure I looked hilarious walking around in my socks, one of them visibly slimy and gross and with a hole at the end where you could see my big toe.

When I hit the forecourt, I came to an abrupt halt and my mouth dropped open in surprise as comprehension dawned. No fucking way.

Rose.

"Payback's a bitch!" she called merrily, hanging out the driver's side window of her SUV. "*Now,* we're even."

She yelped in surprise and scrambled back in the window as I started jogging toward her. But before I could reach the car, she was already pulling away, spitting gravel as she fled.

"Man," Will said, watching the whole thing unfold from one of the garage bays. "I told you she'd get ya back. What'd she do?"

"She put fucking pudding in my boots," I growled back, dropping them onto the gravel.

Will's head jerked as his eyes widened. "Seriously? You musta really pissed her off."

"I put her ass in the kiddie pool during a fucking water fight," I snapped back. "And that was *after* she'd sprayed me with water."

His lips twitched and he rubbed his hand over his mouth, trying to hide his smile. "My baby sister has never done anything halfway in her life." He paused. "It's good to see her back at it. She's been moping around for a month."

"She coulda picked a better way to show everyone she's done moonin' over Copper's idiot ass," I bitched, peeling off my socks. "She took it too fuckin' far."

"Pudding in your boots is nothin'," he replied in surprise. "Have you even checked your bike yet?"

"Sonofabitch," I yelled, running as best I could toward the row of bikes parked along the building. I must have looked like a complete idiot as I jerked and swayed, the gravel biting into the soles of my feet.

I ignored Will's laughter as I checked my bike over, making sure she hadn't scratched anything or taken anything out of my saddlebags. I knew she wouldn't have messed with the tires or anything else that could get someone hurt, but everything else was fair game. When I reached into my saddlebag, I found an envelope that I hadn't put there and pulled it out.

You needed new ones anyway was scrawled across the front. Inside was a gift certificate worth a grip to the shop where most of us bought our leathers and had them repaired.

"Well, shit," I murmured, my anger dissolving instantly.

"Seriously, Dad," Kara asked me that night as I grabbed a box of rubber gloves off the shelf. "What the heck are we buying all of this for?"

"Sometimes, baby, you have to fight fire with fire," I replied distractedly.

"Okay, now you really need to clarify," she said, skipping to catch up with me as I headed to the front of the store.

"Don't worry about it."

She scoffed.

I had no idea how to give Rose back the gift certificate she'd left on my bike. She and I had never been close, but even I knew that she was crazy stubborn. Problem was, I just couldn't accept it. She was right—it was time for new boots, anyway. I just hadn't gotten around to buying any because it took a long ass time to wear them in to the point that they were actually comfortable, so I'd been lazy about making the change.

Right now, I was on a different mission. Her gift didn't change the fact that she'd put pudding in my boots. Luckily, I'd had a pair of flip flops at the club for when I took Kara swimming, so I hadn't had to ride home barefoot—but I may as well have. It wasn't a big deal to me, but I'd had to listen to Kara bitch for the last thirty minutes about how I didn't let *her* wear open toed shoes on the bike. That thirty minutes of whining had cemented the retribution that I was planning for Rose.

Plain and simple, she shouldn't have escalated shit. I wasn't one of her brothers that tucked his tail between his legs when she got a little crazy for fear that the next prank would be far worse. Fuck that. I could take anything she threw at me and send it right back.

Which was why me and Kara were gathering supplies at the drugstore, instead of at home barbequing the steaks I'd had marinating all day.

"Can I get a candy bar?" Kara asked, bouncing on her toes. "I'm starving."

I looked at my daughter and I couldn't help but grin. The braids she'd put in her hair that morning were a tangled mess, and she had a streak of dirt on her neck from God knew what. Sometimes it was easy to forget how young she really was. Twelve seemed to be right in the middle of little girl shit and teenager shit. So, she may have been wearing makeup when we left the house that morning, but by the time I'd picked her up, she was covered in dirt and had proudly showed off a long scratch on her knee that she'd got riding bikes with the kids.

"Sure," I said, laughing as she did a little dance. "Grab me one, too."

I watched the clock as we headed home. It was still a few hours before Rose left for work, so we had some time. I wasn't positive that she'd be bartending tonight, but there was a pretty good chance. I'd noticed that she worked a lot. Unless there was something going on at the club or her family had plans, by seven o'clock, she was slinging drinks somewhere. Last time I'd counted, she had two regular jobs and another where she picked up shifts when someone called in sick.

After a whole lot of grumbling, Kara went up to shower off the day's sweat and sunblock while I put dinner on the grill. God, I loved summer. Even when I worked a full eight hours, we still always had at least a few hours of light when we got home to hang outside or go do something fun. Plus, it was nice to grill when it wasn't raining—not like a little rain had ever stopped me.

My phone rang as I was flipping a couple of corncobs, so I answered, holding it with my shoulder as I continued what I was doing.

"Hey, Ma."

"Cubby," my mom said fondly, using my childhood nickname as an endearment. "How are you and my granddaughter doing?"

"We're good," I replied, glancing over my shoulder as Kara came outside in her pajamas and headed straight to the swing hanging from an old oak tree in our back yard. "Working like always and soaking up this sun when we can."

"How's Kara enjoying her summer? Does she have anything fun planned?"

"She's lovin' havin' no school," I replied making my mom laugh. "But she's not too happy that she still has to get up before noon."

"It's good that she's got somewhere to spend her days while you're at work," my mom said, a tinge of remorse lacing her tone.

"You and Dad did the best you could," I said. "I just got lucky with the friends I've got. She's got somewhere to hang with kids her age, and Trix doesn't mind having extra monsters running through her house all day."

"That's awesome," she replied.

"And she's got camp coming up, too. She's pretty psyched for that."

"The sleep-away camp she was so excited about?"

"Yep. Did some side jobs so I'd be able to swing it. It's next month."

"Only twenty-seven days!" Kara yelled from the swing with a whoop.

"Twenty-seven days," I repeated to my mom, making her chuckle.

"But who's counting?" she said dryly.

"How are you and Dad doing? Still enjoying tripping all over each other?" My parents never had any extra cash while I was growing up, but the plant my dad had worked for had a hell of a pension. When he retired, they'd sold the little house I'd grown up in and bought a tiny RV outright, and they'd been travelling ever since. They always made it home for Christmas and Kara's birthday in January, but during the winter months, they were usually somewhere down south, making their way north in the summer. They stopped where they wanted, left when they wanted, and generally had the time of their lives. I couldn't have been happier for them.

"The RV had a water leak," she griped. "So we've been stuck in this little town in Iowa for a week, but I think your dad finally figured out the problem, so we should be hitting the road soon."

"Why didn't he just take it into a shop?" I asked, going inside to get the steaks.

"You know your dad, he wasn't going to waste money taking it to someone else if he could do it for free."

"Understandable," I replied, grabbing the meat out of the fridge. "But you guys have the cash now. Don't scrimp when you don't have to."

"I know, I know," she mumbled. "But letting your dad do his thing is easier than arguing about it. I pick my battles."

"Since when?" I teased.

"Since we started tripping all over each other, as you put it."

I laughed.

"Fighting with someone in a space this small is worse than getting a root canal," she said, a smile in her voice. "There's nowhere to escape."

"Sounds terrible," I said in mock seriousness.

"Ha!" she laughed. "You'd be right here with us if you could."

"Damn straight," I replied instantly.

I was pretty sure that my love of the road came from my parents. My dad's hips were too bad to ride for any length of time, but when I was a kid, he and my mom used to take off for hours on his old, piece of shit Harley. Knowing what I knew now, I had no idea how he'd kept the thing running—but he had. It was the only escape they'd had when times were tough.

"Well, I was just calling to check in," she said. "We miss you guys."

"We miss you, too. Be careful on the road."

"We always are. Love you."

"Love you, too. Tell Dad I love him."

Holding the phone out, I called for Kara. "Your nana's on the phone."

Mom always took the time to have a one-on-one conversation with Kara when she called. I knew they hated missing out on their only grandchild's life, but they made a concerted effort to stay close with her.

As Kara walked away, talking a mile a minute, I threw the steaks on. They only took a couple minutes, so I went straight in to get plates and silverware. When it was nice, we always ate outside. Why bother to be cooped up in the house if you didn't have to be?

"Gram said to tell you she loved you and she'll call again soon," Kara said as she came out to the patio table and handed back my phone. "What do you want to drink?"

"Ice water, please," I replied, hurrying over to flip the steaks. "Before you ask, yes, you can have a soda."

"Sweet," she sang, skipping into the house.

Life was hard sometimes. It threw curveballs and knocked you on your ass. But nights like this, when it was just me and my girl, grilling, relaxing, and creating a little mayhem after dinner, made every shitty day worth the effort.

Chapter 3

Rose

"You don't pay me to shake my ass," I called to my boss, Matt, as I lifted a tub of dirty glasses onto the counter. "You pay me to tend bar."

"I'm just saying, if you wore something…"

"Careful what you say," I warned, pointing at him. "Sexual harassment will get you sued." I grinned as the patrons of the bar *ooohed*. "Besides, you tell me to wear anything but this comfortable shirt and jeans, my brothers will serve you your own nuts on a platter."

"Now, why would you say something like that?" he grimaced, pausing what he was doing so he could drop his hands to cover his junk.

"You know it's true," I said as I poured a couple of beers for some regulars I could see walking in the door.

"Yeah," Matt said as he walked closer with his arms full of tequila and whiskey. "Your brothers already gave me the speech."

I laughed. "It pissed me off the first time they did it," I confessed. "But I couldn't stop them, so…" I shrugged.

"*Barkeeeeeeep!*" my brother Tommy yelled from the front door.

"Speak of the devil," I muttered.

"You can wear whatever you goddamn want," Matt said quickly as Tommy strode toward us, his arm slung over Heather's shoulders.

"Good to know," I said out the side of my mouth.

"Did I ever tell you that I *love* the fact that you have to pour my drinks when you're working?" Tommy asked as he and Heather slid onto a couple bar stools.

"About a hundred times," I muttered back. "What do you want?"

"Damn," Tommy replied, wrinkling his nose. He looked at Matt. "You really need better service."

"Don't look at me," Matt said, raising his hands out in front of him. "I just sign the checks, you know she runs the place."

"And I'm damn good at it, too!" I said loudly, making everyone on the bar stools cheer.

"Beer. You know what I like," Tommy replied. "What do you want, baby?"

"Vodka cran, please," Heather said, leaning forward to rest her elbows on the bar top.

"Ew," I said, quickly. "Don't do that."

Grabbing a wet rag, I wiped it over the bar top. "There, now you won't stick to it, at least."

"Thanks," she said, leaning forward again and propping her chin on her hands. "Go heavy on the vodka, I had a shit day at work."

"Oh, yeah?" I said, handing Tommy his beer and starting on Heather's drink. "What happened?"

"My boss is an asshole."

"Her boss is an asshole."

"Jinx," Tommy said, saluting Heather with his beer.

"I've had plenty of those," I replied, handing Heather her drink.

"Who?" Tommy said darkly.

"No one around here," I replied, rolling my eyes.

"It's fine," Heather said. "Someday, I'll be the boss and I'll eat douchebags like him for lunch."

"Hell, yeah, you will," Tommy said, kissing the side of her head.

"I don't know how you do it," I replied as I moved down the counter to pour a beer for someone who was waving at me. "I couldn't sit at a desk all day. I'd go nuts."

"Same, little sister," Tommy said.

"I like the work," Heather grumbled. "It's the people I work with that suck."

My brother and Heather wandered toward the pool tables as we got busier, and the night flew by, like it always did. I loved my job, even when I had to deal with drunk idiots and shitty tippers. I knew it wasn't for everyone. Hell, my parents had been on me for years to go to college and get a higher paying job—but I just couldn't make myself do it. There was something about the energy in a bar that called to me. I wasn't much of a drinker, but I liked making drinks for other people. I liked watching their lives play out one snippet at a time. First dates, groups of friends shooting the shit, old timers watching the TV along the wall with a beer in their hand—all of it. Plus, I was on my feet, and I got to visit with people all night long, but I still had time during the day to do whatever I wanted. It was a win-win as far as I was concerned.

By the time last call was announced, I'd already cleaned up behind the bar and I only had to wait for a few stragglers to leave before I could. Matt usually locked up and walked me to my car, but I was surprised to see Tommy and Heather waiting for me after I'd grabbed my jacket and purse from the back office.

"What are you guys still doing here? I thought you left."

"We had a quickie in the parking lot," Tommy said easily.

As I cringed, Heather reached over and pinched him.

"Why don't you have a filter?" I asked as I led the way outside. "Seriously. No one else in our family is as disgusting as you."

"Because all of you are prudes?" Tommy asked. He'd parked his bike right next to my Jeep, and my Spidey senses started tingling.

"What's going on?" I asked, looking at them suspiciously.

"What?" Heather looked confused, so I relaxed.

"I'll see you guys later," I said, opening my door. "Is there still a party at the club on Friday?"

"Yep," Tommy said, climbing on his bike. "Just like every other Friday at the club."

"I'll see you then."

"Love you," he called as I started up the Jeep.

"Love you, too," I called back.

The ride home didn't take long, and as we got closer to my apartment, I started to wonder what the hell was going on. Tommy and Heather's place was clear across town, but they still followed me all the way to my parking lot. It wasn't unheard of for one of my brothers to follow me home if we were both on the road at the same time, but it something seemed off about tonight.

When they drove on past the apartment complex, I relaxed a little. If there was something I needed to know, someone would have told me. My dad and brothers didn't lead the safest lives as part of a motorcycle club, but it had been a long time since any of their shit had affected me.

I wasn't paying close attention to my door when I reached it, because I'd been taught—rightly so—to be hyper aware of my surroundings. So when my hand slid off the doorknob, it startled me. What the hell?

I touched the doorknob again and pulled my hand away to stare at it. Then I looked at the door as a whole.

Someone had covered the entire door, from top to bottom, with Vaseline. There wasn't a single inch that wasn't coated with the stuff. I gritted my teeth as I shoved the key into the lock, and my hand slipped at least four times before I could grip it hard enough to turn it and let myself inside.

I was going to kill Mack.

When my phone started ringing in my purse, I nearly threw it across the room, I was so irritated. How did you even clean that shit off a door? It was so *greasy*.

I locked up behind me and went to the kitchen to wash my hands, ignoring my ringing phone. By the time I was done, I'd heard the text message alert twice. When I pulled the phone out of my purse, I saw that it was Tommy trying to reach me.

Don't clean it tonight.

Wait until the morning.

I *knew* there was something off about him following me home. Had they parked and snuck back to watch my reaction? If there was a video of me making some dumb face, I was going to throw his phone in a toilet.

You're a fucking TRAITOR, I texted back.

Love you too.

I tossed my phone onto the couch and growled. I really wanted to open the door and see how bad the damage was, hoping it wasn't as bad as it had seemed at first—but I knew Tommy was right. It wasn't smart for me to be hanging outside with my door wide open at one in the morning, no matter how irritated and ready to kill I was. That was just asking for trouble that I didn't need.

I stomped toward the stairs, then felt like shit because I had downstairs neighbors and walked normally again. It wasn't their fault that Mack actually had the balls to keep this little prank war going. For a minute, I wondered if Mack was actually mad about the pudding in his boots—a spectacular prank, if I did say so myself—but I was pretty sure he wasn't. If he was angry, he would have called and said so, not kept the war going.

I peeled off my clothes and hopped in the shower, wondering what I should do to pay him back. There were tons of pranks that sounded good, but I had to be careful. I didn't want Kara caught in the crossfire—I may need her to help me get her dad later.

By the time I'd climbed in bed with a book and a glass of ice water, I still wasn't any closer to finding the perfect way to pay Mack back for the slimy door, but I had figured out how to clean it. Apparently, it was going to take a lot of paper towels and some dish soap.

I had to admit, his prank was pretty good—even better than mine since I'd actually ruined a pair of his shoes. I was kind of embarrassed about that, actually. I'd seen how ratty his boots were getting, so it had seemed like the perfect opportunity for him to get some new ones. I'd even gotten him a gift certificate to get a new pair. I would've done the same thing to my brothers, complete with the gift—it wasn't unusual for us. One time, Will had taken my makeup and thrown it all in the toilet so I'd had to fish it out, but he'd gotten me a huge gift certificate to replace it. The ruined makeup hadn't been the prank—fishing it out of the toilet had been. It was the same with Mack's boots. I'd wanted him to stick his foot into a boot full of pudding, but ruining the boots had just been a casualty of war.

Now, I was wondering if paying for new ones made me look like a lunatic.

I wished I could text Lily to get her opinion, but it was way past her bedtime. She'd be up at the ass crack of dawn with Gray, and she'd be working from home all day doing the accounting books for like five different companies. Yet another person who loved sitting at a desk all day, even if her desk was at home and she got to pick her hours.

I sighed and opened my book. Maybe if I stopped thinking about it, the perfect payback would come to me.

※ ※ ※

CLEANING OFF THE door hadn't been as bad as I'd expected, but it had taken forever, so I'd still bitched about it to anyone who could hear me. This wasn't my first rodeo, after all. Smugly declaring that someone's prank was weak was just asking for them to up their game, and I wasn't about to egg Mack on. By Friday, I still hadn't figured out what I was going to do to pay him back, but I wasn't worried about it. I was known for taking my time before I struck, and the longer I waited, the more nervous my opponent usually got. It worked out perfectly.

When I showed up at the club, I was glad to see that they'd decided to barbecue. Sometimes it was strictly booze and whatever snacks you could pilfer from the kitchen, but usually during the summer, all the old ladies got together and made a huge meal. I was starving. I'd spent the afternoon cleaning my house from top to bottom, trying to ignore the nervous anticipation that I absolutely refused to acknowledge.

I'd partied with Mack a hundred times. We were cool. Friendly. Tonight wasn't any different from any other party, even if we were in the middle of a prank war. Nothing had changed. Nothing was going to change.

I still took my time applying my makeup and ironing my hair, though, telling myself that I wanted to appear completely unconcerned with our new relationship. No, not relationship. Our new... shit, I didn't even know the right word for it. Relationship implied something of a romantic nature, and that was not this. New friendship? No, that wasn't right, either. We'd been friends before all of this started.

I was so busy arguing with myself that I walked straight into a muscular chest and almost fell flat on my ass.

"Whoa there, space cadet," my cousin Cam joked, catching me before I fell.

"Sorry," I said, returning his smile. "I wasn't watching where I was going."

"Clearly." He laughed. "What's up? Something wrong?"

"Nothing's wrong," I replied quickly, my voice coming out all high and shaky, like I was lying.

"Uh huh," he murmured, unconvinced.

"No, really," I said, shaking my head. God, what was wrong with me tonight? "Nothing is wrong. I was just thinking."

"That's never a good thing."

"Ha-ha," I said dryly.

"You planning out your next attack?" he asked curiously, lighting up a joint and offering it to me.

"No, thanks," I said with a wave of my hand. "Attack?"

"Yeah," he said, his voice raspy with smoke. "You know, that thing you've got going with Mack."

"Does everyone know about it?" I asked in annoyance.

"Kind of hard to miss it when you're comin' into the club to put pudding in his boots," he said with a laugh.

"I gave him a gift certificate to replace them," I pointed out. It wasn't like I was an asshole.

"He'll never spend it," Cam said easily.

"What? Why not?"

"A man's not going to accept a gift like that."

"My brothers do!"

"They're your *brothers*," he replied, like I was an idiot. "That's different."

"I don't see how," I argued, my voice going high again.

Now, I was kind of panicking. If Mack wasn't going to use the gift certificate to replace those boots, then I really *was* an asshole. I'd ruined an expensive pair of boots. I mean, they were old, but they were still expensive.

"Don't worry about it," Cam replied with a wave of his hand. "Doesn't seem like he's pissed."

"Shit," I mumbled, reaching out and wiggling my fingers so he'd pass me the joint. I was going to need the calm it brought if I was going to face Mack.

※ ※ ※

THREE HOURS LATER, I was feeling no pain. After a few shots with my brothers and a couple trips outside to smoke, all of my anxiety was gone. So what if Mack didn't use the gift certificate? He could throw it away for all I cared. It was the intent of the gift that mattered, and I'd had nothing but good intentions.

"I'm glad you came out tonight," I told Lily as we walked toward the small bonfire behind the building. "I barely see you anymore."

"You see me all the time," she replied, bumping me with her hip so I stumbled to the side.

"Not like this," I argued, pointing at her. "Not like...like *Rose and Lily*."

"We're always Rose and Lily," she said, throwing her arms in the air.

"You know what I mean," I replied, laughing as she tripped over some grass.

"It is nice to have a night out," Lily sang. "And I'm going to have drunk sex later."

"Good for you," I said seriously.

"It always is," she replied.

We found a couple of chairs and dropped into them.

"I haven't seen Mack tonight," she said slyly as we stared into the fire.

"You're like the fiftieth person to bring him up."

"Well, we're all just waiting to see what'll happen next."

"I'm so glad we could amuse you guys."

"Oh, come on," she said, rolling her eyes. "You guys are doing some weird mating ritual that—"

"It's not a mating ritual," I hissed, widening my eyes at her.

"Oh, my God," she whispered, her mouth dropping open. "You're *embarrassed*!"

"I'm not embarrassed."

"Yes, you are! Your eyes are all squinty and you keep glancing around, like you're afraid someone will hear me."

"Then why aren't you shutting up?" I asked.

"Because this is hilarious!" She leaned toward me. "You actually like him. I know you get all flustered around him—"

"I do not."

"—but I didn't realize you were actually into him."

"I'm not *into him*," I replied, keeping my voice low. "He just flusters me."

"Flusters you," she said flatly, raising her eyebrows. "No one flusters you. You're unflusterable."

"Not a word."

"You are the coolest person I know," she said, ignoring me. "You don't get flustered. You're a freaking ballbuster. Guys are scared of you."

"They are not."

"You're intimidating," she continued. "And aloof. And I've never seen you act as goofy as you do when Mack's around."

"Gee, thanks," I muttered.

"It's like your mouth isn't connected to your brain or something," she said, waving her hand in the air for emphasis. "I don't remember the word for it."

"He rattles me," I admitted.

"Why?"

I thought about it for a second, trying to find a way to put the feeling into words. "He's quick," I said, glancing at her before looking back at the fire. "Anything I say, he has a response, like—" I snapped my fingers. "And I swear to God, Lil, every single word out of his mouth is laced with innuendo. He could tell me he was headed to the grocery store, but it would sound like he was taking a trip to pound town."

Lily burst out laughing, and I felt my lips twitch.

"I've never noticed that," she said through her giggles.

"His voice is all deep and gravelly," I replied defensively. "He's like the male version of a phone sex operator."

"Imagine that voice in bed," she teased. "Oh, Rose." She groaned. "Right there, Rose."

"Would you shut it?" I snapped, swatting at her.

"Suck me harder, Rose," she continued.

"You have a filthy mind."

"You're just as bad as I am," she shot back, grinning.

"No, I'm not," I retorted, getting to my feet. "I'm going to get another drink. You want one?"

"Sure," she said, getting more comfortable in her lawn chair. "I'm gonna stay here."

"Thank God," I mumbled under my breath as I headed back toward the clubhouse.

My cheeks were hot as I made my way through the darkness. Maybe Lily was right and I did have a thing for Mack—but that didn't mean anything. It wasn't as if I'd do anything about it. He was older than us, more responsible than us, and way more experienced than I'd ever be.

I was so busy thinking about all the things I'd say to Lily when I got back with our drinks that I walked right into someone for the second time that night. This time, the collision was a lot harder, and I ended up flat on my ass.

"Damn, you okay?"

Jesus. Of course it was Mack. *Of course.*

"I'm okay," I replied, getting quickly to my feet. "Totally fine. Right as rain."

Right as rain? Was I sixty-four years old? What was wrong with me?

"I hit you pretty hard," he said, his voice laced with concern. Of course, all I heard was *hard* and I immediately flushed.

"My fault," I squeaked, lifting my hands in the air. "No harm, no foul."

Shut your mouth, Rose. Shut it right now.

"You're not going to fake an injury so your brothers will beat my ass, are you?" he said with a chuckle. "Payback for the door?"

"I wouldn't do that," I replied, offended. "That's not a prank, that would be a total asshole thing to do."

"Right," he said. Even though it was pitch black outside, I could tell by his tone that he was smiling.

The silence between us stretched while I stood there trying to think of something clever to say. I wasn't ready to walk away yet, but Lily was right—when I was around Mack, my mouth seemed disconnected from my brain.

"Did you use the gift certificate?" I finally blurted out.

"I was meaning to talk to you about that—"

"It's nonrefundable," I said, cutting him off. "And I gave it to you so you would *use* it."

"Rose," he said softly. "That's a big gift, yeah?"

"I ruined your boots," I replied.

"Needed new ones, anyway, babe."

"Doesn't matter," I said stubbornly.

Mack was quiet for a long moment. "You're sweet."

There wasn't anything wrong with his words, exactly, but the way he said them—like I was a little kid—made me narrow my eyes in irritation.

"I'm not sweet," I said flatly. "It's the rules of a prank war. If you ruin something, you replace it."

"Can't take that much money from you, Rose," he replied.

"That's bullshit," I snapped.

"That's the way it is," he said with a shrug.

"Fine, then, I'm done," I replied, with a little wave of my hand. I moved to go around him, but I didn't get far when his arm wrapped around my waist.

"You're givin' up?" he asked.

"If you're not wearing new boots tomorrow, then yeah, I am," I shot back.

His arm tightened around my waist as I tried to walk away, and I swallowed hard as his front pressed against my back.

"Baby, I've got new boots on now."

I was so busy letting the word *baby* roll over me that it took me a minute to put the pieces together, but when I did, a mixture of annoyance and guilt filled me. If he hadn't used the gift certificate, he'd just paid a shit load of money to replace something that I'd broken.

"You're kidding me," I snapped turning my head to look up at him.

"Did you think I'd ride in my flip flops all week?"

"I thought you'd use the gift certificate I gave you to replace them," I practically shouted.

"I'm not takin' money from you."

"It was a gift!"

"It was too much!"

The words were like a slap in the face. How often had I heard that? I was *too much*. I was *always* too much. I couldn't even reply as I jerked away from him. Why had I harbored this ridiculous crush for so long?

"Come on, Rose," he said, following me toward the building. "Why are you so pissed?"

"Not pissed," I said, shaking my head. "You won. Congratulations."

"Jesus," he muttered.

He followed me all the way to the back door, but as soon as I'd reached it, grabbed my hand and yanked me toward the side of the building.

"You're just going to leave it," he said incredulously. "You're gonna let me win."

"Yep," I replied emotionlessly. I could feel tears burning at the back of my eyes and I wanted to get as far from him as possible before the waterworks started.

"Damn," he said, taking a step backward.

I wasn't sure if it was the alcohol, or the fact that I was so frustrated that I could barely see straight, but I never intended my next words to fall out of my mouth the way they did.

"I'm *not* too much," I said, glaring at him.

"What?" he asked in confusion.

"I'm not too much. So fuck you." I could feel my chin starting to tremble, and that frustrated me even more.

"I didn't—"

"I don't even know why guys say that," I said, cutting him off. I lowered my voice. "*You're too much, Rose. Too sarcastic. Too loud. Too emotional. Too mean.* Fuck that." I jabbed him in the chest with my pointer finger. "Maybe you're not fucking *enough*."

In the space of a heartbeat, I was against the wall, Mack's hand pressed firmly against my sternum.

"I'm enough for you," he said, his nose almost touching mine.

"I doubt it," I scoffed.

His lips made contact as soon as the words left my mouth, and it wasn't like any kiss I'd ever had before. His beard was soft, but it was the only thing that was. His mouth was firm against mine, and his lips were chapped, and as I dug my fingers into his back, I realized that our kiss was just an extension of our argument. I pushed and he pushed, and my head swam as his hand wrapped around my jaw and positioned it how he wanted.

Burrowing my hands under his cut and t-shirt, I dug my nails into his skin and he groaned deep in his throat. His thigh pressed between mine as our tongues dueled, and I had just enough presence of mind to spread my legs to accommodate him. Then it was my turn to groan.

I wasn't sure how far we would've gone if the door hadn't swung open beside us and my cousin Cam's voice hadn't brought us back to reality like a burst of cold air.

"Trix's gonna be pissed she missed that," he said to Leo as Lily's other half came out the door behind him. "She didn't feel like comin'."

"Her turn to keep the kids, anyway," Leo replied.

Me and Mack stood frozen except for his leg slowly sliding from between mine, the friction making my eyes roll back in my head. I barely stifled a gasp.

They either didn't notice us, or deliberately kept their eyes averted as they walked toward the fire pit.

"Enough for you?" Mack asked, his hands sliding away.

My tongue felt glued to the roof of my mouth.

"The gift was too much," he said, taking a step back. He ran a hand over his face. "But any man that says you're too much has a small dick and an even smaller brain."

I swallowed hard and met his eyes.

"You hear me?"

"I hear you," I rasped.

"Good." He cleared his throat and gave me a nod, then he walked toward the edge of the building like he hadn't completely just rocked my world.

"What the fuck was that?" I whispered to myself, reaching up to rub my fingers against my sore lips. They were swollen and tender, and my chin stung from beard burn.

"Where did she go?" Lily's voice carried through the night as she and Leo came toward me. "She went to get drinks forever ago."

"Didn't see her inside, Dandelion."

"Well, I'm thirsty," she replied.

"Let's get you a drink, then," he said. His voice dropped, Lily giggled, and I knew if I didn't make my presence known, there was a good chance they'd find a place in the darkness beside me to do whatever he was whispering in her ear.

"Hey," I said, taking a step forward.

"Shit," Leo said as Lily yelped. "Where the fuck did you come from?"

"I think I'm gonna head out," I replied, ignoring his question.

"But it's early still," Lily replied, obviously forgetting that she and Leo had just been on their way to spend the next couple of hours alone.

"I know," I said, letting her tow me toward the back door. "But Will said he'd give me a ride home and I don't want them to wait on me."

"Fine," she replied as we strode inside arm-in-arm. "But you're coming over tomorrow, right?"

"Why do I have to help you paint your bedroom?" I grumbled. "Why can't Leo do it?"

"Leo doesn't paint," Leo said from behind us. "Leo will demolish and remodel whatever his woman wants, but painting is where he draws the line."

"It's creepy as hell that you're talking in the third person," I said, glancing at him over my shoulder.

"Nice beard burn," he replied, grinning. "Where'd you get it?"

I narrowed my eyes at him, glad that Lily was rambling on about something and hadn't heard his question. I wasn't quite ready to talk to anyone about what had happened with Mack—especially not my drunk best friend, who couldn't keep her voice at an acceptable level.

"Will's by the bar," Leo said as we walked into the main room, his voice laced with amusement.

I scanned the bar and found my big brother at the far end. Talking to Mack. Sonofa…

"Look at Molly," Lily laughed, pointing at my sister-in-law. "Good thing you're ready to leave, or Will probably would've left without you."

My sister-in-law was clearly hammered. She was leaning heavily against Will, looking up at him with stars in her eyes, and her hand was up his shirt all the way to the elbow. Even though I really didn't want to face Mack yet, I headed their way, laughing. Molly was seriously the best drunk I'd ever been around. She went from prim and proper to wild and dirty in the space of a few drinks, and I swear to God, she could never control what came out of her mouth and barely remembered anything the next day. It was fantastic. I couldn't wait to tease her about molesting my brother in plain view of my parents.

"Hey, you ready to head out?" Will asked, calmly placing his hand over Molly's roaming one on his chest. "Need to go get Reb and head home."

"Yeah," I replied, refusing to look to his left, where Mack was standing. "Let me say goodbye to the 'rents. Where's Tommy?"

"He and Heather pitched a tent outside and disappeared an hour ago."

"No need to say more," I said quickly. "I'll be right back."

"If you want to stay later," Mack said, making my heart jump, "I can give you a ride when I leave."

Half of my brain was stuck on the fact that he'd just offered to give me a *ride,* and the other half was screaming silently at him to stop looking at me while my brother watched us.

"I'm ready to go now," I said as we made eye contact, my voice squeaky and high. Before I could start rambling, I spun and headed toward my parents to say goodbye.

Good grief. If I thought being around Mack was hard before, I was kidding myself. Looking at him now, knowing the feel of his skin and the taste of his mouth, was infinitely more mind scrambling. I was just glad I hadn't stuttered or blushed.

"I'm leaving," I sang when I got close to my parents, internally shaking my Mack fog away.

"Not drivin'," my dad replied.

"Of course not." I leaned forward and gave him a hug. "Will's giving me a ride."

"Probably a good thing he's taking Molly home," my mom said in amusement.

"Amen," I replied as I hugged her, too. "Are you coming over to help us paint at Lily's tomorrow?"

"Yeah." She glanced across the room. "It's going to be fun dragging your Aunt Farrah's hungover ass out of bed."

"Good luck with that," I replied, grinning at the sight of my aunt shaking her ass while my uncle laughed.

Thankfully, Mack had disappeared by the time I caught up with my brother and Molly outside, and the car ride to pick up Rebel at Trix and Cam's was short. Will didn't have time to grill me before we got there, and once Reb was in the car, I knew he wouldn't. My niece was the sweetest person on the planet, and because she was so sweet, she didn't really understand the whole don't-repeat-this-conversation-or-you'll-embarrass-your-aunt thing.

I practically bolted from the car when we got to my apartment with a thank you and a wave. Eventually, he was going to ask me why I'd been goofier than normal around Mack, but that wasn't a problem for tonight. No, tonight was for reliving that kiss and figuring out what the hell I was going to do about it.

Chapter 4

Mack

THE CHURNING OF my stomach woke me up, and I groaned as I rolled onto my back and stared at the cement ceiling. I'd slept at the club after Kara had done me the favor of asking to stay the night with Casper and Farrah's daughter Charlie. It was a good thing, too, because I'd needed almost an entire bottle of tequila to erase the taste of Rose from my mouth.

I probably shouldn't have kissed her. Not like that. But when she'd stared at me, full of bravado with her lower lip quivering, I'd lost all sense of reason. She was gorgeous—a fact that had been harder to ignore lately—and she'd been giving me shit, even though I could tell she was really upset. The combination had been hard to resist.

I had a thing for strong women. Mouthy ones. The women who didn't know when to stop. My mother was that way. My dad always said *she didn't know when to say when*. Kara's mother had been that way, too, before Kara. I hated thinking about the personality change that had happened after our daughter was born. The way I'd listened when people called it the baby blues, and said it would fade away. How I'd picked up the slack when she couldn't, thinking I was doing the right thing, instead of getting her the help she'd needed.

Doctors knew a whole lot more about that shit nowadays. They didn't ignore it when a mama spent hours thinking of all the things that could go wrong, fearful to drive or cook or bathe their own babies. They didn't let it go on forever, until those mothers killed themselves in some misguided attempt to keep their families safe.

I shook off the memories and pushed myself up. No use reliving the past. There wasn't anything I could do about it now, no way to go back and change things. I'd keep the knowledge tucked away until it was time for Kara to have babies, so I'd know what to watch for, but until then, thinking about wasn't good for anyone. I'd fallen into my own pit for a while after we lost Mia, and I'd never go to that place again. Kara deserved better.

"Yo," Will called, banging on my door. "You up, brother? Church in five."

"I'll be right out," I called back, wincing as my own voice made my head pound.

I pulled on some fresh clothes in a hurry and headed to the main room of the club for some coffee before heading into the war room. I'd only had a seat at the table for a couple years now, even though I'd been a member since before Kara was born. I'd been busy proving myself in the beginning, and then I'd had so much shit on my plate when I'd lost Mia that the boys had known I'd be no use to them. They'd let me come into work bleary eyed and pass up parties for movie nights with Kara, and they'd slapped me on the back and asked if I needed anything almost daily.

By the time I had a grip on my new reality of single parenting, old Samson's wife had gotten sick, and he'd chosen to give up his spot to take care of her. I was voted into the man's seat, and the rest was history.

"All here?" Grease asked, leaning back in his chair. He looked almost as bad as I felt.

As soon as Dragon smacked the gavel on the table, Casper started speaking.

"We're getting a lot of fuckin' chatter and nothin' concrete," he said, scowling. "Not sure what's goin' down yet, but somethin' is happenin' down south."

"How far south?" Hulk asked.

"San Diego, as far as I can figure," Casper replied. "Our eyes and ears are shit these days. But the boys in Sacramento are already dealing with missing shipments, so it's makin' its way north. A big fuckin' cloud of trouble."

"How many missing shipments?" Dragon asked.

"Just two, so far."

"That's two too many," Will muttered. This morning, his hair stuck straight up, like he'd just rolled out of bed, and he oddly resembled the moose that he was nicknamed after.

"No shit," Grease spat.

"We're all good so far?" Dragon asked me.

"Haven't had a single issue," I replied, knocking wood on the tabletop. "Been quiet as a Sunday morning."

"Run an extra guard, anyway. It'll be quiet until it ain't."

"Done," I agreed. I felt eyes on me and glanced to my left to see Leo staring, his mouth tipped up at the corners.

Shit. That didn't mean anything good.

"We got a run comin' up," Grease said, scratching at his beard. "Nothin' big. Children's hospital charity. Should be an easy ride, Seattle and back."

"Women and kids?" Hulk asked. "Don't know what Trix has got planned for the boys this summer."

"Just women," Grease replied. "Party with the boys in Seattle that night."

"So we'll be shittin' and pukin' our way south the next mornin'," Tommy said with a laugh. "Awesome."

"You can't handle your liquor, might as well stay home," Casper shot back.

"I'm good," Tommy said quickly, raising his hands in the air with a grin.

"Amy and Poet have offered to keep the kids," Dragon said, glancing at me. "That includes Kara."

"Appreciate it," I replied.

"I'm sure we've got Reb covered," Will said. "That ain't really Molly's scene."

"Probably a good thing," Tommy joked.

"You just worry about keeping your woman conscious on the way back down," Will shot back. "We've all seen Hawk after a bender."

"She's a fuckin' Amazon," Tommy argued, making us all laugh.

"That poor girl has some nasty hangovers," Casper said in amusement.

"Fair point. Maybe we'll stick to smoke," Tommy mumbled.

"If we're done here?" Dragon asked, unamused. He looked around the table, and when no one spoke, slammed the gavel down, signaling the end of our meeting.

I stretched my neck from side to side as we shuffled out of the room. I needed a new mattress for my room at the club. The thing was so uncomfortable that I couldn't even make myself sleep on it unless I was too drunk to ride.

"What were you doin' last night?" Leo asked, his tone insinuating that he knew exactly what I'd been up to.

"What are you talking about?" I asked easily, pouring myself another cup of coffee. "After you and Lily came back out here, I spent the night drinkin' you under the table."

"Earlier than that," he said, tilting his head to the side with a smile. "Spend any time outside?"

"A bit," I replied slowly.

"Long enough to cause some whisker burn on a sensitive skinned woman?"

"Did you just say *sensitive skinned woman?*"

"I've been livin' with Lily too long," he replied, waving his hand dismissively.

"No shit," I replied. "Must be why you're askin' me who I was with last night."

"She'll tell my woman all about it," Leo said. "Just a matter of time."

"Nothin' to tell."

"Guess I was way off base, then?" he asked, fishing. I ignored the question.

"Good chat," I muttered, walking away as he chuckled.

I didn't give a shit if anyone knew I'd kissed Rose the night before. It wasn't some big secret, and we were both single adults. But I knew that even if no one really cared, they'd all have plenty to say about it, especially her brothers. Rose was their little princess, and from what I'd seen, they were even more protective than her dad. Where Grease gave Rose enough rope to hang herself, if it were up to the boys, she'd never even catch sight of the rope.

I wasn't at all interested in having a sit-down with Will and Tommy about my intentions toward their sister, when all I'd done was kiss the woman.

Instead of riding over to Hulk and Trix's, where Kara had spent the night with Charlie, I decided to walk. I needed the time to clear my head.

I needed to figure out what I was doing, messing around with Rose. Was I really going to go there? It was probably stupid that I was just now thinking about the ramifications of seeing a woman who was so tangled up in my day-to-day life that it would be impossible to escape her should things go sour.

Rose had her shit together, lived on her own and worked like a damn machine—but she was young. Damn young. I'd been changing diapers while she was in elementary school. The thought of that made my nausea worse.

She was beautiful and fun as hell. I knew we'd have a good time together. That didn't worry me. What worried me was the decision I'd eventually have to make if we had a little too much fun, got a little too close, and I had to cut her loose.

Hell, maybe I was overthinking things. It was shaping up to be a beautiful day, and when I got to Trix's, the kids were already outside. They'd built a ramp in the front yard and were taking turns jumping it on a couple of dirt bikes. I smiled as I watched Kara double check her helmet and tug on her borrowed gloves.

Stopping far enough away that they didn't notice me, I watched as Kara took the jump, landing beautifully on the other side.

"I got higher than both of you!" she yelled, pointing at Curtis and Draco. "Ha!"

"No, you didn't," Curtis argued.

"Yeah, she did," Draco said with a laugh. "It's because you weigh less than us," he told Kara, reaching forward to gently help her with her helmet.

My entire body tightened as I watched how carefully he pulled her hair from the buckle, but relaxed again when I realized Kara was oblivious.

"It's because I'm better and you know it," she said easily, grinning. "Pay up."

"This is bullshit," Curtis mumbled as he put a crumpled bill in her hand.

"Language, C!" Trix scolded from where she was sitting on the front porch. I hadn't even noticed she was there. "Kara, your pop's here."

"Dad," Kara said, turning toward me. "Did you see me? Nailed it!"

"Yeah, ya did," I replied, walking toward the group.

"I need a dirt bike," she said as she peeled off her gloves and handed them to Charlie.

"We'll see," I replied noncommittally.

"Just a pit bike," she continued, pushing her hair out of her face. "I don't need anything big."

"We'll talk about it later."

"Aw, man," she complained, the faintest hint of a whine in her voice.

"You can come ride ours whenever you want," Draco said, smiling at Kara until he got a look at my face. "I—uh, I mean, if your dad's cool with it."

Trix laughed, and I looked up to see her watching us from the edge of the porch.

"Want a cup of coffee?" she asked as I walked toward her.

"Wouldn't turn it down."

I followed her into the house as the bike started up behind us.

"I wouldn't worry too much about that," Trix said, motioning toward the front of the house. "Draco's just like his Grandpa Casper—he'd cut off his arm before he hurt her."

"That's not helping," I grumbled.

"Now, Curtis," she said, drawing his name out. "He's the one I'd worry about. The kid's got girls calling the house already, and he talks to every single one. Boy's going to give me gray hair."

"They're too young for all that shit," I said as she handed me a cup of coffee.

"Time's passing quick, man. It won't be long."

"Bullshit," I shot back, making her laugh.

We walked back onto the porch and sat down in a couple of chairs, where we could see the kids riding. Draco was currently the one with the helmet, and he was listening intently to whatever his twin was saying, nodding his head and smiling.

"I don't know how you do it with two of them," I said, glancing at Trix. "I can barely get Kara to school on time."

"Boys are easier," she said with a wave of her hand. "And I've got help."

I nodded.

"I don't know how *you* do it. Cam's good at taking over when I'm at my limit. I can't imagine doing it alone."

"You just do it," I said quietly, watching my girl jump up and down while she cheered for Draco. "When there's no other option, you just do."

"Yeah," she replied. "I guess so."

"She's pretty easy," I said, relaxing into the chair. "When she's not whining about something she wants or doesn't want, or both."

Trix laughed. "Sounds about right. I wouldn't want to go back to that age. The *angst*. The *drama*. Yuck. It's only going to get worse."

"I wish I could keep her a little girl," I said ruefully.

"No chance of that."

"Guess not." I watched as Kara and Charlie did some weird handshake and whooped.

"Though," Trix said thoughtfully, "maybe you've got some time."

I chuckled.

"You ever think of finding someone?" she asked nonchalantly.

"You, too?" I complained, making her smile. "My mother asks the same thing all the damn time."

"Well," she said, smiling, "you're a good guy, you have a good job, you don't look like an ogre—"

"Thanks."

"It's not like you couldn't get someone."

"I'm good."

"I could hook you up—"

"No, thanks," I said quickly, cutting her off.

"You already have someone," she said accusingly, leaning forward in her chair. "Who?"

"I'm free as a bird," I replied, lifting my hands in surrender.

"I don't believe you," she muttered, turning toward the driveway.

I cursed inwardly as I followed her gaze, watching Rose's Jeep creeping toward the house. Something in my face or body language must have given me away, because Trix started laughing.

"Leo was right?" she said in surprise, looking back and forth between me and the Jeep. "When did that start?"

"Your brother gossips like an old lady," I snapped. "And nothing has started."

"Bullshit," she replied. "I knew something was up with that prank war."

"Rose has prank wars with people all the time."

"Her brothers," Trix clarified. "Not you."

"I pissed her off."

"I'm guessing you did more than that," she said in amusement as Rose parked and climbed out of the Jeep.

She was wearing a pair of old Levi's cut-offs that were baggy and faded, and they shouldn't have been attractive. On anyone else they would've looked ridiculous. But on Rose, they were hot as hell. I couldn't fucking figure it out.

"Hey," Rose greeted, her eyebrows rising as she realized I was on the porch.

"Hey back," Trix said as I gave Rose a nod. "Did I invite you over and forget?"

Rose laughed, and I felt the noise deep in my gut.

"No, I'm just here to get Charlie. We're painting over at Lil's today," she said, making her little cousin groan.

"Can you come back later?" Charlie pleaded. "We're riding."

"I see that," Rose replied. "But no can do. I've been sent by the parentals."

"I totally forgot that was today," Trix said, leaning over the porch railing. "But I can head over in a couple hours."

"No worries," Rose said with a wave. "We can use the help whenever."

"Can I come?" Kara asked, throwing her arm around Charlie's shoulders. "I'm a fantastic painter."

I knew for a fact that my daughter had never painted a bedroom in her life.

"It's up to your dad," Rose said with a smile. "But I don't care."

"Dad?" Kara asked, bouncing up the porch steps. She wrapped her arms around my waist and leaned back to look at me, smiling so wide that I could see her back molars. "Please?"

"You sure she won't be in the way?" I asked, meeting Rose's eyes.

Damn, I probably shouldn't have done that. Not if I wanted to play shit cool. Looking at her, really looking, brought every single memory from the night before to the surface. The way she smelled and tasted and felt. I could feel a smile pulling at the edges of my mouth.

Rose's eyes widened and she quickly looked away. "Yeah," she said, trying and failing to seem unaffected. "She's more than welcome."

"Then it's okay with me," I replied.

"Yes!" Kara let go of me and danced away.

"Kara, grab your bag," I reminded her before she could jump off the porch.

"You, too, Charlie," Rose said.

"I'll help them grab their stuff," Trix murmured, grinning.

As soon as they'd gone into the house, Rose practically ran for her Jeep.

"See ya later, Mack," Draco called as he and Curtis rolled the dirt bikes around the side of the house. I guess it wasn't as fun to show off when no one was there to watch you do it.

Once they were gone, I walked over to the Jeep.

"Uh, hey," Rose said again as I reached her window. She watched me closely as I leaned in, crowding her a little.

"What time should I pick Kara up?" I whispered, rubbing my thumb down her bare arm.

Rose laughed and pushed at my shoulder. "Get the fuck out of here," she joked, rolling her eyes.

I chuckled and braced my elbows on the door. "Is this an all day thing?" I asked, my gaze roaming over her face. She wasn't wearing any makeup and her hair was pulled up in a knot on top of her head. Jesus, I wondered what it would look like if I pulled that hair tie out. Would it be wild and sexy as hell, or look like she'd stuck her finger in a light socket? And while I was thinking of that, my mind wandered to what it would look like after I'd fucked her so hard she screamed my name.

"Stop looking at me like that," she said, shaking her head.

"Like what?" I asked distractedly.

"Like you're picturing me naked," she said bluntly.

"I wasn't picturing you naked." Yes, I was.

"Yes, you are," she said with a laugh. "Newsflash," she whispered. "It's better than you're imagining."

And that's the moment I got hard.

"You—" my words were cut off by Kara and Charlie whooping and yelling as they ran down the porch steps toward Rose's Jeep.

"You were saying?" Rose teased as the girls climbed in the Jeep.

"Time," I muttered roughly, rubbing my hand over my face. "What time should I pick Kara up?"

"Why don't I just drop her off?" Rose asked with a laugh.

"Works for me," I replied, taking a step back.

"Love you, Dad," Kara said, leaning up between the front seats.

"Love you too, princess."

I took another step back and lifted my hand in a dumbass wave as Rose backed up and turned around. As soon as they were headed back down the driveway, Trix spoke up from the porch.

"You've got it bad," she said in amusement.

She had no fucking idea. I flipped her off as I walked back toward the clubhouse.

Chapter 5

Rose

"I SAY YOU go for it," Lily said as she dipped her brush into a plastic cup of paint. "I bet he knows exactly what he's doing in bed."

"Obviously," I replied, glancing at her. "Was that ever in question?"

"Well, then, what's the problem?"

"The problem is, after I rock his world," I said dryly, "then what?"

"You worry too much."

"Says the girl who ran away from Leo for years."

"I didn't run—" she said, making me laugh. "I made a strategic retreat."

"Whatever." I waved my brush at her and then got back to edging around the window. "It's just that I can't escape him. He's everywhere."

"I don't even see Mack that often," she argued.

"I do," I muttered.

"Probably because you're looking for him."

"And you think I won't be looking for him after I sleep with him?"

"Who said anything about sleeping?"

"What are you two whispering about?" my Aunt Farrah asked from the doorway, making me jump.

"Boys," Lily sang with a laugh.

"No time for boys," Farrah replied. "We need to get these rooms finished so I can go home and sit on my ass."

"How did we get roped into painting two rooms?" I asked as my aunt left the room again. "You said one."

"I lied," Lily replied with a laugh.

Our discussion on whether or not I should throw myself at Mack was postponed by the trio of tween girls that joined us. At some point, Kara and Charlie had added Rebel to their girl squad, and the three of them giggled and whispered as they started painting along the baseboards on the far side of the room.

"Where's your mom, Reb?" I asked.

"Auntie Rose!" Rebel said, gasping dramatically with a hand pressed to her chest. "I didn't even notice you there."

"I see how it is," I complained with a smile as she came toward me.

"I was just teasing," she replied, grinning. "I always notice you."

"I always notice you, too," I whispered in her ear as she leaned down to give me a tight hug. Reb's hugs were always firm. She said soft touches hurt, like bee stings.

"I wasn't lying," Rebel said as she pulled away. "I was teasing. Dad says sometimes they're the same, but they're not always the same."

"Right," I said with a laugh. "Teasing is just supposed to be funny."

"Funny, not mean," she replied, looking over my shoulder. Reb had come a long way from the non-verbal toddler she'd been when I first met her, but she still didn't like to make eye contact or accept hugs when she was upset. "Mom is downstairs with Gram. She said she needed coffee and a hundred aspirin."

"She's not going to take a hundred aspirin," I said seriously, knowing that she didn't always realize when someone was exaggerating.

"I know that," she said as she crossed the room. "Two aspirin is the recommended dose."

Lily snorted. "She told you."

"She was teasing me," I said proudly, shooting Lil a grin. "Did you hear that?"

"Sure did."

"Draco is *not* cute," Rebel said loudly, making the other girls shush her. "Tell her, Charlie. Dad says he's stinky."

I choked on the spit in my mouth, and coughed like a lunatic as I tried to hide how interested I was in their conversation.

"He's not stinky," Kara said furtively, glancing over at us.

"That's because he always showers before you come over," Charlie replied easily. "When it's just me, they smell like wet dogs."

"That's because you're their aunt," Kara said, her cheeks rosy. "I don't shower when my grandparents come to visit, either."

"You don't shower?" Rebel hooted.

"I do shower!" Kara replied with a laugh, poking Rebel in the side. "I just don't shower especially for them."

"But you do shower especially for Draco," Rebel replied, like she was finally figuring out how it all went.

"No—" Kara shook her head. "Let's talk about something else."

It was quiet for a few moments while me and Lily tried not to laugh.

"Mom said I can get a new bike," Rebel said nonchalantly, glancing at the girls to see how impressed they were. "A purple one."

My throat got a little tight as Charlie and Kara *oohed* and *aahed*.

"Lucky," Kara said. "Are you gonna put stickers on it?"

"Maybe a couple," Rebel said seriously.

"I'd definitely do stickers," Charlie commented, pointing her wet brush at Rebel. "Really customize it."

"Yeah," Reb said quietly, nodding. "Customize it."

"Do you know if you're getting light purple or dark?" Kara asked.

"I'm glad none of the kids are assholes," Lily said quietly, drawing my attention back to our side of the room. "Remember how shitty people were to me when I couldn't see?"

"Of course I do," I replied grimly. "I was the one throwing punches and getting suspended."

"Punches?" Lily said, her lips twitching. "I can distinctly remember a baseball bat."

"That kid was huge and the bat was just sitting there," I replied defensively. "I had to get creative."

"You're lucky his parents didn't press charges."

"They're lucky I didn't aim for his face," I shot back. "That douche deserved worse than getting the wind knocked out of him."

"You always looked out for me," she said, straightening out her leg so she could nudge me with her toes.

"Watch it," I warned. "I've got wet paint here."

"Are we having a paint fight?" Rebel asked in wonder.

"No!" Me and Lil yelled at the same time, making the girls giggle.

<hr />

THANKFULLY, KARA HAD gone home with Molly and Reb, because I really didn't want Mack to see me sweaty, dusty, and covered in light green paint. What I'd thought would only take a couple of hours had turned into a massive project and I was exhausted.

After showering off the funk and cleaning dried paint out from under and around my nails, I sat down on the couch with a cup of instant noodles and a beer. I didn't plan on moving again unless there was an emergency of natural disaster-like proportions.

When someone knocked on my door a couple hours later, I groaned in frustration. I didn't have work or any family events for once. Why couldn't everyone just leave me alone for a single night?

"Just a minute," I yelled when they knocked again.

I wasn't wearing a bra, so I threw a hoodie on over my tank-top as I walked toward the door. When I looked through the peephole, I froze. What the hell was Copper doing at my apartment?

"What are you doing here?" I asked flatly as I opened the door.

"Come on," he replied, giving me a small smile. "Don't be like that."

"Seriously," I said, standing my ground as he moved as if to come inside. "Why are you here?"

"I thought maybe I'd left a couple t-shirts here," he said, stuffing his hands in his pockets.

"You didn't."

"Are you sure? I thought I might've left 'em in the laundry."

"I've washed all the laundry," I replied. "No t-shirts."

"Did you check under the bed?" he asked, smiling.

"No," I said honestly. "But you didn't leave anything here."

"Could you check?" he asked, leaning against the door frame. "I don't have a lot of clothes to spare, ya know?"

"Fine," I muttered, stepping back so he could come inside. "Stay here and I'll double check."

I left him in the living room and jogged up the stairs, eager for him to leave. It was so strange. I'd missed him so bad when he left that I'd felt physically ill. I'd laid in bed wondering what I'd do if he came back and said it was all a mistake and he loved me and wanted to work things out. I'd even planned what I'd say to him, how I'd make him understand how badly he'd hurt me, and then force him to jump through hoops for a second chance.

But now that he was standing downstairs, smiling and asking me to check my room for shirts that we both knew weren't here... I felt nothing. No sadness or regret. No anticipation. No butterflies. Nothing. I just wanted him to leave again so I could get back to watching *Dirty Dancing* for the thousandth time and dozing on the couch.

"They're not here," I said as I made my way back down the stairs.

"You got a new TV," he said, looking around the living room.

"Yeah," I replied. "I did. Your shirts aren't here."

"Trying to get rid of me?" he asked teasingly.

"Well," I tossed my hands in the air. "Yeah."

"Ouch."

"There's no reason for you to be here," I said, not unkindly.

"I've missed you—"

"I'm going to stop you before you say something and embarrass us both," I muttered, cutting him off. "There really isn't any reason for you to be here, okay?"

"You're a real robot, huh?" he asked. The words were light, but I recognized the look on his face. He was far from calm. "Don't even give a shit that the guy you said you loved came to see you."

"You left," I replied, crossing my arms over my chest. I really wished I would have gotten fully dressed before letting him in.

"I wonder why," he snapped.

"It doesn't even matter," I said. "It's in the past. Okay? No hard feelings."

"Oh, shut the fuck up," he shot back, making the hair on my neck stand straight up. "No hard feelings," he scoffed. "You were fuckin' begging me to stay, and now all of a sudden, you don't even want to be around me?"

I wanted to point out that *this*, what he was doing right this moment, was the reason I didn't want to be around him. Time apart had given me some clarity, and the things I'd used to find attractive about him weren't appealing anymore. Maybe he was insanely sweet once in a while, but it didn't outweigh the way he spoke to me when he was angry. It didn't excuse the way he looked at me or flew off the handle. I didn't say anything, though. I just stood there, hoping that if I didn't engage, he'd stop.

"You fuckin' lied when you said you loved me. You're a liar."

I bit the inside of my cheek to keep from responding. It wouldn't help. Nothing helped when he was like this.

"You said you were in it for the long haul. That there wasn't anything that would make you leave." He laughed nastily. "Fuckin' liar."

He had no idea how ridiculous he was acting, but I knew from experience that nothing I said would make him see it. It didn't matter that he was the one who left—not me. It didn't matter that I still loved him, in a way that made me hope nothing bad would happen to him, but didn't make me want to actually *be* with him.

"I told you not to use sex as a weapon. I told you not to do that from the very beginning, and you did it, anyway." He glared at me. "And now you're acting like it's my fault that shit didn't work out. Such bullshit."

I dug my fingernails into the fabric of my hoodie and kept my mouth shut, even though I wanted to scream my denials at him. The way he was twisting things and making me feel defensive was something he *did*. I couldn't have an opinion different from Copper's, or be angry with him about anything without it somehow getting spun around until I had to defend myself.

"Fuck you, Rose," he said, leaning toward me.

For a split second when he was in my space, I felt actual fear. My baseball bat was across the room, and even though he wasn't a huge guy, I knew I'd never stand a chance if things got physical.

I startled as another knock came from my front door.

"Who the fuck is coming over here this late?" Copper asked, scowling.

I had no idea who it was, but I was really hoping one of my brothers had decided to stop by. I didn't bother checking to see who it was before I flung the door open.

I'm not sure what Mack saw when he looked at me, but his expression instantly darkened as he put his hand against my belly and pushed his way into my apartment.

"Didn't know you were back in town," Mack said as he wrapped one arm around my shoulders and closed the door with the other. "You just get here?"

"So it's like that, huh?" Copper said in disgust as Mack kissed the side of my head. "Fuckin' figures."

"You got a problem?" Mack asked, his arm tightening around my shoulders. "Pretty sure you two have been done for a while."

"No, man," Copper replied, looking me up and down. "No problem."

I quickly wrapped my arm around Mack's waist to keep him from tearing Copper's head off. I held him there, next to the stairs, as the other man strode past us and out the front door. It wasn't until I heard the door latch that I finally let go. My hands were trembling.

"You alright?" Mack asked, using both hands to cup my face. "You looked freaked as fuck when you opened the door."

"I'm okay," I replied, shaking my hands out at my sides. "He was just being an asshole."

"He put his hands on you?"

"No," I shook my head. "No, he's never done that."

"Good thing," he said seriously. "I'd bury him."

"You'd have to get in line," I said ruefully.

"He always like that?" Mack asked as he let his hands slide away from my face.

"When we were alone? Sometimes." I moved away and leaned against the back of the couch. "He was always careful not to act like that in front of people."

"Looks like the mask's slippin'."

"He's not my problem anymore."

"Why'd you let him in?" Mack asked. There was no censure in his voice, just curiosity.

"He thought he'd left some t-shirts here," I mumbled.

"Rose," he chastised with a laugh.

"I know," I replied, an embarrassed laugh escaping my mouth. "I know. But he wasn't going to leave until I checked."

"That joker would've been back the next day if he'd thought he forgot somethin'," Mack said. "The man wears the same four t-shirts constantly."

"There's five," I corrected, my lips twitching.

"Well, hell," Mack replied. "Color me surprised."

I couldn't stop my laugh or the tears that came immediately afterward. I didn't even know why I was crying. I hadn't felt sad when Copper showed up. I hadn't felt anything. But now my chest ached like crazy, and I just wanted to bawl my eyes out.

"I'm sorry," I said, wiping at my face. "I don't know what's the matter with me."

"Adrenaline crash," Mack said knowingly. "You're okay."

"I'm sorry," I said again as my chest heaved. Pulling my hoodie up so the neck was near my forehead, I hid my face and used the fabric to dry it.

"Stop apologizing," he replied.

"This is so stupid," I said, pulling my head out of my sweatshirt once my tears were finally under control. "I don't even give a crap that he showed up."

"Because he was screamin' at you?"

"I didn't give a crap *before* he started screaming," I replied. "That's why he was screaming."

"Motherfucker," Mack muttered.

"No shit," I said unsteadily, lifting my hands to show him how they shook.

"Damn, baby," Mack's voice softened. "He really freaked you out."

"I don't even know why," I replied. "He was just being his normal asshole self."

"Come here," he ordered softly.

Without hesitation, I walked into his arms and relaxed into him.

"He won't bother you anymore," he said, leaning his cheek against the top of my head. "He thinks you're with me now, and I outweigh him by at least forty pounds. He might be an asshole, but he doesn't have a death wish."

"All he has to do is say something at the club and he'll know we're not together."

Mack laughed. "You really think he has the balls to say your name at the club? He might be stupid enough to show up there, but he sure as hell won't give your brothers any more reason to kick his ass."

"True," I mumbled.

"Let me know if he bothers you again," he said, rubbing my back. "I'll take care of it."

I huffed and pulled away. "I'm not answering the door if he shows up again."

"Plenty of places to run into him," Mack replied.

"I'll handle it," I said, looking up into his eyes. "I'm glad you showed up tonight."

"Me, too."

"But what are you doing here?" I asked with a laugh.

"Kara's spending the night at Will and Molly's," Mack replied, a small smile tugging at the corners of his mouth. "Thought I'd see what you were up to."

"I was watching a movie."

"You want some company?"

"No," I replied. His face fell. "I mean, I don't think I could sit through a movie now."

"Then let's get out of here," he said. "Go put some clothes on."

"Are you asking me to ride on the back of your bike?" I asked, fluttering my eyelashes.

"Offer expires in three, two—"

"I'm going!" I yelped, hurrying toward the stairs.

"Gettin' chilly out," he called. "Should probably layer up."

"This ain't my first rodeo," I called back, smiling so hard my cheeks hurt.

I'd never been the little girl who asked to go for rides on her daddy's motorcycle. I'd been too busy competing with my brothers and begging for my own. But there was something to be said about flying down the highway on the back of a man's bike, no responsibilities or worry beyond holding on tight. The summer air and the sound of the road relaxed me in a way nothing else could have.

By the time we came to a stop, all of my worry and anxiety was gone.

"What are we doing here?" I asked, climbing off the bike.

Mack shrugged. "Nice spot for a break." He motioned to the left. "Bathroom if you need it."

I glanced through the darkness and scoffed. "If I wanted to pee in the woods, I'd go a hundred feet off my back deck."

"Always bustin' my balls," he said with a smile.

"And you like it," I shot back, pulling my helmet off.

"Go for a walk?" he asked, putting his hand out, palm up.

"Sure." I laced my fingers with his and let him lead me off the pavement onto a little trail that wound through the trees.

"I love the quiet," I said with a sigh.

"Love it, but have to fill it, huh?" he teased.

I elbowed him in the side, making him laugh.

As we ventured further into the woods, I held his hand a little tighter. It was so dark that, even with the full moon, I could barely see where I was walking. Eventually, though, the sky lightened and we reached a clearing with a lone bench facing in the opposite direction.

"This place is nice during the day," Mack said as he led me to the bench. "Used to take Kara here to run her energy out."

"Oh, yeah?" I replied, sitting down with one of my legs pulled up so I could face him.

"She had a lot of energy, and I was never real good at playing."

"I find that hard to believe," I replied. "I've seen you with her."

"Well, yeah, *now*," he said with a laugh. "I figured it out. But these days, she doesn't really play."

"I remember when she was little," I argued. "I used to see you chasing her around and stuff. You played with her."

"*You* were little," he said with a laugh.

"Oh, good grief," I replied, seeing where the conversation was going. "I'm not that much younger than you, and I'm a fully-grown adult."

"Fully grown, huh?" he said, his lips twitching.

"Let's not play that game," I said seriously. "You know I'm old enough, or I wouldn't be here right now."

"Against my better judgment," he said ruefully, pissing me off.

"Then take me home," I snapped, getting to my feet.

"Hey." He grabbed my wrist before I could storm off into the darkness.

"I didn't ask you to stop by my house," I ground out. "And I'm not interested in screwing around with someone who doesn't even know if they want to be doing it."

In less than a second, my wrist was free and his hands were wrapped around the backs of my thighs, half tugging and half lifting me until I'd straddled his lap.

"Are we screwin' around?" he asked, jerking me toward him until we were notched together like a couple of puzzle pieces.

"You tell me," I whispered, our noses almost touching.

"Not sure you're a woman I can screw around with," he said softly, his eyes searching mine. "Not without gettin' all tangled up."

"Would that be so bad?" I whispered back.

"Fuckin' worth it," Mack muttered.

Then his lips were on mine and my mind went blank beyond the taste and feel of him. Touching Mack, feeling his beard against my cheeks and his fingers digging into the cheeks of my ass was a high I knew instinctively I'd never grow tired of.

"That's it," he encouraged, his hands sliding under my sweatshirt as I started grinding my hips against his. The long ridge of his erection pressed perfectly against my clit, and I whimpered as he started directing my movements, his hips countering mine.

Wrapping my fingers around the back of his skull, I pulled his mouth back to mine and pressed my tongue inside. I wanted to get closer. We were covered from neck to toes, dry humping like a couple of teenagers, and I couldn't get enough.

My breath caught and we both groaned as his hands slid up and cupped my breasts over my bra.

"Off," he ordered, dropping his face against my collarbone. "Let me see you."

Grabbing my sweatshirt and tee by the neck, I pulled them over my head and off my arms, dropping them on the ground behind me.

"Fuck, you're beautiful," he said, staring. His thumbs ran lightly over the lace of my bra and I shuddered. Without conscious thought, I reached behind me and unclasped my bra, making it sag between us.

As Mack pulled the lace away from my skin, I let my head drop back, watching the stars as I heard him let out a heavy breath. I wasn't prepared for the moment his tongue swept over my nipple, and I jerked in response, making him chuckle. Then his lips wrapped around it and he sucked hard. From that point on, laughter was the last thing on either of our minds.

I tore at his cut and the thermal beneath it, determined to reach any skin I could as I felt him pulling at the laces of my high tops. My shoes hit the ground and his hands went into the air, giving me the opportunity to pull his shirt over his head. I got almost dizzy the moment our bare chests touched.

"Damn," he said huskily, his hands sweeping down my spine and into the back of my jeans.

"Please tell me you have a condom," I replied, licking along the tendon on the side of his neck. Jesus, he even tasted good there. I bit the top of his shoulder, leaving marks, and his fingers tightened against the skin of my ass.

"Yeah?" he said, his hand sliding out of my jeans so he could use my hair to pull my head away and make eye contact.

"Did you think this was headed anywhere else?" I asked.

"I've learned not to assume," he said roughly.

Then we were up and I was wrapping my legs around his waist as he stepped forward onto the grass. Keeping one arm firmly around my back, he knelt and laid his thermal on the ground, then lowered me onto it.

Our hands collided as we went for each other's pants. I didn't complain when his fingers wrapped around mine and firmly pressed them to the cool grass beneath me.

"I'll let you explore later, baby," he said as he unbuttoned my jeans. "But I'm on a hair trigger, here."

"You have five minutes," I joked, my breath catching as he pulled my jeans down my hips, his knuckles dragging along my skin.

"I'm gonna need more time than that," he murmured when he realized I wasn't wearing underwear. His gaze never wavered from between my thighs as he dragged the pants off my legs. His hands were on me in the next moment, and I shuddered as the cool night air hit humid flesh.

I kept my hands at my sides, my fingers tangled in the grass, for as long as I could as he stroked and circled, pinched, and finally slid one finger inside me. Then, as he leaned over me and pressed his open mouth to the underside of my breast, I lost all willpower. My hands found his belt buckle as my hips began to roll. I lost his touch as he grabbed a condom from his wallet, but it didn't matter, because at the same time, my hand found his cock, and I wrapped my fingers around him.

In a million years, I'd never forget the first time he slid inside me. The stretching sensation, the unique smell that only came from condoms, the way his hand tangled in my hair as he groaned into my mouth, the scratch of his jeans against my inner thighs and the feel of his chest hair against my nipples. It was nirvana. A revelation. I wasn't sure what I'd been doing wrong before, but sex with Mack was like nothing I'd ever experienced. I was solely there, in the moment with him, all thoughts focused on where our bodies met and the sound and taste of him.

I came first, unable to stop the loud whimper that escaped my lips. My orgasm was both startling in its intensity and felt like a natural progression of every brush of skin that had led to that moment. *Of course* I'd come so hard that my scalp tingled. How could I have expected anything less?

My hands were everywhere as Mack continued to thrust, his movements growing jerky. I ran them over his muscular arms and down his back until I could dig my nails into his ass, making him groan. When his mouth dropped to my shoulder and begun to suck hard at the skin there as he came, my entire body tightened, instinctively trying to hold him inside me.

"Jesus," he breathed when he finally stop gliding in and out.

"Yeah," I replied, staring into the night. Once again, my mouth seemed to have disconnected from my brain. How could I adequately express what I was thinking without looking like some sort of nutcase? I couldn't. Sex with Mack had been so much better than anything else I'd ever had, that it was almost embarrassing.

"You good?" he asked, pushing himself up on his arms to look at me. He peeled some sweaty hair away from my neck and cupped my cheek in his hand.

"I can't feel my legs," I muttered jokingly, making him chuckle.

"No shit," he said, his smile so fucking gorgeous that I could've cried. "I was afraid I was gonna pass out and squish you."

"I would've rolled you off of me and climbed on top," I replied, smiling back.

"You ever wanna wake me up like that, you go on ahead, sweetheart," he said with a hum.

I shivered and Mack cursed quietly. "Sorry, baby, you must be freezing."

"Well, now I am," I complained as he leaned up on his knees and I lost his body heat. "Geez, when did it cool off so much?"

He stood, pulling his jeans up in almost the same movement, and quickly gathered my clothes as I got to my feet. When he turned to face me, clothes in hand, he froze.

"Goddamn," he rasped, his gaze working its way up my body. "It's a damn shame you have to cover any of this up." He handed me my bra and shirts, then reached out to pinch my nipple, making me sway toward him.

"Fuck," he groaned, leaning down to suck my nipple into his mouth.

"Again?" I asked, dropping my clothes on the ground.

"Again," he confirmed.

I got to be on top that time.

Chapter 6

Mack

I WAS PULLING my boots on when Rose rolled toward me, reaching out across the bed. When she didn't find me lying beside her, she opened her eyes and gave me a sleepy smile.

"Leaving already?" she asked, curling her arm back under her pillow.

"Gotta pick Kara up at Will's," I replied, reaching out to touch her bare shoulder.

After a couple of rounds at the park, I'd brought Rose back to her place, and we'd spent most of the night playing with each other's bodies until we passed out. I couldn't remember how many times she'd come, but I'd been completely wrung out with number four. Of course, that hadn't stopped her. I grinned.

"You're looking very smug," she said with a laugh, nudging me with her toes.

"I had a good night," I replied, catching her foot.

"Me, too."

We sat there looking at each other, neither of us sure what to say. It was easy in the dark, when the day was winding down and possibilities seemed endless and the night stretched out in front of us. Shit got more difficult when sunlight and reality came into play.

"I'd like—"

"We should—"

Rose laughed. "You first," she said.

"I'd like to see you again."

"Yeah?" she said softly, her voice almost surprised.

"Yeah." I leaned down and pressed my lips to her shoulder.

"I thought you had to leave," she said huskily as she rolled to her back, the sheet falling down to her waist.

"I do," I murmured, reaching out to run my finger over her nipple. I shook my head to clear it. "See? Tangled up already."

She grinned.

"I'll—"

"Don't say you'll call me," she ordered. "It's cliché, and I don't want to wonder when you'll do it. Just say goodbye."

"Goodbye," I replied, kissing her softly.

I got up reluctantly and left her all naked and drowsy on the bed, kicking myself for telling Kara I'd pick her up early from her sleepover.

On the ride to Will's, I couldn't get his little sister out of my head. It had been years since I'd had that much fun with someone. It was easy—and shit didn't come easy to me, ever.

I'd been single since Mia died. It wasn't like I was opposed to finding someone, exactly, but I'd just never found someone I wanted to stick around for. I had enough responsibility on my plate, and adding another person to the mix sounded goddamn exhausting. Plus, I had Kara to think about. I wasn't going to bring another person into our life if I thought they'd leave. My kid had lost enough already.

As I pulled into the driveway at Will's and shut off my bike, I called myself every kind of idiot. Because even though I'd gone over every reason why I shouldn't make things with Rose bigger than they were, I knew without a shadow of a doubt that I was in too far with her already. No excuse, rational or otherwise, was going to stop me from taking it further. In short, I was fucked.

Molly answered when I knocked on the door and waved me inside.

"Hey, Mack," she said sweetly. "The girls are just finishing breakfast."

She led the way into the kitchen and moved toward the counter where Will was standing, wearing a pair of reindeer printed pajama bottoms. I couldn't hold back my snicker.

"They're comfortable as fuck," he said, pointing at me. "Don't say a word."

"I wasn't going to say anything," I replied with a laugh, walking over to Kara so I could give her a kiss on the head.

"Hey, Dad," she said, tilting her head back to look at me upside down. "I'm almost done."

"No worries," I told her with a smile.

"Mack, you want some coffee?" Molly asked.

What I'd really like was a shot of whiskey, but I nodded as I walked toward the adults. "That'd be great, thanks."

"Thanks for letting Kara sleep over," Molly said as she handed me a mug. "Reb loves having the girls stay the night."

"She behave?" I asked.

"They were perfect angels," Molly replied, making Will choke on his coffee.

"If by *perfect angels,* you mean they kept us up until one in the morning with shitty karaoke, then yeah. Fit 'em for some wings and halos."

I smiled as Molly rolled her eyes at Will.

"They had fun," Molly said firmly. "And Kara's always a sweetheart."

"Good," I replied. My girl was a good kid, but I'd had groups of pre-teen girls at my house before, and I'd seen the way mob mentality made them rabid. They were loud and obnoxious and sometimes mean as hell. I should've known it wouldn't be that way with Kara, Charlie and Rebel, though. Putting three sweet, easygoing girls together didn't usually have the same affect.

"I'm done!" Kara said, jumping up from her spot at the table.

"Clear your plate," I ordered as she started to walk away.

"It's okay," Molly started to say before her mouth snapped shut.

"I'm guessin' she didn't cook breakfast," I said, turning to look at her. "But even if she had, she could at least bring her plate to the sink. You ain't her maid."

"Point taken," Molly said ruefully, smiling at Kara as she rinsed her plate. "Thanks, K."

"Welcome," my daughter sang as she skipped away.

The other two girls brought their plates to the sink and rinsed them, making my lips twitch, because I was pretty sure they were only doing it for my benefit. Then they followed Kara out of the room. Once it was just the adults, Will turned to me.

"What you got goin' on this week?" he asked easily.

"Rebuilding that old Chevelle," I replied, nodding when he whistled in appreciation.

"You ridin' out at all?"

Molly walked away as the conversation turned. She probably knew more than she'd ever let on, but she made a deliberate choice to keep her nose out of club business. She didn't want to know anything.

Most of the old ladies didn't know much about the shadier side of the business, but all of them knew a little. It was hard to keep so many secrets, even if they never knew specifics. Molly was different, though. She didn't want to know anything, and Will made sure that her wishes were followed.

"Got a short run to Corvallis," I murmured, drinking my coffee. "But nothing big until next month."

"You goin' to Seattle this time?"

"If I can find somewhere for Kara to stay," I replied.

"She can probably stay here," Will said. "I'll talk to Mol about it."

"I'm ready," Kara announced, peeking her head around the corner.

"Alright," I replied.

"Let me know if you need another pair of eyes this week," Will said as I started to leave. "I have a bad feelin' shit's about to get squirrelly."

"Will do."

❦ ❦ ❦

KARA AND I spent the day doing nothing. I took a nap in the hammock out back for a couple of hours, she painted her toenails and half her fingernails—I had to paint her left hand because she'd never gotten the hang of painting with her right hand. We did some laundry and I swamped out the bathroom. There was nothing quite as disgusting as pulling long, tangled hair out of a shower drain, but someone had to do it, or we were showering in ankle deep water, which was pretty nasty, too. It was an easy day—nowhere to be and nothing to do—my favorite.

The day was so easy, in fact, just me and my girl, that I started wondering if I really wanted to add someone into the mix. Kara and I were comfortable by ourselves and adding another person would upset the balance. Did I really want that?

It wasn't until after Kara had gone to bed and the house was quiet that my thoughts shifted. I liked that it was just us, I did, but sometimes it would've been nice to have a partner. Like late at night when I was laying in bed watching a movie by myself, instead of rolling around naked with a woman until I passed out from exhaustion.

Grabbing my phone from my nightstand, I texted Rose.

Hey gorgeous

I set the phone back down, refusing to watch for a response. I wasn't going to be that guy. I was too old and too fucking busy to wait on a text from—my phone beeped and I immediately reached for it again.

Hey! You're up late.

I smiled.

So are you.

Yeah, but I'm working.

I glanced at the clock. It was already after midnight, so her shift had to be almost over. I stared at my phone for a few minutes.

Stop by on your way home?

Is this a booty call? ;)

I laughed as I texted back. *If you want it to be.*

Count me in.

Let me know when you're on your way.

As soon as I set my phone down, I climbed out of bed and started cleaning up. I never let things get too messy around the house, but my bedroom was a different story. There were boots, bags of clothes that I'd never unpacked from different camping trips, mail from months earlier, even a row of empty beer bottles on my dresser. If I was honest, the place was a pit.

As quietly as I could, I stuffed shit into the closet and carried the empty bottles into the recycling bin in the kitchen. When I got back into my room, I quickly made the bed and kicked my boots under it. Looking around the room, I sniffed. Damn, where was that smell coming from?

My phone beeped as I frantically searched the room for whatever was causing the funk. Nothing under the bed, dresser and nightstand were clear, floor was mostly clear. I strode toward a bag propped up in the corner and grimaced. Yep. That's where the smell was coming from. I picked up the bag of dirty clothes as my phone beeped again. Shit.

Fuck it. I opened my window and tossed the bag into the backyard. I'd grab it in the morning. Flipping on the fan to get some air circulating, I grabbed my phone. Rose was in the driveway already.

It only took me a minute to get to the front door, and I held my finger to my lips as I opened it.

Damn, she was gorgeous.

"Is Kara asleep?" she whispered as I pulled her inside.

I nodded and locked the door behind her before towing her to my room. As soon as the bedroom door was shut, I pulled her in for a kiss. It felt like forever since I'd had my hands on her, not just that morning.

"I kind of like sneaking around," she said, grinning. "I feel like a teenager."

"So, what? Last year?" I joked, making her scoff.

"You have a real problem with my age, huh?" she said as she stepped backward, pulling her shirt off. "I mean, you keep bringing it up."

"I'll never say another word about it," I vowed as she started unbuttoning her jeans.

I was practically drooling as Rose pushed her jeans down her hips, kicking off her shoes so she could discard the pants completely. Her movements were sure and easy, she wasn't trying to put on a show—but it was far sexier than anything I'd ever seen.

Then, just as she stepped backward toward the bed, all hell broke loose as a moth the size of my fist flew right into her face. I jerked in surprise as Rose yelped, swinging her arms in front of her, trying to swat the moth away. It didn't help. If anything, it seemed to freak the thing out. Then a couple of his friends joined him.

"Get them off," she hissed, dropping down to her knees. "Are they in my hair? Check my hair!"

I tried hard not to laugh as I reached back and hit the light switch, blanketing the room in darkness.

"Now, you won't be able to see them," Rose said fearfully, her voice wobbling.

"They're attracted to the light above you," I replied, reaching for her. She shuddered as I pulled her against me. "No light and they'll leave."

"Please check my hair," she said quietly. "It feels like they're crawling all over me."

"They're gone," I murmured, running my fingers through her long, dark hair. "Nothin' is in your hair."

"I hate moths," she grumbled.

"My fault," I replied, kissing the top of her head. "I left the damn window open."

"You should have a screen," she said seriously.

"I'll get right on that."

"Please close the window."

"On it," I said. She was naked except for her bra, and it was downright painful to let her go. I hurried to the window and slid it closed just as Rose began to laugh.

"Jesus," she gasped through her giggles. "That must have been sexy as hell, watching me freak out because of a bug."

"I'd pay to see the show again," I replied seriously, trying to hide my smile.

"Wait," she said, cocking her head to the side. "I could get *paid* for this?"

I couldn't stop the loud guffaw that left my mouth. She was a fucking trip.

"It's a sliding scale," I said as I wrapped my arms around her and lifted her off her feet. "Moth fights don't pay much."

"What about naked moth fights?" she asked, smiling as I tossed her onto the bed.

"Depends on who's naked."

Rose laughed again, but the sound cut off as I pulled off my t-shirt. There was enough moonlight that I could see her pretty clearly as she licked her lips and folded her arms behind her head, watching me.

"I'm the naked one," she said huskily as I pushed my shorts off.

"Not yet," I pointed out, nodding toward the bra she still had on.

"Easily remedied."

It was my turn to stare as she rolled a little to the side and reached back to unclasp her bra. Without fanfare, she pulled it away from her skin and dropped it on the far side of the bed.

"I'll turn the light back on and you can earn some cash," I said, my mouth suddenly dry as the Mojave.

"Touch that light switch and you're a dead man," she warned, smiling.

I'd seen every part of her the night before, traced every hill and valley more than once, but that didn't seem to matter as I stood frozen beside the bed trying to decide which part of her I wanted to touch first. Every shadow was like a hidden treasure, and every inch highlighted by the moon was damn near mesmerizing. Every part of her was gorgeous, from her full lips to the way her thick hips tapered to muscular legs and small feet. She looked like a fucking painting. One of the really old ones where the women were curvy and smooth in all the right places.

"Well, if you're just going to watch," she said, the last word drawn out. Her arm slid from behind her head, and I damn near had a heart attack as her hand slid between her legs.

"Oh, fuck that," I muttered, climbing onto the bed.

She laughed as I jerked her legs apart and knelt between them, and in the back of my mind, I realized that I liked when she did that. Rose was prickly and she didn't take shit from anyone, but when she was happy—you knew it.

Her laughter stopped as I scooted down the bed, and she gasped as I put my mouth on her. I liked it when she made that noise, too. Rose tasted good everywhere, and I groaned as she grew wetter against my mouth.

I'd been with plenty of women, all shapes and sizes, and I'd realized a long ass time ago that none of that surface shit mattered. The only thing that mattered was participation. The difference between a woman who let sex happen and one that actively participated was like the difference between gas station food and a steak hot off the grill. There was no comparison.

Rose didn't let anything happen to her. She rolled her hips and scratched at my shoulders, gripped the sides of my head with her thighs and pulled my hair. There wasn't anything passive about her. After she came, she pulled at my shoulders, urging me up the bed so she could kiss me and run her lips down my neck.

"Condom?" she asked, her hands reaching between us, one hand wrapping around my cock and the other cupping my balls. I shuddered as I blindly reached for a condom in the drawer of my nightstand.

Rose only moved her hands long enough for me to roll the condom on, and then they were back, guiding me inside her. The hum she made as I bottomed out gave me honest-to-God goosebumps, and I gritted my teeth against the urge to groan my reply.

Then we were both moving. The slow, leisurely, sex we'd had the night before was a distant memory as we both fought toward orgasm. Her hands were everywhere, never stopping as she scratched at my back and squeezed my ass, pulled at my hair and gripped my shoulders. Mine weren't any less busy. Leaning on one elbow, I played with her nipples and pulled her leg further up my side, changing the angle and making her whimper. I wrapped my hand gently around her throat and she moaned. When I slid my finger into her mouth and she bit down, sucking as she came, it took every ounce of willpower I had to wait until she was finished before I blew.

I rolled onto my back and pulled Rose against me, my chest heaving as I struggled for air.

"I didn't think it could get better," she said with a sigh. "I was wrong."

"It's always better once you know what the other person likes," I said, tipping my head down to look at her.

"Not true," she said, raising one eyebrow. "I've had really good sex before, and it got progressively worse. It was just the excitement in the beginning that made it good."

"The man you were fuckin' clearly didn't know what he was doin'," I replied, making her snicker.

"Well, I'm glad you do," she said, patting my chest.

"Baby, I haven't even had your ass," I joked. "You haven't seen my skills yet."

"Oh, come on," she said, drawing out the last word as she smacked me. "Why'd you have to go ruin the moment?"

"We were having a moment?"

"Ass," she joked, relaxing into my side.

"I'm just givin' you shit," I said, running my hand up and down her back.

"But only half-joking, right?" she replied.

"Well, yeah."

She huffed out a laugh.

"This was a good way to end the night," she said sleepily. "Work was shit."

"What happened?"

"Nothing for the first few hours," she replied. "Then a couple of douchebags came in and wouldn't fucking leave."

I didn't like the sound of that. "What kind of douchebags?"

"The harmless, think they're God's-gift-to-women, kind." She turned her head to look at me and rested her chin on my chest. "They kept talking to me, even though I made it perfectly clear that I found them annoying."

"You got someone working with you?" I asked.

"Yeah." She grinned. "Tonight was Wren."

"Wren?"

"He's this super hippie dude that can name any of our beers by taste with his eyes closed. It's awesome."

"Sounds like good protection," I replied dryly.

"Yeah, well, one of my regulars was there, too. Old Larry likes to tell anyone bothering me about how he killed Charlie in 'Nam with just the knife he still carries around on his belt."

"That right?" I asked.

"I don't think he's kidding, either," she mumbled.

"You like bartending, huh?"

"I love it," she said, her eyes lighting up. "I mean, I know pouring drinks isn't rocket science, but it's fun. It's always different, you know?"

"Hey, don't knock doin' somethin' you like," I replied. "People spend their whole lives doin' jobs that suck. Who wants to live like that?"

"Not me," she said, raising her hand.

"Yeah, me, either."

"You like working on cars?"

"Wouldn't be doin' it if I didn't."

"What's your favorite part?"

"Restorin' old ones," I said, the answer coming easy. "I like makin' the old ladies purr again."

"I swear to God," she said, shaking her head a little, "everything that comes out of your mouth sounds like an innuendo."

"Not everythin'," I argued.

"See!" she pointed at me. "Even *that* sounded dirty."

I laughed and her head bobbed with every shake of my chest.

"Probably sounds like that to you 'cause you want my dick all the time," I said reasonably.

"Not all the time."

I just looked at her.

"Okay, most of the time," she grumbled.

She blew a piece of hair away from her face, then crossed her eyes and smiled at me. Jesus.

"Are we doin' this?" I asked quietly. "Me and you?"

"Do you want to?" she replied, just as quiet.

"Yeah." I was beginning to think there wasn't even a choice to be made. That train had left the station when she sprayed me with water through the kitchen window.

"Me, too," she said with a sigh.

"Alright."

"Alright."

I was pulling her up to kiss her when a loud thump came from inside the house.

"Fuck," I said, jumping off the bed. I quickly pulled on my shorts and grabbed my pistol from inside the nightstand, checking to make sure it was loaded. "Stay here."

Rose nodded, her eyes wide and worried.

I checked the living room and kitchen first, but nothing was out of place. Just as I started back down the hallway, Kara called for me. My stomach sank as I ran toward her room.

"I'm okay," she said tearfully as soon as I reached her doorway. She was sitting on the edge of her bed, holding her hand to her head. There was blood everywhere.

"What the fuck happened?" I asked, flipping on the light as I hit the safety on my pistol.

"I fell out of bed," she cried. "I think I might have hit the rocking chair."

I glanced at the tiny rocking chair that she'd had in her room since she was a baby, and decided I was going to burn the fucking thing.

"Let me see," I said gently as I dropped to my knees, setting the pistol on the floor.

As she pulled her hands away from her forehead, the bleeding got a fuckton worse.

"Shit. Put 'em back." I sure as hell wasn't going to touch her face when I hadn't had a chance to clean up.

"Rose," I called making Kara jerk.

"Rose is here?"

"What do you need?" Rose asked, coming to the door in her jeans and t-shirt.

"Can you grab me a towel? They're under the sink in the bathroom."

"Rose is here," Kara said in understanding, her eyes wide.

"She'll be around a bit," I replied, my cheeks hot.

"Sweet."

"Here," Rose said, holding a whole pile of towels. "I didn't know if you wanted a washcloth or a hand towel or a big one."

"Hand towel works," I said, grabbing it off the pile. "Thanks."

"No problem." She looked at Kara. "Damn, what happened?"

"I fell out of bed," Kara said miserably as I moved her hands away and pressed the towel to the cut. "Ow, Dad!"

"You need to keep pressure on it," I said, letting her take over. "Or it's not gonna stop bleeding."

"Head wounds are the worst," Rose said. "They bleed like crazy."

"You okay?" I asked Kara, squeezing her knee.

"Yeah." She sniffled. "It just scared me."

"I bet. It scared the shit outta me."

We all grew silent, then, none of us sure what to say. In all the time I'd had Kara, she'd never dealt with me and a woman in her room in the middle of the night. I knew she probably suspected when one slept over if they were still at the house when she went to bed, but she'd never come face-to-face with it. My face grew even hotter, and so did the back of my neck.

"Is it slowing down?" Kara finally asked. She pulled the towel away and I grimaced. The bleeding had slowed a little, but she definitely needed stitches.

"Here, honey," Rose said, handing Kara a washcloth. "Use a new one."

"I'm gonna get dressed, princess," I said, getting to my feet. "Need to go get that stitched up."

"No," Kara whined. "Can't you just tape it? Or use super glue?"

Rose laughed.

"This ain't your knee, Kara," I said. "It's on your face."

"I don't care."

"Well, I do. You need someone to stitch it up so the scar ain't bad."

"It's *my* face!"

"And I gotta look at it," I replied as I walked out of her room.

It didn't take me long to throw on some clothes, and I was putting my boots on as Rose walked back into my room.

"Sorry for the way tonight ended," I said ruefully. "Duty calls."

"Oh, quiet," she said, waving her hand like she was brushing me off. "I had a good time. I just wish Kara hadn't hurt herself."

"Yeah, me, too."

"I helped her put some sweats and a zip-up hoodie on over her pajamas," Rose said as I stuffed my wallet and keys in my pockets. "So she's all ready to go."

"Thanks, baby," I replied, pausing so I could kiss her.

"You better wash your hands," she said, pulling my fingers away from her cheek so she could kiss my palm. "You smell like you, me, and a faint whiff of condom."

"Shit," I muttered.

"Do you need me to drive you guys?" Rose asked as she followed me to kitchen. "She can't ride on the back of your bike like that."

"Nah, I'll take the Mustang."

"You have a Mustang?" she asked, grinning.

"1964, fully restored, flat black," I said, glancing at her as I washed my hands. "I told you I like making the old ladies purr."

"We're so getting down in the backseat of your car," she whispered as Kara came down the hallway.

"Sounds good," I replied.

"Okay, this is really starting to hurt," Kara complained.

"You ready, princess?"

"Yeah."

I herded the women toward the front door, turning off lights as we went.

"Send me a picture of your stitches," Rose told Kara as we walked outside. "I have a gnarly pic of the stitches I got when I was little and we can compare."

"I'm gonna say I was doing something cool," Kara replied. "Like jumping off the roof."

"Why, so you can look like an idiot?" I mumbled, locking the front door. Rose snickered.

"I tripped over my brother's shoes," Rose said out the side of her mouth. "And hit my head on the coffee table."

"Dang," Kara muttered.

"But I told everyone that I got in a fight."

"No way," my daughter said, her eyes wide.

"No one believed me," Rose said with a shrug. "They won't believe you, either."

"Why not?" Kara asked.

"Because they know your dad would kick your ass if you did something like that," Rose said easily. "I'll see you guys later."

I waved as Kara called out her goodbye.

Rose drove away as I opened the garage door and ushered Kara toward the Mustang.

"So," she said. "You and Rose?"

"Me and Rose," I confirmed, opening her door.

"I like it."

I chuckled as I closed her in and rounded the hood.

"She's fun," Kara said as I climbed in the car. "And she's really cool."

"Oh, yeah?"

"She doesn't care what anyone thinks," she said, watching me as I maneuvered us out of the garage. "You know? She just does her own thing, and that makes her even cooler."

"Yeah, I've noticed."

"I can't believe she's with you," Kara said, her surprise a shot right to the gut.

"Hey," I complained. "I'm cool."

"You're like the least cool person I know," Kara murmured, closing her eyes as she relaxed into the seat.

I wanted to argue, but what could I say? Of course I was the least cool person Kara knew—I was her dad. I didn't let her do all the fun shit she wanted, and I made her go to bed on time. I glanced at her and smiled.

I was pretty sure that Rose and I were equally matched.

Chapter 7

Rose

"I AM THE champion!" Kara crowed, doing a little dance in her seat.

"I should have never taught you how to play," I replied, gathering the cards from the table.

"Sore loser," she said with a grin.

"Poor winner," I shot back, sticking my tongue out.

"You have a concussion," Mack called as he came into the room, wiping his hands on a rag. "You're supposed to be resting."

"I am," Kara argued. "We're just playing a game."

"And I can see by the look on your face that you feel like shit," he said, shaking his head. "Go in and lay down for a while, yeah?"

"Fine," Kara grumbled. "See you later, Rose."

We watched her walk through the main room and disappear through the archway that led to the guys' rooms. "I'm sorry. I just thought I'd keep her company for a while."

"Nothin' to be sorry for," he said in surprise. "She woulda been bored outta her mind without you here. Clubhouse is pretty quiet during the week."

"I didn't even notice that her head was bothering her."

"You haven't been lookin' at her face every day for the last twelve years," he said easily. "She's alright. The rest'll probably help, though."

"Yeah. I better head home, anyway," I said, grabbing the card game as I stood. "Will you give this to Kara? Maybe she can find someone else to beat later."

"Sure," he replied.

It had been two days since the last time we'd touched, but neither of us made an attempt to change that. I hadn't exactly been spreading the news that we were, what, dating? I guessed that was as good of a label as anything. No one knew we were dating, and I wasn't sure if I wanted to broadcast it yet.

The club was really tight knit, and the men gossiped almost as much as the women. I was kind of enjoying flying under the radar for once.

"You wanna come over for dinner tonight?" he asked as he walked me outside. "I'm grilling."

"You're always grilling," I teased.

"Gotta take advantage of the nice weather while we have it," he replied. "Plus, it's the only way I can make somethin' decent."

"I'm a good cook," I boasted as we reached my Jeep. "Like, seriously good."

"Oh, yeah?"

"Yep." I nodded. "I have no idea how it happened. My mom says it's in my genes. My great gram was crazy good, too."

"I look forward to getting a taste," he said, his lips curving up at the edges.

My skin warmed. "Everything you say sounds dirty."

"That time I was tryin'," he said with a laugh as he stepped backward. "Stop by around six."

"I'll be there."

As I drove away, I let out a huge breath. Jesus, I'd nearly jumped him standing out in front of the garage where anyone could see us. I had no idea how we'd keep our relationship to ourselves. I had a feeling that anyone that saw us together would notice the chemistry between us in less than two seconds. It was impossible to ignore.

On that thought, I pulled out my phone and called Lily.

"Thank you," she answered with a sigh. "I needed to take a break."

"You work too hard."

"Yeah, yeah, tell that to my clients. Whatcha doin'?"

"I'm headed to your house," I replied.

"Then it looks like I'm on lunch," she said happily.

"Don't forget to clock out," I teased.

"See you soon," she said before hanging up on me.

It only took a few minutes to get to Lily and Leo's house. Just like the rest of the kids, they hadn't strayed too far from their parents. Only Lily's older sister Cecilia had cut the apron strings and moved all the way to California. Some of us had wandered a bit, but we'd eventually found our way back to the ten-mile radius surrounding the clubhouse.

"I'm here," I yelled, letting myself in.

"Kitchen," Lily yelled back.

"Woman, you better be making me lunch," I announced as I made my way through the house.

"You're lucky I'm hungry," she joked as I reached her.

"Ooh, ramen. Lunch of champions."

"It's easy and fast," she shot back. "Cut up some green onions and we'll make it fancy."

"Aye, aye, captain," I replied as I opened the fridge.

"I'm glad you came to visit," she said, looking at me over her shoulder. "But you usually leave me alone when I'm working. What's up?"

"Well," I said, pulling out a cutting board. "Me and Mack have been fucking like rabbits, and I figured you'd want to know before the whole club was talking about it."

Lily's jaw dropped as she stared at me. "No fucking way."

"Way." I nodded. "Wait, aren't we missing a certain three-foot tall gentleman?"

"Gray's at my mom's. Now, spill."

"He showed up at my house, we went for a ride. Then went for a *ride.*"

Lily chuckled.

"He stayed the night at my place," I said with a grin. "And then the next night, he asked me to stop by after work and we broke in his bed."

"Holy crap."

"Seriously," I murmured.

"Is this just banging, or is it a relationship?" she asked, grabbing some bowls out of the cupboard.

"A relationship, I think," I said, tossing some onion on top of our bowls of ramen. "I mean, Kara fell and busted her head while I was at his place, so she knew I was there. He didn't ask me to hide or jump out the window or anything."

"Well, that's good," Lily said as we started eating. "Because that would've been a dick move."

"He says he's all tangled up in me," I told her quietly, unable to hide my smile.

"Oh, nice," she breathed. "I like this. I like Mack. He's a good guy."

"He is a good guy," I agreed. "But I'm just taking each day as it comes, you know? I always fall head first and then when the dude leaves, I feel like shit."

"I think that's good," Lily replied. "Have some fun. See how you guys mesh before things start getting messy."

"Exactly."

"But he is *all tangled up in you*," she said, happily. "So don't play too hard to get."

"I think that ship has sailed," I joked. "I'm pretty sure he's already gotten me...multiple times in multiple positions."

"Yes," Lily yelled, raising her fork in salute.

⚜ ⚜ ⚜

THAT NIGHT, I packed a small overnight bag just in case, mixed up a batch of macaroni salad, and headed over to Mack and Kara's for dinner. Mack hadn't told me to bring the clothes or the food, but I'd been raised to never go to dinner empty handed. Different levels of association meant different offerings. If I didn't know a person well, wine was always a winner. If I was headed to a friend's house, I brought a side dish that went well with the main dish. And if it was family, I didn't bring anything unless they asked me to.

I left the overnight bag in the car and brought the salad with me as I strode up the front walkway.

"You're here!" Kara said excitedly through the screen as I stepped onto the porch. I laughed as she did an awkward ballet pose with one leg extended out behind her.

"Don't let your dad catch you doing that," I said as I opened the screen door. "How's your head feeling?"

"It's fine," she said with a sigh, wiggling it from side to side.

"It wont be for long if you keep doing that," I warned, pointing at her.

Kara grinned. "Dad's out back," she said as she led me through the house. "I have to go take a shower." She pirouetted and pranced down the hallway, leaving me at the entrance to the kitchen.

I took a minute to look around. I'd been in Mack's house a few times before, but never had a chance to actually pay attention to it. There was something undeniably sexy about a guy who *didn't* live like a bachelor. Mack didn't half-ass anything, and his house was no different. He'd made a home for him and Kara, complete with curtains on the windows and photos on the fridge. I took a step closer to check out the photos. There were a few different ones of Kara with an older couple that had to be Mack's parents, if the uncanny resemblance between the man and Mack was anything to go by. Kara's school photo was front and center, and beneath it was her latest report card—all A's. There was even a picture of my niece, cheesing for the camera in her own school photo. As I leaned in to look at the slew of magnets from different cities down the west coast, Mack came up behind me.

"I always bring Kara home a souvenir when I'm on the road," he said, making me nearly jump out of my skin.

I spun around to face him. "I was just—"

"Snooping?" he asked in amusement.

"Putting this in the fridge," I argued, lifting the bowl a little for emphasis.

"What's that?"

"Just macaroni salad."

"You brought food?" he asked, his eyebrows rose in surprise.

"Just a side dish," I said as he strode toward me. "It goes with anything off the grill."

My last word was garbled as his lips pressed to mine. I barely registered as he took the bowl from my hands and placed it on the counter behind me. I was too caught up in the feel of him, the soft scratch of his beard and his tongue sliding against mine. He tasted like beer and mint, and it was a surprisingly good pairing. I slid my hands into his hair as his fingers dug into the cheeks of my ass, and both of us groaned. It felt like it had been years since I'd last touched him. An eternity.

We stood there in the kitchen having a PG-13 make-out session until Mack suddenly ripped his mouth from mine and took a full step backward.

"What?" I asked dazedly, reaching for him again.

"Shower just shut off," he replied, clearly frustrated as he slicked his hair back with his hands. "Kara'll be out in a minute."

"Then we still have a minute," I said, taking a step toward him.

"I'm gonna need one," he replied ruefully, backing away. He slid the heel of his hand down the erection tenting his jeans and my mouth watered.

"We could hide," I said hopefully.

"She's twelve, not six," he said with a laugh. "She'd know exactly what we were up to."

"Oh, God," I muttered, shuddering at the thought. I remembered hearing my parents go at it when I was Kara's age. I'd run completely out of the house and nearly vomited when I'd realized what the noises were.

"You're lookin' a little green," he said, his lips twitching.

"We need to be quiet," I said seriously. "Like, really quiet."

"What the fuck are you talkin' about?" he asked, trying and failing to hold back his laughter. "She's gonna be out here in about thirty seconds. We aren't startin' shit *now*."

"I mean always," I replied, starting to panic a little. Had we been too loud the other night? Is that why she'd fallen out of bed? I shuddered again.

"What's your deal?" he asked in confusion.

"Do you think she heard us the other night?" I whispered as the bathroom door opened. I froze, then let out a breath of relief as Kara's door closed.

"Hell, no," he said easily. I must have looked as freaked out as I felt because he pulled me into his arms. "You mighta been outta your mind," he murmured into my ear. "But I'm always conscious of that shit. We weren't loud."

"How can you be sure?" I asked.

"Number one, because I'm a parent, and I'm always aware of where my kid is and what she can hear and see me doin'," he replied. "And number two, Kara woulda given me a ration of shit and gagged every time she saw me for at least twenty-four hours afterward."

"She knows we're together, though?" I asked, tipping my head back to look at him.

"Hard to miss when you come outta my room in the middle of the night," he said, his voice laced with amusement.

"And she's okay with it?"

"Yep," he replied. "She said you're way too cool for me, though."

"That's because I am," I replied instantly.

"Is that right?" he asked, his fingers going to my ribs to tickle me. I jerked and snorted, trying to get away, my laughs coming out in big guffaws, and that's how Kara found us.

"Ew," she said, strolling into the kitchen. "Child in the room!"

"You want some of this?" Mack asked her, letting me go so he could lunge for his daughter.

Kara screamed as he wrapped his arms around her, his hand going straight into her armpit.

"Careful now," he said breathlessly, laughing as Kara screamed and giggled. He hugged her tight and kissed the top of her head before letting her go.

"I kept the shampoo off my stitches," Kara said, tilting her head back to show them off to her dad. "Like a boss."

"Good job, princess," he said. "Why don't you grab some plates and silverware. Burgers are almost done."

"Need help?" I asked as Mack pulled condiments out of the fridge.

"Sure," he said, shooting me a smile. "Take these to the back deck?"

I took the bottles from his hands and brought them outside to the table on their back porch. They had a nice little set-up back there, with a barbecue off to the side and an umbrella shading the table. Kara followed me outside and set out all the place settings, turning things just so.

"You guys eat out here a lot?" I asked as we went back inside.

"Every day in the summer," she replied. "Except last year, when the bees were bad."

"It was a shitshow," Mack said, carrying my bowl of macaroni salad and a plate of burger fixings toward us. "I had to call a damn exterminator."

"You aren't supposed to kill bees, you know," I said.

"They were wasps," he replied, smiling. "Little bastards weren't pollinating shit. Grab us a couple beers?"

His shoulder brushed mine as he walked outside.

"You want something?" I asked Kara.

"Dad, can I have a soda?" she yelled.

"You've already had two," he yelled back. "Get somethin' else."

"I'll get ice water," she said with a put-out sigh.

"You should freeze some lemons and limes in ice cubes," I told her as I grabbed a couple beers out of the fridge. "For your water."

"That's a good idea," she said, pulling an ice tray out of the freezer. "You could do cucumber, too. Or mint."

"Ooh, mint sounds good."

"I can't wait until I'm an adult," she said, filling her glass with water. "I'm going to eat crap and drink whatever I want."

"You'll also have to pay bills," I pointed out dryly. "And cook your own food, and do your own laundry."

"I'm not going to cook," she replied as we walked back outside. "I'll eat out all the time."

"You can't eat out all the time," Mack said reasonably, joining the conversation with a sentence that made my cheeks heat with embarrassment.

"Watch me," Kara muttered as she sat down at the table.

"Get your mind outta the gutter," Mack whispered to me as he set the hamburgers on the table.

"Stop putting my mind in the gutter," I hissed back. I sat down as he laughed at me.

It was one of the best dinners I'd had in my entire life, and it made me imagine all sorts of things. I wanted this. I wanted to sit down to dinner and listen to Kara and Mack tease each other. I wanted to pass the ketchup, and add in my two cents when they were discussing dirt bikes, and kiss Mack in thanks when he grabbed us another round of beers without asking. Suddenly, my easy ramen dinners in front of the TV didn't seem so relaxing. They just seemed sad.

When we were done, we all worked together to bring the food and dishes inside.

"Load the dishwasher before you watch a movie," Mack said to Kara. "And don't forget to wipe down the counters."

"I can help," I said easily.

"Nope," Mack replied just as easily. "It's part of her chores. Even if we've got company."

"I'm on it," Kara said.

"Sorry," I murmured as Mack led me out the back door. "I didn't know it was a thing."

"Nothin' to be sorry for," Mack replied, leading me across the yard. "Bein' polite's always nice."

"Where are we going?" I asked, lacing my fingers with his.

"Hammock," he said with a grin.

They had a blue and green striped hammock strung between two trees, and I eyed it with trepidation as Mack pulled the edges apart and sat down sideways in it, his feet flat on the grass.

"You want me to get on that?" I asked.

"Lay with me for a bit," he replied. He spun easily and lay back, the hammock gently swinging from side to side.

"If I try to climb on, I'll tip us both over," I said, laughing nervously.

"Nah," he said, pulling one leg out and setting his foot back on the ground. "Come on, baby, I'll make sure we don't tip."

I really didn't want to get on that hammock. When I was eight, me and Lily were screwing around on a hammock, and I'd busted my face so hard when I fell off that it knocked out one of my teeth. I'd been lucky the dentist was able to put it back in, and the ensuing root canal was no fun. I rubbed my tongue over that tooth as Mack reached his hand toward me.

"This is a terrible idea," I said as I let him help me onto the hammock.

It was a snug fit, our bodies plastered together with one of my arms around his waist and my head on his shoulder, but we made it sort of comfortable.

"See?" he said, letting out a long breath. "Easy."

"Don't move," I said nervously as he shifted.

"We're not gonna tip over," he said with a chuckle.

We laid there quietly for a long time as the sun started to set. It took a while, but I eventually relaxed against him.

"Finally," he murmured, running his fingers up and down my arm.

"I'm glad I didn't have to work tonight," I said, tilting my head up to look at him.

"Me, too," he said, smiling. "How'd you manage that?"

"I knew it would be a slow night, so I called in sick this morning," I confessed.

"Such a rebel," he said with a chuckle.

"Worth it," I replied, laying my head back down.

"I'm glad you're here," he said, kissing my forehead.

Kara didn't seem phased a few hours later when she told us goodnight and headed to her room. It was like she'd assumed I'd be sleeping over. After she was gone and Mack and I were curled up on the couch watching some treasure hunting show, Mack spoke quietly.

"See," he said. "If she woulda heard something the other night, she wouldn't have been so cool about you stayin' over."

"Jesus," I muttered. "You had to bring it up again, didn't you?"

Mack laughed. "You were so freaked."

"Uh, yeah," I said, pulling away from him so I could see his face. "I don't want her hearing us having crazy monkey sex!"

"She's cool," he replied.

I looked at him incredulously.

"I mean, she's cool—she isn't gonna hear anything," he said with a shake of his head. "Shit, I don't want her to fuckin' hear us, either."

"I've never had to worry before," I said, leaning back against him.

"You never dated a guy with kids?" he asked.

"Not that I knew of," I replied.

"That gonna be a problem?" That's when I noticed that he'd gone completely still.

"Of course not," I replied quickly.

"If it is—"

"Mack," I said, cutting him off sharply. Grabbing his chin, I turned his face toward mine. "I knew you were a dad long before we started this. It's not like it was a surprise."

"Still," he said, watching me closely. "Different when you're in it."

"It's not any different for me," I argued. "I like that you're a dad."

"Oh, yeah?"

"Don't make it weird," I said, lightly slapping his chest. "I like you, okay? Being a dad is part of who you are."

"You like me?" he said, lips twitching. "You askin' me to go steady?"

I sat up straighter. "You should be so lucky," I replied, narrowing my eyes.

"You're so full of shit," he said with a laugh. "You've got it bad for me."

"Whatever." I threw myself against the back of the couch.

"You can't get enough of me," he continued, yanking me down until I was flat on the couch. He leaned over me, grinning. "You're fuckin' crazy about me."

I stared at him, refusing to reply.

"It's all good, baby," he said in a whisper, closing the distance between us until our noses were practically touching. "'Cause I'm fuckin' gone for you."

"Yeah?" I said, searching his eyes. A lump got caught in my throat as I tried to swallow.

"All tangled up," he confirmed.

We didn't talk anymore, but at some point, we made our way to the bedroom. And later, the words between us were spoken in whispers because they were too filthy for anyone else to hear.

※ ※ ※

THINGS BETWEEN MACK and I heated up quickly, no matter how hard I tried to keep myself from becoming too attached. I knew how these things went, and I knew how easily they could go sideways. It was easy to fall in headfirst, riding the high of a new relationship, until you slammed back to earth with a heavy dose of reality. I'd made a promise to myself that I wouldn't let myself fall into that trap again. That I'd take my time and keep what little distance I could so that when it ended, I wouldn't fall apart like I had the last time.

I knew within the first two weeks that all of my plans and promises meant nothing. How could they, when Mack looked at me like I was the most beautiful woman in the world? How was I supposed to keep my distance when he stopped by my work just to give me a kiss, or when he picked me up in the middle of the day to take me out to lunch, even though I knew he'd be working late to make up the time? I couldn't stop the butterflies in my stomach when he smiled any more than I could stop the sun from rising. Our relationship wasn't like anything I'd ever had before—it was effortless, and I was falling hard and fast. I should have known that nothing so good lasts forever, but I couldn't see any scenario where I wouldn't want to wake up to Mack's bleary eyes and morning breath.

I was in my bathroom getting ready for work when my phone rang.

"Hey," I said, putting the phone on speaker as I worked on taming my crazy eyebrows.

"Kara started her period," Mack replied, forgoing any pleasantries. "And I've got no idea what I'm supposed to get her."

"Get her?" I asked, drawing a blank.

"You know, pads or whatever," he shot back, the panic evident in his voice. "There's like five hundred fucking choices."

"Oh," I said, leaning back from the mirror and picking up my phone so I could pay closer attention to our conversation.

"I've bought this shit before," he said, his voice kind of high. "But usually, you get sent to the store with specifics, and I'm flying fuckin' blind here."

I ignored the pang I got at the idea of Mack buying period products for another woman. "Okay, it's not rocket science. We'll figure it out."

"What brand, though?" he asked. "And I'm not buying her tampons." His voice got even higher. "She's fuckin' *twelve*. Isn't this too early? I thought I had more time before we dealt with this shit. Should I take her to the doctor? What if something is wrong?"

"Whoa," I replied, trying not to laugh. "No, twelve's a pretty normal age to start having periods. And don't take her to the doctor unless you want to embarrass the hell out of her."

"She's at the house and she won't come out of the bathroom," he said, curtly. "Pretty sure she's already embarrassed." His tone immediately put me on edge.

"Why don't you go home, and I'll run to the store and get her some supplies?" I offered, trying to calm him down a little.

"I got it," he replied. "I just need to know what to get."

"I don't know without looking at the selection," I replied, trying to imagine the store in my mind. The supplies I used weren't necessarily what a twelve year old would need, and I didn't want her ending up with some diaper-like pad that had her hating her life. "I can just run down—"

"Rose," he snapped. "I said *I got it*. You know what, I can just call my ma."

"Mack," I said, trying to keep my voice even. What the hell was his problem? He called me for help, and was being an ass when I tried to give it. "Just get her regular pads," I said finally. "Ones with wings. Unscented. Try and find some with colorful packaging."

"Regular. Wings. Unscented. Pretty," he repeated. "Thanks."

He hung up without saying goodbye, and I forced myself to set my phone calmly on the countertop instead of tossing it across the room. It shouldn't have been a big deal that he was short with me. People had bad moods. Intellectually, I knew that. But my stomach churned with anxiety, anyway.

Chapter 8

Mack

I LEANED BACK in bed and finished my beer in one huge swallow. I didn't bring the twelve-pack into my room like I wanted to, but I'd already made my way through four out of the six I'd set on my nightstand. Still wasn't relaxed. Still didn't know what the fuck I was supposed to do about my daughter, who'd barely looked in my direction during dinner because she was so damn embarrassed about something that shouldn't be embarrassing at all. Still felt like shit about how I'd snapped at Rose.

I cracked open another bottle and set it on my chest, the glass cool against my skin. I was out of my fucking depth and I knew it. I'd been banking on Kara being able to talk to my mom about all the woman shit, periods and makeup and boys, ignoring the fact that my parents were out of state most of the year. Stupid, yeah, but how the fuck was I supposed to prepare for that shit? I'd had the sex talk with Kara when she was ten and came home spouting off bullshit she'd heard at school. Both of us had been uncomfortable as hell, but I hadn't wanted her believing all the wrong shit kids her age pieced together from overheard conversations and crap on the internet.

Kara hadn't wanted me tonight, and that burned. I took another drink of my beer and stared at the ceiling. She'd wanted to be anywhere but at home, talking to anyone but me, and I was pretty sure her tears had been more about asking me to get her supplies than the fact that she'd started her period. I didn't know what to do. She'd always been my little sidekick. If she was hurt, she wanted her daddy. If she was happy, she wanted me. Hell, if she was pissed, she wanted to take it out on me. But this wasn't something that she wanted me anywhere near, and that fucking killed me.

It meant things were changing, and I wasn't fucking ready for that.

When Rose had offered to get Kara some stuff at the store, for a split second, I'd considered taking her up on it. Hell, it would've been easy to let Rose come in and save the day, with her no-nonsense attitude and knowledge of shit I had no idea about. But then I'd been pissed for even considering it, and irritated that she'd asked.

Rose was my woman, and I had a lot of fun with her. I was crazy for her, if I was being honest. But she wasn't Kara's mother, and never would be. I didn't want her stepping into that role. There was no way in hell I'd ever give that kind of power to someone else, not after what we'd already been through.

I still felt like an asshole, though, for the way I'd handled things earlier in the day. I should've said thanks, but no thanks, and instead I'd snapped at her and hung up on her. Fuck. I'd be lucky if she even answered her phone when I called. Rose wasn't exactly the forgiving type, not if her prank wars were anything to go by. I'd seen her refuse to talk to Tommy for an entire month once because he'd eaten the pizza she'd left in her parents' fridge.

Screw it. I wasn't going to spend all night wondering if Rose was pissed at me. She could be pissed all she wanted, but she'd still come back. The chemistry was too good for her to stay away. I huffed and took another drink. I knew firsthand that this thing between us was too hard to walk away from.

※ ※ ※

WHEN I WOKE up the next morning, Kara was already dressed and ready downstairs.

"Hey, princess," I greeted, running my hand down her ponytail as I walked toward the coffee pot. "You're up early."

"Can I go to Charlie's today?" she asked, pausing with her spoonful of cereal halfway to her mouth. "I called her last night and her mom said it was cool."

"She did, huh?" I asked. I'd been contemplating calling in to work and taking my girl for some fun, but I could tell by the stubborn set to her chin that wasn't going to fly. If I was reading her right, she wanted to get away from me. Wasn't that some shit.

"Please, Dad," she said, trying and failing to keep the whine out of her voice. "I don't want to hang at the clubhouse all day. *Please*."

"Fine with me," I said as I poured my coffee.

We both went silent, and I had no fucking clue what to say.

"You feelin' okay?" I finally asked.

Kara's face went beet red. "I'm *fine*."

"It's nothin' to be embarrassed about," I replied, making her blush even harder.

"I'm not embarrassed," she lied.

"Women have been bleedin' once a month for thousands of—"

"Jeez, Dad!" she yelled. "I'm fine."

"It's gonna happen again," I continued. "And I don't want you thinkin' it's somethin' you gotta hide, or—"

I stopped talking when she stood from her chair and raced out of the room.

Well, that had gone fucking fantastic.

I kept my mouth shut for the rest of the morning, and things were almost normal by the time I dropped Kara at Casper's place.

"Bye, Dad," Kara said quickly, not even bothering to take off her helmet before dashing up the porch steps.

I followed her at a more reasonable pace and reached the doorway just as she went inside.

"Hey, Mack," Farrah said, meeting me at the door.

"Thanks for having her over," I replied as she gave me a sympathetic look and stepped outside. "She didn't want to hang at the club today."

"Charlie told me," she said, giving me a look. "How you holding up, Papa?"

I laughed. "I'm not ready for her to grow up," I said seriously.

"Well, you can't stop it," she replied, smiling. "Believe me, I've tried."

"Yeah." I shook my head. "She was embarrassed. Because of *me*."

"I'll talk to her today about shit, see if I can get a read on her," Farrah said. "First periods are weird when you've got a mom to talk to, I'm sure it's worse when you're dealing with a dad. Hell, I don't think Cody's ever even acknowledged that our girls have a monthly visitor."

"It's a fuckin' natural event," I said in frustration. "It's not a big deal."

"Well, aren't you progressive?" Farrah teased. "Don't worry. The girls didn't even like talking to me about it at that age."

I huffed and Farrah laughed. "If it's that bad, why don't you let Rose take the lead on this one? The girls never wanted to talk to me, but they did talk to Trix. And Lily went to CeeCee, if I remember right."

"Nah." I shook my head.

"So, it's like that, huh?" Farrah replied knowingly.

"Like what?"

"She's in your bed, but that's it?" There was an edge to her voice that hadn't been there before, and the hair on the back of my neck stood straight up. Farrah was Rose's aunt, they were as close as mother and daughter, and I had to tread carefully.

"That's not how it is," I replied. "But we aren't to the point where Rose is makin' decisions about my kid or steppin' into that role."

"Will she eventually?" Farrah asked.

"Don't know," I said, lying through my teeth.

"Well, you better figure that shit out," Farrah shot back. "Because my niece isn't gonna sit on the sidelines for long, not when she's spending most nights at your house, eating dinner and hanging out like a family with you and *your* kid."

I looked at her in surprise.

"I hear everything, man," she said, her eyes on mine. "And just saying, I know where to bury a body that no one will ever find."

"Message received," I muttered.

"Take this as it's meant," she said seriously. "I like you for Rose. You're good for her, and I think you guys work. But don't fuck her around. Because, full disclosure, I'd be the least of your worries if you do."

"We're dating and shit is good," I replied, growing irritated with the whole conversation. "That's where we're at right now."

Farrah nodded.

"Thanks again for keeping Kara today." I walked down the steps calmly, even though I wanted to jog away from Farrah's knowing gaze. As I got to my bike, she walked to the edge of the porch and crossed her arms over her chest.

"People look at Rose," she called out, making me pause, "and they see what a badass she is. They remember that she never lets anything go, she gives as good as she gets, and she's got no problem going toe-to-toe with a man twice her size. But that girl has a soft heart, soft as hell. They remember how she protected Lil when she couldn't see—but they didn't see her sleeping in Lil's bed for months so she wouldn't wake up afraid. They didn't see how she cut up Lil's food, or made sure every fucking day that Lil's clothes matched for school and she didn't have food in her teeth or anything else that would embarrass her."

"I hear you," I replied.

"Rose is a born caregiver. She thrives on taking care of the people she loves." She paused. "Don't you dare shit on that."

I nodded and climbed on my bike. I heard what she was saying, but that didn't change anything. Farrah hadn't counted on someone to parent her kids, only to have them disappear. And yeah, Mia had been sick, and I knew it wasn't her fault—but it still happened. Shit like that happened all the time. Rose was an even worse bet when it came right down to it, because she could just bail, and then where would that leave Kara? Grieving for another lost mom? Fuck that shit. I wasn't going to put my kid through that ever again. Rose would find her place in our family. I was beginning to think that she'd be my partner in every other way, eventually. But she'd never be Kara's mother.

"WHAT THE FUCK happened?" Dragon yelled, throwing a wrench across the garage. He looked over Grease's shoulder and met my eyes. "Mack!"

I strode toward him, dread pooling in my belly.

"—Ham was knocked out and Rocky's laid up with a broken femur. His bike's toast."

"Where were Bro and Charles?" I asked, dreading the answer. The prospects were a couple of our best, but they were green as hell.

"They were there," Grease said. "They're fine. Shook up, but fine."

"They took the entire motherfuckin' truck," Dragon spat, his hands fisted at his sides.

"Jesus." I closed my eyes and forced myself not to lose my temper. Didn't look good for the officers to lose their shit, and Dragon had already met our quota for the day throwing that wrench.

"Gotta ask Casper how much that'll set us back, but it's not good," Grease said.

"I'm goin' on the next one," I replied. "Four men shoulda been plenty. Somethin' ain't right."

"Rock says they ran him and Ham off the road—he didn't see how they stopped the truck," Grease said.

"And the prospects?"

"They said they kept goin', but the fuckers got ahead of them and created some type of roadblock," he answered.

"You trust them?" Dragon asked me.

"I did," I shot back. "Don't now."

"We can't be makin' that type of mistake."

"Won't happen again," I replied. "Shouldn't have sent prospects in the first place, but I figured Ham and Rock would have a handle on it."

"No more prospects drivin' trucks," Grease said firmly. "I get what you were doing, and I woulda done the same, but no more unpatched members on any run while we deal with this shit."

"Understood."

I went back to work, but had a hard time focusing, I was so fucking pissed. It looked like shit was about to get squirrely again, and I didn't have the goddamn time for it. I wished we knew who this new player was, stealing shit instead of making their own contacts and doing their own business, but Casper and Poet hadn't heard a word. Things were so quiet on the street it was eerie. After a while, I gave up trying to figure out what was wrong with the Nissan I was working on and walked outside to take a break and call my parents.

"Hello," my mom sang happily when she answered. "How's my favorite son?"

"Your only son is fine," I replied. Even with all the shit going down, I couldn't hold back a smile. "How're you two?"

"We're good. On the road."

"You headed this way?" I asked, mentally crossing my fingers.

"At the moment, we're headed to Montana," she replied. "Should we be headed toward you?"

"Kara started her period yesterday," I blurted, dropping my ass onto one of the picnic tables out front. "And she's bein' super fuckin' weird about it."

"Of course she is," my mom said knowingly. "She doesn't want her *dad* to know about it."

"I've known about everythin' else her entire life."

"Sorry, son," she said with a chuckle. "You don't have the right parts to be in on that particular conversation."

"Yeah." I sighed. "I'm beginning to realize that."

"She'll come around. I'll call her tomorrow and see how she's doing."

"On top of that, I'm gonna have to start travelin' a bit," I said, staring at my boots. "And I hate to ask—"

"You need us to come home?"

"If you can. I'll figure somethin' else out if that fucks with your plans too much," I said quickly.

"Honey, the whole point is that we don't make plans," she said easily. "Howie, Jacob's asking if we can come help with Kara for a while."

She was quiet for a second.

"Should take us about two days to get there," she said when she came back on the phone. "Will that work?"

"That works just fine." I let out a huge sigh of relief. "Thanks, Ma."

"Of course," she said easily. "I've been wanting to meet your girlfriend, anyway."

"Shit," I muttered, making her laugh.

"I'm not that bad."

"Nah, you're not bad *at all*," I replied jokingly.

"It'll be great. Make sure you clear out that space for the RV, so we have someplace to park." She grew quiet for a minute. "Never mind," she said with a sigh. "Your dad says we're going to get a camp spot."

"I don't mind if you guys park it at the house."

"You'll be doin' your own thing," my dad yelled so I could hear him. "We'll take Kara for a bit and give ya some time alone with your woman."

I grinned.

"Apparently, we'd be cramping your style," my mom said ruefully.

"Either way," I replied. "Can't wait to see ya."

"Me, either. Love you."

"Love you. Dad, too."

"I'll tell him. Bye, son."

I dropped the phone to my side and felt like a huge weight lifted off my chest. I had a lot of help with Kara, the club family was awesome that way, but there was nothing like having my parents in town.

"Yo, you gonna work today or what?" Will called from the garage. "In case you hadn't noticed, we're fuckin' swamped."

"I'm on my way," I hollered. "Untwist your panties."

"Fuck you," he shot back. "Molly likes me commando."

"No one wants to hear that," I said as I reached the garage.

It was going to be a long ass day, working on that Nissan and figuring out what the hell had happened on the run I'd planned and, like a moron, had left others to execute.

I also I needed to figure out what the fuck I was going to do about Rose. She hadn't texted or called since the day before—which wasn't like her. She was pissed, for sure, and I was going to have to fix that on top of everything else.

For a second, I contemplated just letting it lie. She could be pissed all she wanted—if she wanted to be done, that was one less thing on my plate. But I dismissed that train of thought almost immediately. There was no way I was giving Rose up.

By the time I left the garage, I was tired, sweaty, and had a throbbing tension headache. Kara had called, asking to spend the night with Charlie, which wasn't a surprise. I was actually thankful that my kid was trying to escape me, because I still hadn't heard from Rose and I needed to fix that shit. Letting it fester would only make things worse.

I took my time in the shower, letting the cool water run over my tired shoulders and arms and while I figured out how to smooth things over with Rose. Twenty minutes later, I was walking into the shop where she'd bought my gift certificate. Thirty minutes after that, I was walking into the bar where Rose was slinging drinks.

I stepped aside as someone came in behind me, taking a minute to look at her before she noticed me. She was wearing a black t-shirt and her hair was piled on top of her head in a bun, and I grinned at the fact that she didn't seem to give a shit that the man leaning toward her at the bar was definitely trying to pick her up. She laughed and rolled her eyes at whatever he said, then moved away, forgetting he even existed. Jesus, she was hot. Especially when she was in her element, chatting with people and pouring beers like it was her favorite thing in the world to do. I moved toward her.

When she noticed me at the bar, she raised one eyebrow and went back to what she was doing, which automatically made me want to catch her attention again. Instead, I waited.

"What can I get you?" she asked as she finally made her way toward me.

"You," I replied, holding back a laugh when she scoffed.

"I can't even tell you the number of times someone has said that to me," she said. "Or some version of it."

"But I actually have a shot," I replied.

"Debatable," she said, crossing her arms over her chest.

"Sorry I was a dick," I said quietly. Better to get that out first. I didn't like apologizing a whole lot, but I knew she deserved that first thing.

"Forgiven," she said easily. "What are you doing here?"

"Brought you a present," I said, setting the box in my hand on the bar top.

I knew the moment she realized what I'd done because her eyes widened.

"You didn't," she murmured.

"Open it."

She pulled the box toward her and lifted the lid, her smile lighting up the damn room.

"These are gorgeous," she said, pulling the black Harley boots out. "Holy shit."

"Gonna need somethin' better than the high tops you've been wearin'," I said, grinning.

"How did you know my size?" she asked, running her fingers over the leather.

"I notice shit," I replied.

"Wait," she said, pausing to look at me. "Why do I need boots?"

"Wanna ride up to Seattle next week?" I asked, holding her gaze.

"Hell yes," she said, her smile growing bigger. "But if you get one of those t-shirts that says *if you can read this, the bitch fell off*, I'll nut punch you."

A startled laugh fell out of my mouth. "I hadn't even thought of that," I said honestly.

"Tommy did that the first time Hawk went with him on a charity run," she said ruefully. "I thought she was going to murder him in his sleep."

"I give you permission to murder me if I ever act like your brother Tommy," I replied.

"Deal." She leaned across the counter and crooked her finger at me so I'd lean in and kiss her.

"You smell good," I said against her lips as her fingers slid down the side of my throat.

Rose laughed. "I haven't even showered today," she said, pulling away. She pointed to her hair, like that was supposed to mean something.

"Still smell good," I said with a shrug. "You wanna shower at my place tonight? We could make it a group activity."

"A group?" she teased. "How many people you plan on inviting over?"

I took the joke as it was meant and chuckled, but it still made my stomach lurch. There was no way in hell I'd ever share Rose, with a man *or* a woman.

"Just me and you, baby," I replied.

"I get off at midnight."

"Probably again at 12:30," I said, making her grin. "We'll see how it goes from there."

"Sweet talker."

"Always."

CHAPTER 9

ROSE

"STOP FUSSIN'," MACK ordered as I fidgeted with my hair. "You look fine."

It was nine o'clock at night, and we were expecting Mack's parents to pull up at any moment. Things had gone back to normal after Mack had apologized, and if I was honest with myself, I knew that I'd been testing him. Sure, I'd been pissed when he'd snapped at me on the phone, but it hadn't really been that big a deal—not if I looked at it logically. But we all have baggage, and part of mine was a history of relationships with men that treated me like crap. I was determined not to let myself fall into the familiar habit of letting things go just to keep the peace, so I'd stood my ground and given him the silent treatment until he'd said he was sorry. It wasn't my finest moment, but oh, well. His apology had given me the reassurance I'd needed.

Of course, a new pair of hotshit boots hadn't hurt, either.

But now, Kara was bouncing around the house with excitement and Mack was looking out the screen door every five minutes, and I was freaking out. The three of us had a good thing going, we'd formed a little unit that worked. Now, we were adding two more people to the mix. People Mack adored. People who could change everything if they didn't like me.

I had never been so nervous to meet someone's parents in my life.

"They're here!" Kara squealed suddenly, bolting out of the house.

"Showtime," Mack said to me, smiling as he grabbed my hand and tugged me out the door.

By the time we reached the front steps, Mack's parents had parked and were climbing out of a mid-size RV, stretching their arms above their heads and grinning from ear to ear.

"Nana!" Kara yelled, heading for Mack's mom first.

"Holy cow," his mom replied as Kara flung herself into the older woman's arms. "You've grown at least a foot since we saw you in April!"

"Two inches," Kara said proudly.

"You're going to be as tall as me soon," Mack's mom said indulgently.

I didn't think that would be happening, ever. If I guessed right, Mack's mom was nearly six feet tall. Slender and angular, with cheekbones that looked like they could cut glass, she may have been the most striking woman I'd ever seen. She also kind of looked like someone who gave great hugs.

"I thought men went for women who reminded them of their mothers," I said under my breath, making Mack chuckle.

"What about me?" Mack's dad called to Kara, swinging her up in his arms with a laugh.

Where Mack's mom was all angles, Mack's dad was not. He was big and barrel chested, and even though he was in his sixties, he didn't look like he'd lost a bit of muscle. The man was built like a tank, and now I knew exactly what Mack would look like in thirty years.

"We're here!" Mack's mom called, striding toward us. "I swear, the last few hours are always the longest when you're headed home."

"Hey, Ma," Mack said, meeting her at the bottom of the steps for a hug.

"You look good," she said, kissing his cheek.

He took a step back and gestured to me. "This is Rose."

"Hi, Rose," she said, reaching out to shake my hand. "I'm Louise."

"It's nice to finally meet you," I said, as she used her opposite hand to pat the top of our shaking ones.

"I'll save your kisses for when you know me better," she said with a smile.

"Thank Christ," Mack mumbled.

"Hey," I said, elbowing him in the side as Louise let go of my hand. "I like kisses."

"I'll give you all the kisses you need," he shot back, making my face go red as his mom laughed merrily.

"Lou," Mack's dad called as he came toward us with Kara hanging on his back like a monkey. "Have you seen Kara? I can't find her anywhere."

"Grandpa," Kara said with a sigh. "That stopped being funny when I was five."

"Did you hear something?" his dad joked as he reached us. "You must be Rose. I'm Howie."

"Nice to meet you," I said, shaking his hand.

"Lou try to kiss you yet?" he asked, his eyes twinkling. "She's a kisser."

"Not yet," I replied. "But the night is young."

"You're gonna scare her off," Mack said, moving forward to give his dad a hug as Kara dropped from his back. "Good to see you, Dad."

"Likewise," Howie said gruffly, patting Mack's shoulder.

We followed Mack's parents back into the house, and I felt the tension in my shoulders fade away. I wasn't sure if Howie and Louise would like me, but I already knew I liked them.

❦ ❦ ❦

"Give me that sound I like," Mack murmured against my ear as his fingers found my clit. His hips slapped against my ass as he thrust, and I pressed my cheek against the bed, my hands fisted in the sheet. "Come on, baby. No one can hear you."

I stubbornly refused to give him what he asked for and felt him chuckle against my neck. Sliding my hand underneath my hips, I reached back as far as I could and cupped his balls, using my middle finger to rub the spot right behind them.

I smiled as Mack groaned.

"Playin' dirty," he muttered, his hips moving faster.

"You like it dirty," I gasped back. I held my breath for just a moment, and that's when my orgasm hit hard. I couldn't have stopped the moan that fell from my lips if I'd tried.

"That's the noise I wanted," Mack said through gritted teeth. Seconds later, he was coming, too.

I fell onto my belly as Mack's hands slid around my sides and swept feather-light up my back.

"Gonna take care of this condom," he said as he pulled out. He leaned down and kissed the space between my shoulder blades before crawling off the bed. "'Cause as soon as I lay down, I'm gonna pass the fuck out."

"Water," I mumbled, reaching blindly for my glass on the nightstand.

I leaned up and took a sip, then sighed as I pushed myself up to find my underwear. I was all about sleeping naked, but not with Mack's parents and Kara sleeping right outside in the RV. They were planning on camping in one of the local parks, but by the time we got done visiting, it had been too late for them to go looking for a spot.

"Whatcha doin'?" Mack asked as he walked back into the room.

"Putting some clothes back on," I replied, staring as I stepped into my underwear. "But feel free to sleep naked."

Mack laughed. "Nah, I'll put some shorts on. You want a shirt?"

"I can use this one," I said, lifting the shirt I'd stripped him out of.

I sputtered as he smacked it playfully out of my hand.

"That one reeks," he said, laughing. "I was sweatin' in it all day. I'll get you a fresh one."

By the time we climbed into bed, I was yawning.

"Told you they'd like you," Mack said as he pulled me against his chest. "They're cool."

"Cool is an understatement," I replied. "Your parents are freaking magical."

He chuckled. "How so?"

"They just wander around the US, no destination in mind, living like freaking vagabonds," I said in wonder. "And they make friends everywhere. Did you hear your mom telling us about that guy they found in Yellowstone that they're pen pals with now? Who does that?"

"Louise does that," Mack replied. "That guy's probably wondering what the fuck he got himself into."

"He writes her back!"

"Guilt," he said jokingly. "They're lucky they've got a fantastic son that forwards their mail to 'em whenever they stay in one place long enough."

"Well, I think they're awesome," I said firmly. "They love you guys."

"Of course they do," Mack replied easily.

"No, they *adore* you," I insisted, leaning up to meet his eyes. "Your parents think the sun shines out of your ass."

"Your parents feel that way about you, too," he pointed out.

"Well, yeah," I huffed, laying back down. "Because I'm their only girl. They love the boys a lot less."

I smiled as Mack's chest shook with silent laughter beneath my head.

"Howie and Lou dug the hell outta you," he said, rubbing his hand up and down my back. "Don't be surprised if you gain a fuckin' pen pal."

"That would completely make my year," I replied seriously.

"I love you," he said quietly.

I froze, unsure if I'd heard him correctly. If I had, holy shit. If I hadn't... what had he said?

"Could you repeat that?" I asked, swallowing hard.

"I love you," he said louder.

I closed my eyes and let the words wash over me. I'd heard them before. Men had been telling me they loved me since I slept with my bull-faced prom date in high school. Some said it during sex, some said it jokingly, and some were completely serious, but I'd never felt the words all the way to my bones the way I did then. It was like I was covered in a weighted blanket and Pop Rocks were crackling in my belly at the same time.

"You gotta say somethin'," Mack murmured. "Even a *thank you* would be okay."

"I love you," I said quickly, climbing on top of him, my legs straddling his hips. I peppered his face in kisses, and pulled back to grin at him.

"Thought I was tired," he said, reaching up to slide his fingers into my hair. He pulled me down for a kiss. "Feelin' all sorts of awake now, though."

Our kiss was interrupted by Mack's phone ringing loudly on the nightstand.

"The fuck?" he said in frustration. "Who the fuck is callin' at two in the goddamn morning?"

He reached out and snagged the phone, cursing when he saw the name lighting up the screen.

"Yo," he barked. His hand patted my hip, and he was up and out of bed as soon as I'd climbed off his lap. "When?"

My eyes widened as he started dressing quickly.

"Give me twenty," he said before hanging up. He turned to me. "Sorry, baby. I gotta go."

"What?" I sat up in bed, alarm making my stomach twist. "What's wrong?"

"Club shit," he said dismissively.

I scoffed. "That won't work with me," I shot back.

Mack paused from putting on his boots and turned to look at me. "Right," he said with a shake of his head. "Club business. Everyone's fine, I just gotta go take care of some shit."

I let out a breath of relief. Calls in the middle of the night were never good, but if everyone was okay, I could deal. "Should I go home?" I asked quietly, watching him pull on a hoodie.

"Hell, no," he said in surprise. "I'll be back in a while, and I want ya waitin', all warm and sleepy in my bed."

"You know you won't be back tonight," I murmured against his mouth as he leaned down to kiss me goodbye.

"I'll do my damnedest," he said, pulling back just far enough to meet my eyes. "If not, there's pancake shit in the pantry for breakfast and bacon in the fridge. Hang with my parents until I get here?"

"No problem," I said, leaning up to kiss him again.

"Jesus," he muttered. "You're fuckin' perfect."

"Remember that," I ordered as he pulled away.

"Hard to forget," he said with a grin.

"Keep your head on a swivel," I called out as he walked away.

"Say what?" he asked, laughing.

"I always wanted to say that," I admitted with a shrug. "Love you."

Mack's eyes grew soft. "Love you, too, baby. Be back in a bit."

He strode out the door, and I listened to him jog down the stairs. Within moments, his bike started up. As the sound of his motorcycle faded away down the street, I sighed. Then I giggled.

He loved me. He was a fantastic dad, a hard worker, close to his parents, and damn near perfect for me on every level, and he loved me. I'd finally hit the jackpot.

"We heard him leave," Lou told me the next morning while we cooked breakfast. "Hard to miss those pipes."

"They are pretty distinctive," I replied, shooting her a smile.

"But we figured he just had to run to the store or something," she said with a shrug.

"The store?" Why would he go to the store in the middle of the—

"For rubbers," she whispered, glancing over her shoulder to make sure Kara didn't hear her as my mouth dropped open in shock.

"Uh, no," I stuttered. "We have plenty."

"Good," she said with a nod. "Can't be too careful."

What in God's name was happening, and how did I stop it?

"Oh, don't be such a stick in the mud," she teased. "You're red as a tomato."

"I'm usually not," I replied, trying to school my expression. "You surprised me."

"Then I've done my job," she said, smiling. "I'd never want to be predictable."

"You're definitely not that," I muttered, making her laugh. The sound was low and raspy, and I loved it.

"You're good for them," she said, bumping me with her hip. "I can tell. Kara wouldn't stop talking about you in the camper last night."

"I'm pretty popular with the tween crowd," I replied. "It's because I swear so much."

"I'm pretty sure it's more than that," Lou said. Before she'd finished speaking, I heard Mack's bike outside.

"Dad's home," Kara yelled from the living room.

"As if we couldn't hear it," Lou said with a chuckle.

I smiled as I flipped pancakes, but my stomach exploded with butterflies. Mack had left before we could spend any time post-I love you, and I was anxious to see him. Would things be different? Would he say it again? In front of his parents?

"Jesus, I'm wiped," Mack said in the living room. "You guys eat yet?"

"Your mom and Rose are cookin' now," Howie replied.

"You're not helpin'?" Mack asked Kara.

"No, Grandpa said he wanted to kick my butt at checkers, so Nana said I could clean up instead."

"Alright," Mack replied.

Then, he was in the kitchen and I couldn't stop the wide smile that pulled at my cheeks.

"Hey, Ma," Mack greeted as he came toward us. He stopped right in front of me. "Hey, baby," he said, leaning down to give me a sweet kiss. "You sleep okay?"

"Without you taking up most of the bed?" I teased. "I slept like a rock."

Mack chuckled. "Good."

"You get everything straightened up at the club?" Lou asked, watching us with an indulgent smile.

Mack sent a guarded look my way.

"I told her about the fight that broke out," I said, keeping my voice even. "No one's hurt, I hope?"

"Nah," Mack said, catching on easily. "Just a bunch of drunk idiots."

"Sounds like any other party," I said, turning back to the pancakes.

"I'm gonna take a quick shower," Mack said, resting one hand on my hip as he kissed the top of my head. "I'll be right back."

"You have time," Lou said.

After he walked away, we were quiet as we cooked. Then, without warning, Lou wrapped her arm around my waist and squeezed, giving me a kiss on my temple. "See?" she said. "You're good for him."

I smiled at her and shrugged.

Breakfast was loud and fun. We ate on the patio and I got to know Howie a little better. He was a lot like his son, both funny and serious, and I found myself laughing until my stomach hurt as he told me stories about life on the road. He and Lou had planned their entire lives for the moment they could retire and take off, and every word out of his mouth proved how much he loved it. I had to admit, I was a little jealous. I'd gone with Lily to college on the other side of the US, but I'd rarely traveled away from the western states otherwise. Maybe one day Mack would want to do the same thing, just take off and travel for a while.

I glanced over at him and smiled at the way he was laughing at his mom, his body bent at the waist.

"I did not," Lou said imperiously. "I never told you that."

"You did, too!" He looked over at Kara. "She told me that if I didn't pull my tooth out, the Tooth Fairy was gonna come and yank it out while I was sleepin'. 'Cause *the Tooth Fairy ain't got the patience for your shit.*"

"I really didn't say that," Lou said, throwing her napkin at Mack.

"Okay, I'm paraphrasin', but that was the gist of it." He turned to Howie. "Dad? Am I right?"

"I gotta live with the woman in a camper," Howie said, nodding his head. "So I can't confirm that." He continued nodding his head as he looked at Kara.

"You're so full of it," Lou said with a laugh. She glanced down at her watch. "Honey, we better get a move on, or we're not gonna be able to find a good spot before everyone starts showing up for the weekend."

"Yeah," Howie said with a sigh. "You're probably right."

"Can I come with?" Kara asked hopefully.

"Okay with me," Lou said.

"Clear the table and load the dishes first," Mack told his daughter.

"I'll wash the pans for you."

"Thanks, Dad!"

I stood up to help Kara clear and Mack put his hand on my ass to stop me.

"It's part of her chores," he reminded me quietly.

"I don't mind," I whispered back, leaning down to kiss his cheek. "Plus, the sooner they leave, the sooner we can get naked."

He laughed and leaned back in his seat. "How can I argue with that?"

"*Mmhmm*," I murmured.

Fifteen minutes later, we watched as Lou drove the RV away with Kara in the passenger seat and Howie following behind them in the Mustang.

"Do you keep the Mustang so your dad has something to drive when they're here?" I asked, following Mack into the house.

"No," he replied, shaking his head. "I keep the Mustang 'cause it's a hot fucking car and it took me years to rebuild. They could rent a car if they wanted to get around. But I do keep those fuckin' aviator shades in the glove compartment for him."

I laughed.

"Come here," he said, pulling me toward the couch. He dropped down onto it with a sigh and let go of my hand. "Strip."

"What?"

"Come on," he said, smiling as he leaned back into the cushions. "Gimme a show, baby."

I snorted, then realized he was completely serious.

"You want a show?"

"Yep."

"Want me to turn on some music?" I asked dryly.

"I want you to take off your clothes," he replied.

It should have been awkward, but it wasn't. As I slowly took off my clothes, he sat patiently, his eyes never leaving me. By the time I was down to my bra and underwear, his hands were fisted at his sides, but he didn't move.

"Jesus," he murmured as soon as I was stripped bare. "You might be the most beautiful woman on the planet."

"Might be?" I asked jokingly as I moved forward and straddled him.

"Haven't seen all of 'em," he replied, grinning as I pinched his side. "How the hell did I land you?"

"Pure dumb luck," I shot back. "And the ability to make anything sound dirty."

"I knew that would come in handy someday," he said, reaching up to fist his hands in my hair.

Mack kissed me hard, all lips and teeth and tongue, and I lost my mind. I tore at his clothes, barely getting his t-shirt off before his fingers were sliding inside me, hitting just the right spot. We didn't even bother with his jeans, pushing them down just far enough to pull his cock out. I was glad Mack had the presence of mind to roll on a condom, because I wasn't thinking. I was too busy feeling. The rasp of his beard on my neck, the scratch of his jeans against my thighs, and the smooth skin of his shoulders under my fingertips had me on overload. It was fast and desperate and neither of us lasted long.

Later, after we'd moved to bed and fallen asleep, I woke up to Mack's fingers running slowly up my thigh. That time was slow and even better.

※ ※ ※

THE WEEK PASSED quickly, full of visits with Mack's parents between working at both jobs, packing for our trip—when you can only bring a backpack, you have to be strategic about it—and stumbling into bed with Mack in the middle of the night, only to wake up with him a few hours later. By the time we got to the clubhouse Friday morning I was a tired, haggard mess.

"Look at you, riding in on the back of Mack's bike," my sister-in-law Hawk teased out of the side of her mouth. "Someone's an old lady."

"Yeah, yeah," I grumbled, my lips twitching. "Is Tommy wearing his shirt today?"

"Not if he values his nuts," she replied breezily.

"Please don't talk about Tommy's anatomy," Lily said as she strode up to us. "I'd like to keep my breakfast in my stomach."

"His dick is fantastic," Hawk said, jogging away as Lily slapped at her.

"Those two are freaks," I told Lily, watching as Hawk pinched my brother's ass and took off running.

"They're freaking made for each other," Lily replied. "And speaking of made for each other… things look like they're going well with you and Mack."

"They are," I said, grinning. "Sorry I haven't called. Shit has been crazy."

"His parents are in town, right?" Lily said as we walked inside the club. "How has that been?"

"Great," I replied with a shrug. "They're the nicest people ever."

"Not surprising," Lily said. "Look at the kid they made."

"True story."

"You ready for this?" she asked, gesturing at the room full of people.

"What do you mean?" I asked in confusion. "I've been around this all my life."

"Runs are different," she said, throwing her arm over my shoulder. "Riding on the back of your man's bike is different."

"I think I can handle it," I said with a laugh.

"Trust me," she said seriously. "It's one thing going as one of the brother's kids—that shit is tame. This'll be different."

"I'm good."

"Okay." She nodded. "But don't come crying to me when your ass is numb from riding."

"I'm gonna ask you to rub it for me," I said, smiling huge.

"You have Mack for that now," she shot back.

I made my way around the room, saying my hellos, but it didn't take long before we were all headed back outside. Watching the bikes move in a massive group was something to see, but riding in that group was something else. I'd always felt free on the back of a bike, but this time, I felt powerful. People stopped to stare as we rode through town, and other motorists changed lanes to let us pass, watching in awe as the men rode in sync, like one huge entity.

By the time we reached Seattle hours later, my ass was numb, just like Lily had warned me it would be. I was surprised when my legs buckled a little getting off the bike.

"Whoa," Mack said, grabbing me by the hips. "You good?"

"I can't feel my legs," I muttered, pulling off my helmet.

He laughed. "Give it a minute."

"We're staying here tonight?" I asked as I glanced around the property. The club that was hosting us was situated outside the city on a few acres covered in trees. Their clubhouse was an actual house, big, but still a house. I wasn't even sure how we'd all fit inside, there was no way we could sleep there.

"Prospects have some tents in the pickup," Mack replied.

"Well, you better set up far away from everyone else," I said, watching as my parents climbed off my dad's bike. "Because I'm loud when I'm drunk."

"Can't fuckin' wait," Mack said, his hands sliding to my ass to squeeze it.

There was a lot of backslapping and laughing as our members greeted the other club, and I loved watching Mack in his element. He knew everyone, and they all seemed to like him. More than once, I noticed men walking away from conversations to come say hello.

"Grease's kid, right?" a grizzled old man asked me after saying hello to Mack. "Hell, it's been years since I saw you last. Think you had pigtails then."

"That was my preferred hairstyle for a long time," I confirmed, smiling at the way he cackled.

"Well, it's nice to see you, sweetheart. 'Specially with this guy. Good as they come."

"I know," I replied as Mack pulled me against his side.

I glanced over the man's shoulder, and froze as I saw Copper striding out of the house behind him. Sonofabitch.

"All good, baby," Mack said quietly in my ear. "He'll keep his distance."

I wasn't so sure, but I nodded, anyway. Copper was walking around saying hi to everyone like he didn't have a care in the world. Most of them treated him like they'd treat any other member, with handshakes and hugs, but my brothers and parents were far more reserved, and I was pretty sure if my Aunt Farrah could have killed him with her eyes, she would've.

"There's a good spot by the lake," the older man was telling Mack as I forced myself to pay attention to the conversation. "Left of the house, start walkin' and you can't miss it."

"Thanks, man," Mack said. "I'm gonna set us up real quick before things get goin' around here."

"Holler if you need anythin' at all," the old timer replied.

He walked away and Mack tugged me toward the truck.

"Might as well get situated," he said. "We're not gonna wanna be building shit in the dark."

"We?" I joked. "I never said I'd pitch a tent."

"I'll pitch it," Mack said, climbing into the back of the truck. "You just sit there and look pretty."

"Well," I huffed. "That was patronizing."

Mack looked up from what he was doing. "You just said you weren't gonna help."

"Maybe I will help *now*."

"Good," he said, throwing a tent bag over his shoulder. "Because this thing is a bitch to build with only one person. Grab our sleeping bags off the tailgate, yeah?"

"Ooh," I said, picking up the sleeping bags as Mack hopped down. "Are we gonna zip these together to make one big sleeping-bag-for-two?"

"You want to?" he asked as we headed toward our camping spot.

"Hell, yes."

"Then that's what we'll to."

"We should have brought an air mattress," I murmured. He just looked at me like I'd lost my mind.

"We're only gonna be here for two nights."

"Two long nights," I replied.

"Two drunk nights," he shot back.

"Touché," I said with a laugh. "I'm not gonna feel anything when I pass out."

"And I'll let you ride me," he said with a sigh, like he was doing me a huge favor. "So you're more comfortable."

"Such a gentleman," I joked.

"Only the best for my woman."

"The best would be an air mattress," I sang, winking when he scowled at me.

Building the tent and putting our stuff inside didn't take long, and before I could convince Mack to get naked with me for a little afternoon delight, my brothers came to bug us.

"Hey, how'd you find this spot?" Will asked, his eyebrows nearly touching his hairline. "We got stuck near the driveway. It's dusty as hell."

"I know people," Mack said with a chuckle.

"I know all the same people," Tommy said. "This is bullshit. I'm moving our tent over here."

"No, you're not," Will, Mack and I all said at the same time.

"The hell?"

"Think it through," Will muttered. "Three, two, one—"

"Ew, fuck!" Tommy spat, glowering at us.

"My thoughts exactly," I said, flicking his head as I passed him. "Come on, I need a drink."

"You're cute when you're bossy," Mack whispered, throwing his arm over my shoulder. "I could be into that."

"You'd be into anything as long as I was naked," I retorted.

"Fair point."

"It's cool," I said wrapping my arm around his waist. "I'd be into anything with you, too."

"Yeah?" he said, his eyes growing wide as his lips twitched.

"We're not doing any butt stuff while we're here," I replied quietly, pointing at him. "There's nowhere to clean up."

Mack's laughter filled the yard. "Noted."

We grabbed some drinks while the grills heated up, and I found myself in a group of old ladies, listening to my mom tell a story about when my brothers were little. I'd heard it all before, but I loved listening to my mom. From things she'd said over the years, I knew that in the beginning, she hadn't been too excited about my dad's affiliation with the Aces—I couldn't blame her really, since she'd had my brother Will while my dad was locked up—but for as long as I'd known her, she'd fit right in with all the other old ladies.

"How you doin', kid?" my Aunt Farrah asked, running her hand down my hair. "Having fun yet?"

"This is only my first drink," I said, lifting my beer in the air. "Ask me again in about an hour."

"Shit," she said with a chuckle. "I still can't believe you're old enough to drink."

"Hey," I replied. "I've been drinking for years."

"Yeah, yeah," she said. "You make me feel old."

"You have grandchildren," I said, trying to keep my expression neutral. "I'm not the one making you feel old."

Aunt Farrah smiled. "Grandchildren are life's reward for raising your own assholes."

"I'm telling Lily you called her an asshole," I said, jumping away as she swatted at me. "Cam, too!"

"You say that like they'll be surprised," she called as I walked away. "They won't."

"You runnin' from Farrah?"

I scoffed. "I'm not afraid of her."

Mack just looked at me.

"Okay, yeah, that was an outright lie," I admitted.

"Come on," he said, leaning down to kiss me as he grabbed my hand. "I want you to meet some people."

I'd been to plenty of parties at the club, and I'd had fun at almost all of them—but that night outside Seattle was so much better. Mack and I had never really partied *together*, and I was almost giddy as his cheeks grew ruddy and his smile grew wider with every drink he had. My man was serious most of the time, and it was amazing to see him let loose a bit.

The music was loud and the laughter in the yard was even louder. I glanced around the crowd and got a warm feeling in my belly. I was a part of the group of old ladies now, and it was weird, but also pretty cool. My mom sat on my dad's lap like she'd never seen a chair before, Aunt Farrah shook her ass to anything coming out of the speakers while my uncle egged her on, Brenna stood with our President, Dragon, drinking beer and laughing with her hand in his back pocket, Hawk was kicking Tommy's ass at a game of quarters, and Lily... where was Lily? I searched the crowd curiously, and just as I'd almost given up, she and Leo came out of the woods, both of them swaying slightly with huge grins on their faces.

It was a good night, and everyone knew it. No fights had broken out. There'd been no drama. It was just a bunch of people hanging out and catching up with a little help from a kickass sound system and a shitload of alcohol.

"Hey, Mack?" I leaned down and wrapped my arms around his shoulders. "Let's go back to the tent."

"Really?" he asked glancing up at me. The moment our eyes met, I knew I had him.

"I mean, if you want to stay," I trailed off with a shrug.

He turned away for only a second. "Boys," he said with a nod. He immediately finished the last of his beer and stood up.

I had to practically run to keep up with Mack as he led us around the side of the house toward our tent.

"I'm gonna trip," I yelped as I stumbled over a few rocks in the dark.

"Can't have that," Mack replied. He turned and threw me over his shoulder like I was nothing, then kept going as I laughed.

"You have the best ass," I told him, running my hands over it. I tugged his t-shirt up a little so I could push my fingers underneath his jeans.

"Ditto," he replied, smacking my ass.

By the time we reached the tent and he set me back on the ground, I was giggling and pulling at his clothes.

"Shit," he said, running his hand through his hair. "New box of condoms is in my saddlebags."

I groaned.

"I'll run back and get 'em," he said, kissing me. "I'll be right back."

I thought about telling him we could go without, but I knew that wasn't a conversation we should have while we were both drinking, so I kept my mouth shut and nodded instead. "Hurry."

"I'll run like my ass is on fire," he said with a huff of laughter. "Stay put. Don't wanna have to go lookin' for you in the dark."

"Where would I go?" I asked, throwing my hands in the air. "We're in the fucking woods."

He shot me a grin and then jogged off. As soon as I couldn't see him anymore I used my phone to light my way as I climbed into the tent. I'd just pulled my boots and jeans off when I heard him come back.

"You really did run—" I said as I stepped back out of the tent. My words cut off instantly. "What are you doing here?"

"You know, I figured you guys were fuckin'," Copper slurred. "But I was pretty surprised to see ya here."

"You need to leave," I replied, crossing my arms over my chest. Standing there in only my shirt and underwear made me feel vulnerable in a way I really didn't like. "Go, before Mack gets back."

"You think it's cool to just fuck your way through the members?" he said as if I hadn't spoken. "I mean, yeah, club whores do that shit—but I thought you were different."

"Go, Copper," I ordered, trying to keep my voice firm as he sneered at me.

"Daddy's little princess," he mocked. "Drinks with the boys like it's nothin', hangs at the club like she belongs there."

"Seriously, Copper," I snapped. "Get the fuck outta here."

"Your dad know you get on your knees for any dick in sight?" he snapped, taking a step forward. "Maybe he should hear what you're really like."

"Try it," I hissed. My fight or flight response was working overdrive, and I'd never been one to run away. "Say something to my dad. The minute my name came out of your mouth, it would be the last thing you said."

"So fuckin' tough," he said, moving a little closer to me. "When you got your idiot brothers and your dad up your ass all the time, fightin' your battles."

"Fuck you, needle dick," I shot back. "And get the fuck out of here."

He came at me quickly, but I was ready. Adrenaline was racing through me as I braced for impact, knowing that he was either going to hit me or tackle me, and either one would hurt. But before he got within a foot from me, Mack was there, like a wall between me and Copper.

"You motherfuckin' idiot," Mack said darkly. The only sounds after that were the noise a fist makes as it connects with flesh.

It wasn't even a fight. Mack went at him with a singular purpose, and Copper didn't even manage a single swing. I let out a shaky breath as Copper hit the ground, completely knocked out.

"Did he touch you?" Mack asked, spinning toward me. His hands cupped the sides of my head as he searched for injuries.

"No," I said quickly, shaking my head. "No, he was just being an ass."

Mack nodded. "Put some clothes on," he barked.

I flinched at his tone, but didn't say anything as I went for my clothes. Once I was fully dressed again, Mack silently pulled me back toward the party.

"Rose?" my mom asked as we reached my parents. "What's wrong? You're white as a sheet."

"Dragon," Mack said, letting go of my hand. "A word?"

I'd never felt so alone as when Mack strode away from me, my dad and Dragon on his heels. As my mom's face filled my vision, her worried eyes searching mine, my teeth began to chatter and my whole body started to shake.

I was *not* going to cry.

CHAPTER 10

MACK

"HE'S WEARIN' A patch," Dragon reminded me as we stomped back into the woods. "Either of you go off half-cocked, I'll have your heads."

"I fuckin' barely made it in time," I replied through gritted teeth. I couldn't get my jaw to loosen no matter how hard I tried. "If it woulda taken me a few more minutes—"

"Knew that fucker was stupid," Grease muttered. "Didn't know he was suicidal."

Both men went silent at his words.

"Fuck," Grease said. "Sorry, Mack. Poor fuckin' choice of words."

"Forget it," I replied, brushing him off. His words were the least of my worries.

"You heard what he was sayin' to her?" Dragon asked.

"Just the last bit. I started runnin' when I realized he was there."

"What did he say?"

I glanced at Grease and shook my head. "Not repeatin' it."

"Pissed she got shot of him?" Grease asked.

"Pissed he can't take his shit out on her anymore," I replied, increasing my pace. "Pissed she's with a man that won't let him."

When we got to our camping spot, the motherfucker was gone.

"Thought you knocked him out?" Dragon said.

"I did," I confirmed. "Checked his breathin' to make sure he wasn't dead, he was so out."

"Jesus," Grease mumbled. "Where the fuck did he go? We didn't pass him on the way out here."

"He's probably runnin' scared," I spat, checking the tent. "Rose's fuckin' bag is gone."

"He stole her bag?" Dragon asked in surprise.

"What the fuck is wrong with that dipshit?" Grease said in frustration.

"I don't know, but we need a fuckin' sit down," I replied. "From this point forward, he's no brother of mine."

"Hold it," Dragon said warningly.

"How the fuck can I keep Rose safe if he's always lurkin' around?" I said, struggling to keep my voice even. "He came into our camp and started yellin' at my woman while she was half dressed. I get held up for ten minutes, then what? He coulda done anythin' he wanted."

Grease made a sound, and I looked over at him. The veins in his neck were bulging, and he looked ready to lose it.

"We'll deal with it," Dragon said. "Once we're back at the clubhouse. We're not bringin' this shit to someone else's doorstep."

"Know that," I said in disgust. "Why do you think I pulled you away instead of announcin' that shit?"

"Appreciate it."

"You better handle this before I come across him," Grease said quietly to Dragon. "Or I'll deal with it myself."

"Man's stupid enough to get anywhere near you," Dragon said with a sigh, "I won't stop ya."

Grease wasn't gonna touch him. As Rose's man, that fell to me. But I kept my mouth shut as we walked back toward the party. I couldn't imagine some man going at Kara the way Copper had lunged at Rose.

The party raged on, but as we reached the group, our men watched us closely. They knew something had gone down, they just weren't sure what. As Dragon moved toward Cam and Grease headed for his sons, I searched for Rose.

"Callie took her in the house," Hawk said, as she came up beside me. "You might want to go in there."

"Thanks."

"Do I wanna know what happened?" she asked as I started to walk away.

"Go take care of your man," I replied, nodding my head toward where Tommy was rising from his seat. "Calm him down."

"Oh, shit," Hawk muttered as she took off at a jog.

Inside the house was as loud as outside. It took me a few minutes to find the women in a quieter room upstairs, and my stomach twisted when I saw Rose sitting on the edge of the bed.

"I told you I'm fine," she said to her mom, pushing her hands away.

"Sweetheart, you're still pale as a ghost," Callie said, crouched in front of her.

"Would you just tell us what the fuck happened already?" Lily snapped. "This is bullshit."

Rose just shook her head. "It's none of your business."

"Say what?" Farrah asked dubiously.

"Copper showed up," I said quietly, stepping inside the room and closing the door behind me. "Started hasslin' Rose."

"I saw him hanging around," Farrah said. "But he looked like he was keeping his distance."

"Cornered her at our camping spot," I replied.

"Oh, fuck no," Lily snarled.

"It was fine," Rose said, her eyes on mine. "Nothing happened."

"It doesn't sound like nothing," Callie retorted.

"I put a stop to it," I said.

"Well done," Farrah said.

"I was handling it," Rose said stubbornly.

I saw red. "You were handling it?" I ground out. "You think so?"

"I know so," Rose replied, standing up.

"How you figure?" I asked, taking a step forward.

"I would have taken care of it," she hissed back.

The tension in the room amped up as we stared at each other. I wasn't real happy we had an audience, but fuck it.

"By eggin' him on?" I asked. "You think you can take on a grown ass man?"

"I'd do my best," she shot back.

"Your best is shit," I roared. "He coulda done whatever the fuck he wanted."

"No, he couldn't."

"You got a piece you're hidin'?" I asked. "Huh? You got anything to defend yourself?"

Rose just glared at me.

"You got a drunk, pissed off man comin' at you, and you think it's a good idea to call him a needle dick?"

I ignored Farrah's snicker.

"I wasn't just going to stand there and let him talk to me like that!"

"That's all you had to do," I yelled, pointing at her.

"Okay, lets all just calm down," Callie said, trying to defuse the situation.

"I'm her man?" I snapped, looking at Rose's mother.

She looked back and forth between us. "Yeah."

"Then you got no part in this," I said, dismissing her as I turned back to Rose.

"You didn't think to bide your time and keep him calm and *wait for me*?"

"No," she said, shaking her head.

"What the fuck, Rose?"

"I wasn't going to just let him *do that* again," she shouted back.

"Words hurt, huh?" I replied, getting in her face. I was so livid I could barely see straight. "You know what hurts worse? Fuckin' fists."

"Come on, man," Farrah said. "She gets it."

I ignored her.

"You know what hurts? A man twice your size overpowerin' you. Doing whatever the fuck he felt like doin', and havin' it easy because you were already half naked."

"I knew it wouldn't get that far," Rose rasped back.

"How'd you know that?"

"Because I knew you were coming," she said softly, her eyes filling up with tears.

"Jesus Christ, baby," I said, letting out the breath it felt like I'd been holding since the minute I heard Copper's voice in the woods. "You scared the shit outta me."

Rose was in my arms in the next heartbeat. Her legs wrapped around my waist like a vice and she pressed her face into my neck. It was then that I noticed how badly she was shaking.

The other women left the room quietly as I stood there with Rose in my arms.

"I let him talk to me like that for too long," Rose whispered, her body shaking with a silent sob. "I couldn't let him do it anymore."

"Fuck," I muttered, turning so I could drop my ass to the bed.

"What's going to happen now?" she asked, burrowing her arms under my cut like she was trying to get as close as she could.

"Gonna sit down with the boys when we get home."

"What about Copper?"

"He took off before we got back."

"He's still here?"

"He won't be showin' his fucked up face around here this weekend," I assured her, rubbing her back. "By now, every man in the club knows to keep an eye out."

"I braced my legs," she replied, her fingers tightening in the back of my shirt. "I thought if he punched me, I just had to stay standing."

I closed my eyes against the picture that painted. Fuck me.

"Next time," I said, trying to keep the anger from my voice, "you talk him down."

"I thought you said he'd stay away from me." Her voice wobbled.

"He will," I promised. "But if another man, any man, is hasslin' you, you try to calm him down. You keep your smart mouth shut."

"I can't promise that," she said, pressing her head harder against my shoulder.

"You have to," I replied, using her hair to tug her head back so I could look her in the eye. "This ain't about women's rights, or me thinkin' that a woman can't do whatever she wants. This is fuckin' survival, baby. You gotta promise me that you'll do what I'm askin'."

Rose shook her head.

"Listen to me, Rose," I said, tightening my hand in her hair. "You're brave as fuck. You don't back down from a fight and I love that about you. But you've got no chance takin' on a man that's bigger, stronger, and meaner than you are."

"So, I'm just supposed to let them do whatever they want?" she asked, looking at me like I was crazy.

"I'm sayin' let them *say* whatever the fuck they want," I replied. "You figure out how to get away, you do that. You can't, I'll always come for you. Always."

"And what if you don't?"

"Baby," I said, pressing my forehead against hers. "If there ever comes a day that I'm not comin' for you, I'm already a dead man, and you don't have to worry about any promises you made to me."

The night was over for me and Rose. She was too freaked to camp where we'd been, so me and Will moved our shit over to where he'd set up. It was loud and we'd lost the privacy we'd had before, but Rose felt safe, so the other crap didn't matter. We laid there in the dark, listening to the party around us long into the night. I wasn't sure when she fell asleep, but I didn't crash until the sun started lighting the inside of the tent.

"Mack," Rose woke me, running her fingers down the side of my jaw. "Have you seen my bag? One of the old ladies said I could use the shower in her man's room."

Fuck. I hadn't told her. She crawled around the tent, lifting up the sleeping bags to look under them.

"Babe," I said, voice rough. "Copper snagged it."

"He what?" she asked, turning her head slowly to look at me.

"When we got back to the camp, I checked the tent and it was gone."

"He stole my backpack?" she said incredulously. "Why?"

"Who the fuck knows? You remember what was in it?"

"Just my clothes and a bag of toiletries," she said, falling onto her ass. "I left my wallet in your saddlebags."

"Well, at least that's somethin'." I sighed.

"He took my clothes," she said, shaking her shoulders in a mock shiver. "That's creepy as hell."

"He was probably just tryin' to be a dick," I replied, sitting up. "I beat his ass, and there was no other way to get even."

"He's going to be pissed when he realizes I didn't bring anything worth stealing."

"I don't know, babe," I teased, trying to lighten the mood a little. "That fancy shampoo you got costs a grip."

"My mom's a hair stylist," she said, rolling her eyes. "She'd kill me if I used something from the drugstore."

"Come here," I ordered, reaching out and yanking her onto my lap. "You gonna kiss me good morning?"

"You have hangover breath," she replied, wrinkling her nose. She kissed me, anyway.

"Everybody up already?" I asked as she pulled away.

"Yeah, you're the last one."

"Time is it?"

"Two."

"Shit," I grumbled. "I slept late."

"You needed it," she said with a shrug. Her fingers played along the edges of my bruised knuckles.

"How you doin' today?"

"I'm okay. Pissed more than anything. He's always been a shitty drunk."

"Why'd you stay so long?" I asked before I could think better of it.

Rose was quiet for a long moment. "Because I told myself the good outweighed the bad, I guess."

"That's a tough spot to be in."

"It was stupid."

"Nah." I shook my head. "Wantin' to believe that things will get better, or that shit isn't really as bad as it is? Human nature. We all do it."

"You, too?"

"Me more than anyone," I said, Mia's face flashing in my mind. "Come on, this is too heavy for our current digs. We can talk more at home, yeah?"

"Okay," she said, kissing me again.

I followed her out of the tent and pulled on my jeans.

"You realize you just gave everyone a show, right?" Rose asked, hands on her hips.

"Nobody's lookin'," I replied, bending down to snag my shirt.

"Everyone's looking."

I glanced around the property and didn't see a single set of eyes on me.

"I'm jealous," Rose announced. "You need to get dressed *inside* the tent from now on."

I tried to hold back my smile, but it was impossible.

"I'm serious," she insisted. "No more prancing around in your underwear."

"You ever seen me prance?" I asked, shoving my feet into my boots. I threw my arm around her shoulders and led her toward the house. We were still at least fifty yards away when I caught a whiff of bacon. *Yes.*

"You know what I mean," she said as we reached my bike. "I don't want other women seeing the goods."

"Noted," I said in amusement as I pulled my toothbrush and a tiny tube of toothpaste from my saddlebags. "You wanna use this first?"

"Gross," she replied. "I'm not using your toothbrush."

"Grosser than not brushin' your teeth?"

"Just give me some toothpaste," she grumbled, sticking out her pointer finger.

"You've had your mouth a lot dirtier places than a shared toothbrush," I joked as I gave her some toothpaste.

If I hadn't been watching her face, I would've missed the flinch.

"Hey," I said, tipping her chin up with my hand. "I meant on *me*. You've had your tongue so deep in my mouth, I wasn't sure which was yours and which was mine. Sharin' a toothbrush is nothin'."

"I'm still not sharing one," she said with a shrug, stuffing her finger in her mouth to scrub at her teeth.

"Love you," I said softly, watching her.

"Love you, too," she replied, giving me a foamy smile.

The rest of the weekend was pretty uneventful, but by the time we pulled into my driveway Sunday night, I was beat. Sleeping on the ground was fun when I was young, but now it just meant that I could never get comfortable and slept like shit. It didn't help that the night before, I'd had no interest in drinking and hadn't been able to pass out in the tent like I'd planned. Rose had spent the night laughing too loud and pretending that she wasn't bothered by the shit that had gone down, which drove me nuts. Be upset, be angry, be relieved, be *whatever*, but don't fucking hide that crap.

"I'm gonna head home," Rose said with a groan, stomping her feet to get the blood circulating.

"You sure?" I asked. We'd barely gotten our helmets off and she was already trying to bail, which wasn't usually her style.

"No," she said with an uncomfortable laugh. "But I probably should."

"Stay tonight then," I said, as I emptied out my saddle bags. "You can head home in the morning."

"Yeah. Okay." She nodded.

We headed into the house and went directly upstairs, not even bothering to turn on any lights. Since we hadn't been sure when we'd be home, my parents agreed to have Kara stay an extra night. I was glad we had the place to ourselves. I dumped my dirty clothes on my bedroom floor and immediately reached for Rose.

"Let's shower," I said, tugging her t-shirt off.

"Are you saying I stink?" she asked, giving me a tired smile.

"You're fresh as a fuckin' daisy," I replied, making her chuckle quietly. "But I'm ripe."

Rose faceplanted against my chest. "Smell good to me," she mumbled into my shirt.

"Just don't get too close to my pits," I joked.

I stripped both of us down and as I walked her to the bathroom, Rose was unusually quiet. She was somewhere in her own head as I got the shower started and pulled her inside with me, closing the curtain behind us.

"You're gonna have to use the drugstore crap," I said, situating her under the spray as I ran my fingers through her hair. "You don't have any of the fancy stuff here."

"I don't mind," she replied, tipping her head back under the water.

We were silent as she washed her hair, but my hands roamed all over her. I couldn't help myself. Rose's skin was so soft, it didn't seem real. There were no blemishes at all beyond a few stretch marks on her tits that had long since faded into tiny white lines. My mouth watered as I traced them with my finger.

"You have them, too," Rose pointed out, opening her eyes. She reached out and traced the stretch marks where my chest met my shoulders.

"My shoulders grew too fast," I said, looking down at them.

"So did my boobs," Rose said with a shrug. "I've got a few on my hips, too."

"I know," I said with a dramatic sigh. "I love 'em."

"What?" She laughed. "Why?"

"Just do." My fingers found the marks she'd mentioned without hesitation. "You've got four on this side and five on this side."

"It's kind of weird that you know that," she said, trading places with me so I could stand under the spray of water.

"I pay attention," I replied, shrugging my shoulders. I groaned as the hot water poured over my skin. Rose shivered and I tugged her against my chest. "We need two shower heads in here."

"And a bigger shower," Rose joked. She reached for the soap. "I'm going to wash off and get out. I'm freezing."

Without a word, I traded places with her again so she could warm up. She was right, the shower was pretty small for the two of us. Hell, it was small for me. My shoulders made contact with both the shower curtain and the wall when I stood sideways.

I couldn't stop from staring as Rose washed methodically, working her way down her body. She wasn't trying to be sexy, but she couldn't really help it. Everything about her turned me on, from her smart mouth to the way she walked.

"I thought things were supposed to shrink when you're cold?" Rose said, glancing down at my erection.

"Not when you're standin' there, soakin' wet and naked," I replied dryly.

She chuckled as she finished rinsing off, then wrapped her arms around my waist. "Your turn."

"Go get in bed," I said, pressing my lips to hers. "I'll be out in a minute."

As soon as she was out of the shower, I let the weekend's events roll through my mind as I washed up and rinsed off. I was going to have to do something about Copper. Even if the brothers voted to take his patch, he was still going to be a problem. He was probably already back in Sacramento licking his wounds, but assholes like that didn't give up. He'd be back at some point just to fuck with Rose. He wouldn't be able to help himself.

From what Rose had said, Copper had never been violent with her. She'd been adamant about that. But in my experience, if a man was comfortable taking out his frustrations on his woman verbally, there wasn't a whole lot he wouldn't do if he thought he could get away with it. Situations like that escalated all the time.

I flexed my fingers as I toweled off. I'd hit that motherfucker *hard*. I could have easily killed him, probably just a few more blows after he'd gone down and it would've been lights out forever. The only thing that had stopped me was the fact that Rose was watching. She didn't need to see that shit, not from me, not ever. If I had the chance again, though, I couldn't be sure I'd let him live. I'd do whatever I had to in order to protect her.

Rose was still awake as I climbed into bed beside her.

"Sorry, I tried to dry my hair with a towel, but it's still pretty wet," she said, curling up against my side. "It's going to be crazy in the morning."

"I don't mind," I replied. I relaxed into the bed with a sigh. Jesus, I was beat.

"What's happening this week?" Rose asked sleepily.

"Hopefully, absolutely nothin'," I replied, closing my eyes. "Parents'll probably come over for dinner at some point. Maybe have us to their place."

"I'm working every night but Tuesday, but let me know and I'll try to be there."

She fell asleep before I could even reply.

I was tired as hell, but I couldn't shut my brain off. Me and Rose just *worked*. Being with her was effortless. I didn't have to worry about what I was going to say or act a certain way around her; we were comfortable together in a way that didn't need any of that bullshit. If it weren't for the stuff with Copper, our relationship would've been completely drama free. I hadn't realized how important that was until I had it.

When I turned onto my side, she automatically turned in her sleep so that we were spooning. Yeah. I kissed her wet hair. This was it.

And I'd do whatever I needed to protect it.

Chapter 11

Rose

My apartment didn't feel like home anymore. I came to the realization almost a week after we got back from Seattle. I didn't feel relaxed when I sat on my couch or want to veg out in front of the TV. I didn't sleep well in my bed. Everything felt too quiet now. Lonely.

It didn't help that I felt like I was looking over my shoulder all the time. Nobody had heard a thing from Copper in Oregon or Sacramento, which I wasn't sure was a good or a bad thing. I hoped that he was embarrassed by the whole debacle, so he was laying low for a while, but I wasn't counting on it. Copper was a coward. He only said shitty things to me when we were alone, knowing that he could twist the truth if anyone ever called him on it. Now that someone else had seen him being a dick, I wasn't sure what he'd do. It wasn't like he could play it off. Maybe if it had ended before he'd charged at me, he could have apologized, but that wasn't even an option anymore.

My phone rang just as I was pulling a frozen pizza out of the oven.

"Hey," I answered, tucking the phone between my ear and shoulder.

"Hey, yourself. Whatcha doin?" Lily asked. She'd been calling me every day, which wasn't unheard of, but wasn't super common since she and Leo had hooked up.

"Just eating before I have to leave for work."

"I wish our schedules weren't completely opposite," she complained, making me laugh.

"You make your own schedule," I pointed out.

"Yeah, but if I'm working at night, I barely get to spend any time with Leo and Gray."

"Can I just point out, *again*, that it's hilarious that he's called Gray?"

"Yeah, yeah," she muttered good-naturedly.

"I mean, Gray White? Really?"

"His mother named him Gregory," Lily said in annoyance. "Leo told me he was saving up his vetoes for bigger things later on, even though he thinks it makes his son sound like an accountant."

"You're an accountant," I pointed out.

"I'm not a dude," she shot back.

"But Gray?" I teased.

"Well, he wasn't going to call him *Greg*," she replied.

"How about calling him by his middle name?"

"Might be confusing with two Dracos running around."

"Well, at least she got that part right," I murmured. Draco was Leo and Trix's brother that died when he was a baby. Apparently, they'd both named their sons after him.

"Gray suits him," she said, a smile in her voice. "He totally looks like a Gray."

"Like Gray White."

"Shut it, already."

"Are you going to name your baby Black when you guys finally decide to start procreating?"

"You're getting annoying," Lily griped. "Knock it off."

"Fine."

"Maybe I'll come see you at work tonight," she said with a hum. "I haven't done that in a while."

"I don't need a babysitter."

"I'm not going to babysit you."

"Oh, really?" I asked around the pizza I'd stuffed in my mouth. "Yesterday was Tommy. The day before that was Cam and Trix. The day before *that*, it was Will and Molly. And the day before *that*, my parents came in and sat at the bar."

"Maybe we just want to see you," she argued. "You've been hanging out with Mack all the time."

"Pot, meet kettle," I muttered.

"Fair enough." She sighed. "We just feel better when we know someone has your back."

"There's always at least one regular at the bar," I pointed out. "It's not like I'm alone."

"Yeah, and they don't even know what's going on, or who to look out for," she said.

"I'm sure that would be fantastic for tips," I replied sarcastically.

"Just enjoy the company, alright?" she said in exasperation. "Because you're not going to be able to stop us."

"Fine."

"Fine."

"So, I'll see you in a couple hours?"

"Yep."

"Fantastic. Bye." I hung up, knowing it would annoy her.

I packed a bag, just in case I ended up staying at Mack's again, and headed to work. Leaving my apartment was fine, it was still daylight and there were usually neighbors all over, but when I got off work, I dreaded going home. My shift usually didn't end until most people had been asleep for hours, and it was dark even with the parking lot lights. There were too many places for someone to hide.

I hated that I worried about shit like that now.

I'd always been brave to the point of stupid, at least that's what my dad said. I'd never really worried that something would happen to me, because I'd been wrestling and fighting with my brothers my entire life. I knew how to defend myself, and I was good at it. But I'd also never been put into the position where I'd need to fight off more than a drunk frat boy before.

Knowing that Copper was about to hit me, or worse, and planning for that eventuality? It had fucked with my head big time. Even worse had been the look on Mack's face when he'd said that he was scared. Finally, after years of my dad and brothers telling me over and over again that I needed to be careful, all that it had taken was the look of helplessness in my man's eyes to put that fear into me.

Work was slow, even with Lily and Leo there to entertain me. There weren't enough customers to keep me busy, and I could do restocking and cleanup in my sleep. By the time the last customer left, I was yawning into my hand.

"You headed to your place or Mack's?" Leo asked as I waved to my boss across the room. Of course he came in after everything was done, just to lock up and check my receipts. I rolled my eyes.

"Home, I guess," I said, checking my phone for the fifth time. Mack hadn't responded to any of my texts.

Leo and Lily were playing grab-ass as I pushed the front door open and stepped outside, and for less than a minute, I was alone in the dark.

I barely held back a scream when I saw Copper leaning against the building. He had a butterfly bandage on his cheekbone, another on the side of his nose, and the rest of his face was bruised a rainbow of colors.

"Hear me out," he said, raising his hands in surrender. "You gotta say somethin' to—"

"She doesn't gotta say shit to no one," Leo barked as he shoved past me.

"It's none of your business, man," Copper replied, full of bravado. I was comforted to see he'd taken a step backward, though.

"Call your pop," Leo ordered me.

He must have told Lily to stay inside, because the door swung closed behind him and she was nowhere to be seen.

Leo stepped forward and said something to Copper, but I didn't catch it because I was already putting my phone to my ear.

"Rose?" my dad answered. "Everything okay?"

"When I got off work, Copper was waiting outside the bar," I said shakily, staring at Leo's back. His shoulders straightened, and everything inside me went on alert.

"I'll be right there," my dad said immediately. "Leo with you?"

"Yeah."

"Be there soon, baby girl," he said. "Hold tight."

As soon as my dad hung up, I called Mack, almost crying when his phone went straight to voicemail.

"This is bullshit," Copper spat. "Rose, tell them it was just a misunderstanding."

I kept my mouth shut.

"Oh, come on," he said, throwing his hands in the air. "You get up in everyone's shit when they have a fight with their woman?"

"She ain't your woman," Leo replied calmly. "Hasn't been for a long ass time."

"It hasn't been that long," Copper scoffed.

"Rose has a man," Leo said. "Seems like you'd be reminded of that every time you take a look in the mirror."

"Oh," Copper said nastily. "We gonna compare fucked up faces?"

My stomach twisted in disgust, but Leo just laughed.

"Got mine protectin' my family," he said. "How'd you get yours again?"

"Got jumped," Copper snapped.

"Yeah, when you were goin' after a brother's old lady," Leo said. "You're fucked, man."

The sounds of Harley pipes filled the night around us, and when I turned to look, I wasn't surprised to see four bikes pull up. My dad, brother Tommy, cousin Cam and Uncle Cody immediately climbed off their bikes and headed toward us.

"You good?" Tommy asked, pulling me against his side as they reached us. He held onto me as the others moved forward.

"Where's your bike?" my dad barked, his tone so cold that I looked his way in surprise.

"Stashed it," Copper said.

"Good."

"Come on," Copper complained as Cam grabbed him by the neck of his cut and yanked him toward Lily's car.

"Leo, take Lil on the bike," Cam ordered.

"Will do," Leo replied, tossing Cam Lily's keys.

Then the whole thing was over almost as fast as it had started.

"Probably thought he had a shot since there were no bikes out here," my dad said, pulling me away from Tommy for a hug.

"You're a smart fucker," Tommy said to Leo. "Wish I woulda thought of that."

"Good thing you didn't," my uncle said, giving me a soft smile. He looked at Tommy. "We woulda needed a cleanup crew."

"That's fair," Tommy conceded.

"You alright?" my dad asked quietly.

"Yeah." I shook out my arms and stepped back. "He just startled me. Leo was right behind me, so it was fine."

"Jesus," Lily said as she stomped outside. "That guy is a fucking dumbass."

"Tell us how you really feel," Uncle Cody replied with a chuckle.

"Your boss tow ya if ya leave your car here for the night?" Dad asked.

"No, it should be fine."

"Alright." He slung his arm over my shoulders. "You can ride with me to Mack's."

"I'm headed home," I argued as he led me to his bike.

"Mack know what happened?"

"No, I haven't been able to get ahold of him all night."

"Then we should probably let him know, eh?"

I let out a sigh as Lily hugged me, the Harleys firing up around us.

"Aren't you glad you had a babysitter?" she asked, giving me a squeeze.

"Shut up," I replied. "And thanks for bringing your *boyfriend*."

"I swear, he follows me around like a puppy," she joked. "Can't go anywhere without him."

"That must make pooping an event."

"You're so gross," she said, laughing as she pushed me away. "I'll call you tomorrow."

"Have fun pooping," I called as she walked over to Leo. She flipped me off over her shoulder.

"All set?" my dad asked, handing me my mom's helmet.

"Yep." I climbed onto the back of my dad's bike like I'd done hundreds of times before, wrapped my arms around his waist, and let myself relax against his back. All the crap with Copper was over. Finally.

"What happened?" Mack called out several brief moments after we pulled into his driveway, hurrying down the porch steps in nothing but a pair of black boxer briefs. He kept one arm unnaturally still along his side, and I could barely make out the pistol in his hand.

"Idiot showed up at the bar," my dad replied as I climbed off the bike.

"Motherfucker," Mack said, shaking his head. "You okay, baby?"

"I'm fine," I replied, handing my dad mom's helmet. "Leo and Lily were there."

"Why didn't you call me?" he asked, pulling me against him and kissing my head.

"I tried," I mumbled.

"Cam took him back to the clubhouse," my dad said.

"I'll meet you there," Mack replied.

"Alright." Dad stowed mom's helmet and looked at me. "Love you, baby girl. Call your mom when you get inside, yeah?"

"I will. Love you, too."

By the time my dad started his bike back up, Mack had already led me to the porch. We were up the stairs and inside the house within moments.

"I shoulda been there," Mack said, locking the door behind us. "I knew that fucker was gonna show up sooner or later."

"It was fine," I replied tiredly. The night had felt never ending, and now I just wanted to climb in bed and pass out. "Lily and Leo were there."

He strode to the kitchen and picked up his phone, cursing.

"It's dead," he said, shaking his head. Before I could reply, he'd thrown his phone across the room, where it shattered against the wall.

I stood there gaping for a long moment. "You could have just charged it," I finally muttered.

"Can't believe this shit," he replied, coming toward me. He barely stopped walking as he hoisted me up so that my legs were wrapped around his waist. I held on tight as he took the stairs two at a time and brought us into the bedroom.

"You just ran up the stairs," I said in awe as he set me on my feet. "While you were carrying me."

"And?" He pushed his hair back from his face.

"That was the hottest thing I've ever encountered in real life."

Mack's lips twitched as he tried not to smile.

"Seriously," I said, widening my eyes. "Hotter than the guys in kilts that throw those big logs."

"You have a thing for guys with big logs, huh?" he said, still holding back his smile.

"You have no idea," I whispered, fluttering my eyelashes.

He laughed, the sound coming out rough, before it cut off completely. "Shit."

"I was fine," I said, sliding my hands up his chest and around his neck. "Really."

"Can't believe you couldn't get ahold of me," he said, running his hands over my hair until he was cupping the back of my neck.

"Leo took care of it," I replied. "It's all over now."

"Not yet," he said darkly. "But it will be soon."

I dropped my arms as he pulled away from me, watching as he started getting dressed.

"Get in bed, baby," he ordered gently. "Been a long night."

"I don't want to go to sleep without you," I argued, staying where I was.

Mack looked up in surprise. "I gotta run to the club."

"Then I'll wait," I said stubbornly.

"I don't want you stayin' up all night waitin' on me," he said, pulling a hoodie over his head. He came toward me and reached for the bottom of my shirt. Instead of fighting him on it, I let him strip me down to my underwear.

"I can't sleep like this," I said as he ran his fingers down the middle of my chest.

"I'll grab ya a shirt," he replied hoarsely.

"Is Kara home?" I asked as I pulled his t-shirt over my head.

"Yeah," he replied, following me to the bed. When I climbed in, he sat down at my hip. "I'll leave the pistol in the nightstand."

"I won't need it."

"Just wanted you to know it was there," he said, leaning forward to give me a kiss. His lips lingered on mine. "Wish I didn't have to leave ya, but this shit needs to be handled."

"It's fine," I replied. I didn't want him to leave, but I knew how these things worked. I couldn't remember the number of times we'd woken up in the morning, only to find that our dad had left sometime in the middle of the night. It sucked, mostly for my mom, but it was the life we'd lived. The life I was choosing for myself now. I chose him.

"My love," I murmured, tracing my finger over his bottom lip.

"All tangled up," he whispered back, his lips curving up at the edges.

"Go," I ordered, giving him one last kiss.

"I'll be back soon as I can."

"I'll be here."

I listened as he went downstairs and out the front door. As soon as I heard his bike start up outside, I called my mom.

※ ※ ※

KARA AND I were eating cereal the next morning when Mack barreled into the house like a tornado. He slammed the door, tossed his keys against the wall, and cursed as he ripped off his cut and threw it on the couch.

"I'll see what's up," I told Kara quietly, putting my hand on her arm as she started to rise.

"Hey," I said, walking toward him. "Everything okay?"

"Kara awake?" he asked, looking over my shoulder.

"Eating breakfast," I said as he caught sight of his daughter and gave her a head nod.

"Then we'll talk later."

He gave me a quick kiss on the cheek as he went around me into the kitchen.

The rest of breakfast was uneventful as Mack and Kara teased each other and chatted, but I could still feel the tension just under the surface. He was hiding it well, but Mack was more pissed than I'd ever seen him before. He was practically vibrating. As soon as Kara went upstairs to her bedroom, Mack let out a frustrated sigh.

"What's going on?" I asked quietly.

"President from Sacramento is comin' to get him," Mack replied in disgust.

"What?" My jaw dropped open.

"Decision's been made," Mack said, throwing up his hands in defeat.

"And then what happens?" I asked cautiously.

"They decide what happens next," he replied. "Your dad's pissed, but he's tight with the president down there, so he didn't say much."

"Yeah," I murmured. "My mom lived down there when Will was born."

"They won't let him keep his patch, at least," Mack said, standing up. "Your pop would never stand for that."

I nodded as he walked around the table. While a part of me was relieved that I wouldn't have to see Copper at club events ever again, a small voice inside of me wondered if I'd overreacted and just ruined a man's life.

"What's that look on your face?" Mack asked, coming to a stop next to my chair.

"Nothing."

"It's something," he argued. "You still worried?"

"No, it's not that," I said, shaking my head. "I just…I'm wondering if maybe we overreacted?"

"Say what?" he barked, his head jerking back in surprise. "Overreacted?"

"His whole life is over," I replied, getting to my feet. "We just ruined his life."

Mack stared at me. "Rose, he ruined his own life. He knew the moment he went after you that he was done."

"Brothers have done a lot worse shit—" I tried to argue.

"No," he cut me off. "You go after another brother's old lady and you're done. You go after a brother's kid, you're done. You can't be trusted."

"I've seen more than one brother smack his old lady around," I snapped back.

"You're not his old lady," Mack roared. He immediately snapped his mouth shut and glanced toward the bedrooms, but Kara didn't come out. When he spoke again, his voice was level. "You're *my* old lady," he said more calmly. "And just so you know, if an old lady came to the club and asked for help—she'd get it. We'd put a stop to that shit, quick."

"But you'll just sit around and watch it if no one asks for your express invitation," I shot back.

"When's the last time you saw a brother knockin' his old lady around?" Mack asked. "Huh? Been years."

"Right," I said derisively.

"We don't accept bullies into the club," Mack replied. "If a man gets his rocks off goin' after people weaker than he is, he ain't gonna be no help to us."

"This just feels like a lot," I replied with a frustrated sigh.

"Baby, don't," Mack said, cupping my cheek in his hand. "Don't downplay it because the man is facin' consequences of his own makin', alright?"

"Okay."

"Dad?" Kara called from her bedroom doorway. "Is it safe to come out?"

"No," he replied jokingly. "Better stay in there all day."

"Not happening," Kara sang as she skipped down the hallway toward us. "Can I go over to Rebel's today? Her mom said it was okay."

"I'm not drivin' anywhere until I get some sleep," Mack replied.

Kara turned and gave me her best smile.

"She ain't your chauffer," Mack said, reaching out to poke Kara in the side. "You wanna go, you're gonna have to wait a couple hours so I can get some shut-eye."

"Sorry, toots," I said quietly to Kara as I turned to follow Mack down the hall.

"It's okay," she grumbled, throwing herself onto the couch.

I felt kind of weird as I followed Mack into the bedroom. He'd answered for me before I could say that I wouldn't mind driving Kara to my brother's place. Actually, I hadn't seen Molly or Reb in a while, and I was jonesing for some time with them.

"I could've driven her," I said as Mack started undressing. "I don't mind."

"It's not your job to cart her around," Mack replied easily. "She shouldn't have asked. Wanna lay down with me for a bit?"

"Sure." I let him help me take my jeans off, then crawled in next to him.

I didn't expect to sleep, but within moments of my head hitting the pillow, I was out.

<hr />

AFTER ALL OF the drama and upset, life fell into a surprisingly normal pattern. I spent most nights at Mack's, unless Kara was sleeping at a friend's house, and then he'd meet me at my apartment after work. Kara went to camp for a week, and we spent most of the time she was gone naked and having sex on any available surface. We went swimming and barbecued on the weekends, had dinner with my parents and his, and when we could find the time, spent hours riding.

It was one of the best summers I'd ever had, and as fall approached and Kara headed back to school, I found myself more excited about the holidays than I'd been since I was a kid. I didn't even mind the weather getting colder, which usually had me bitching to anyone that would listen. Everything just felt different, the future seemed wide open and full of possibility.

Unfortunately, that only made it worse when it all came crashing down around me.

Chapter 12

Mack

The morning started out just like any other. I woke up with Rose's hair in my face and her leg thrown over my hip, her knee dangerously close to my balls. I wasn't sure how she did it, but the woman could sleep like that all night and had never once made contact unintentionally. I slid my hand up her thigh and sighed.

Kara had spent one last night with my parents before they got back on the road, so Rose hadn't bothered putting any clothes on before we'd passed out the night before, and the bare skin under my fingertips had me feeling all kinds of thankful.

"Morning," Rose mumbled, kissing my chest. "That tickles."

"Oh, yeah?" I swept my hand up her side, barely making contact, and smiled as she squirmed.

"What time do we have to pick up Kara?" she asked, shifting away from my hand.

Glancing at the clock, I groaned. "Little less than an hour."

"Shit," she breathed, dropping her head back against my chest. "I need to hop in the shower. I smell like sweat and sex."

"My favorite scent."

"But I doubt your mom would enjoy it," she replied, propping her chin on my chest and smiling sleepily at me. She was fucking spectacular. Jesus. The way she looked at me hit me straight in the gut every time.

"Move in with me," I blurted out.

"Okay," she replied almost instantly.

"You don't have to think about it?" I asked.

"Hell, no." She sat up in bed and threw her leg over so she could straddle me. For a minute, I was mesmerized by the sight of all that soft skin.

"Eyes up here," she joked, using her middle and index fingers to point at her eyes. "You're serious, right?"

"Course I'm serious," I replied. "I wouldn't say somethin' if I wasn't."

"Just wanted to make sure," she said with a wide grin. "I mean, I haven't even rode bareback yet." She rolled her hips for emphasis and I almost moaned.

"Just waitin' on you to be ready for that," I replied, squeezing her hips.

"Who said I wasn't ready?" she asked. "I was just waiting for *you* to say something."

"Far as I'm concerned, that shit's on your timeline, not mine." I leaned up so we were face to face, and if I hadn't already been sitting, the look in her eyes would have knocked me on my ass.

"Well, I'm ready," she said, wrapping her arms around my neck. "I have an IUD, so we're all safe there."

"Baby," I said in surprise, "I had a vasectomy years ago."

Never in my life had I seen a person's face go from joy to devastation so fast. It was like a switch had been flipped, and no matter how hard she tried to keep her composure, every feeling she had flitted across her face like a movie. Shock, horror, sadness and finally, anger.

"You did what?" she asked quietly, her arms falling from around my neck.

"I had a vasectomy," I replied. Jesus, I thought it was common knowledge. I hadn't been able to ride for weeks and the brothers had given me grief for years.

"And you didn't think this was information I should know?" she asked, finally schooling her expression. It was like a curtain had suddenly fallen between us.

"I thought you knew," I said, letting her go as she climbed off the bed.

"How the fuck would I know?" she snapped, pulling on her underwear. She froze with her hands on her hips and stared at the floor.

"Everybody knows," I replied, getting to my feet.

"No," she huffed. "No, they don't. Someone would have said something to me."

"Why?" I understood that she was shocked, but she was acting like I'd betrayed her somehow, which was complete bullshit. "They probably assumed that you already knew."

"No, they didn't."

"You sure of that?" I asked, pulling my jeans on.

"Yes, I'm sure," she snapped, finally looking at me.

"Right."

"I've wanted kids forever," she said through her teeth. The words were like a punch straight to the groin. "So, yeah. If Lily or my mom or anyone knew that you'd had a vasectomy, that's something they would've brought up."

"You've never said anything about kids," I said cautiously, realizing too late just how badly shit had gone sideways. "Nothin'."

"Well, it wasn't really something I thought we had to talk about yet," she said, throwing her hands in the air. "I'm on birth control, and we were still using condoms."

"If you woulda said somethin'—"

"I'm dating a man who has a kid," she practically yelled, staring at me like I'd lost my mind. "Why would you think I didn't want kids? A huge part of being with you is helping raise Kara—"

"I never asked you to help raise Kara," I said automatically.

I knew the moment the words were out of my mouth that I'd fucked up huge. Irrevocably.

"So you don't want kids with me," she said with a humorless laugh, "and I'm not allowed to claim Kara, either."

"You never said you wanted kids," I snapped defensively.

"You never fucking asked," she yelled back.

She dropped to her knees and started frantically stuffing her clothes into the bag that had been sitting in the corner of the room for over a month.

"What're you doin'?" I asked, reaching for her.

"Don't touch me," she ordered firmly, making me jerk back in surprise.

"You're bailin'? That what this is?"

"There's nothing for me here," she replied dully, getting to her feet.

"Nothin'?" I asked in disbelief. Was she fucking kidding me?

"I thought—" Rose stopped and swallowed hard.

I saw the moment she shut down. It was as if she was suddenly looking through me instead of at me.

"I thought we were building something here." She shook her head.

"We are," I said, reaching for her again.

"No." She pulled her arm out of my reach. "No, we were fucking."

"Knock it off."

"We were fucking," she continued. "And you liked having me in your bed. Which makes total sense, because I'm fantastic in bed."

"Rose, stop," I ordered. She was going to say something she couldn't take back. I could feel it, like bile rising in my throat.

"But you didn't want more than that." She took a step back, and stuck her hand out like she was stopping me from following her. "It's my own fault. I always do this—assume I've found the fairytale."

"I love you," I snapped, running my hands through my hair in frustration.

"I don't want that kind of love," she said woodenly. I would've been less stunned if she'd slapped me across the face.

"I'd fuckin' kill for you, Rose," I shouted. "That's not good enough for you?"

"You'd kill for me," she said, nodding. "But God forbid I help raise Kara, or we have any other kids."

"I made the choice of not havin' more kids a long ass time ago, that's got nothin' to do with us."

"It has everything to do with us," she hissed. "Did you expect me to live on the outside forever? No, Rose, you can't drive Kara to your brother's. No, Rose, you can't help Kara with her chores, or buy her pads, or have any say in her life at all. You can fuck me all night long and hang with us, but you'll never be a part of our very special little group." She held her hands in front of her a foot a part. "We're over here." She shook one hand. "And you're over here."

"Kara's not a part of this conversation," I barked in frustration. "And that's not how it is. Leave her out of this."

Rose shook her head again. "It's like you haven't heard a word I've said."

I followed her as she went to the bathroom and started methodically pulling her bottles of shit out of the shower, calmly and quickly drying them with a towel.

"You're bailin,'" I said, pointing at her. "And you wonder why I said that raising Kara was on me, not you? She's been through enough."

"Don't you dare," she hissed, pausing to glare at me. "You don't get to turn this around on me."

"Then who the fuck is it on?" I asked. "'Cause I'm standin' right here, and you're the one who's leavin.'"

"Fuck you, Mack," she said flatly.

And there it was.

I took a step back into the hallway so she could rush past me. She didn't even bother putting the shampoo bottles into her bag, just carried them in her arms as she hurried away. As soon as the front door closed behind her, I lost it.

The hole in the drywall was going to be a pain in the ass to patch.

⚜ ⚜ ⚜

"Drive careful," I told my mom, hugging her tightly. It didn't matter how many times they hit the road, it still sucked every time they left.

"I will," she replied. "Can't say as much for your dad."

"Real funny," I mumbled, giving her a squeeze before letting her go.

"Jacob, where's Rose?" she said, holding on to my arms. "I thought she'd come with you to say goodbye."

"She had some other stuff going on today."

"Bullshit," she replied, raising one eyebrow.

"Got into it this mornin'," I confessed. "Don't think she's gonna be around much."

"How bad did you fuck up?" she asked sympathetically.

"Who says it was me?"

Mom laughed. "Rose is crazy about you," she said. "And she's insanely polite."

I scoffed.

"When she needs to be," mom clarified. "If she was the one who'd fucked up, she still would've come to say goodbye."

"It's complicated," I replied.

"Good relationships always are," she said sagely. "Fix whatever you did, son. You're just as crazy about her. So is my granddaughter."

"Kara'll be fine," I argued.

"I didn't say she wouldn't be," she said as my dad and Kara came around the front of the camper. "It's you I'm worried about."

"All set?" my dad asked.

"Yep." My mom opened her arms and Kara ran to her. "Be good for your dad."

"I'm always good."

"Sure," my mom said teasingly, drawing out the word. "At least try not to give him any more gray hairs, huh? It makes me feel old."

"You'll call when you get where you're goin'?" I asked as Kara left my mom and tucked herself under my arm.

"Always do," my dad replied. He came in for a hug that squished Kara between us.

"Thanks for comin.'"

"Anytime," my mom called as she walked toward the passenger door.

Kara and I watched as they climbed inside. My dad leaned over to give my mom a kiss before starting the engine. Then they were off, the RV swaying from side to side as he navigated around the potholes in the asphalt.

"I wish they didn't have to go," Kara said wistfully.

"I know," I replied as I picked up her backpack. "But they've earned it."

"I don't understand why they don't want to stay here," Kara said as we walked over to my bike. She took her backpack from my hand and put it on, buckling the strap at her chest. "I'm here. You're here."

"They were stuck in one place for a long time," I said, climbing on the bike. "This is their time to roam."

"Well, I think it's stupid," she pouted.

"Watch it," I warned.

"I didn't say *they* were stupid."

"Kara."

"Fine. Sorry." She buckled her helmet and climbed on behind me.

Before she could say anything else, I started up the bike, making conversation impossible. I was actually a bit relieved that she was so preoccupied with my parents leaving and hadn't said a word about Rose yet, since I had no fucking clue what I was going to tell her.

This was the exact reason that I'd made the decision to keep Kara as detached as I could from any relationship I had. She didn't deserve to be left behind when whatever woman I was seeing decided that she wanted something else. Rose's face as she stormed out of the house flashed in my mind as I pulled out of the camping spot, but I shook it away. She'd proved every point I'd made when she'd walked out on me.

※ ※ ※

"WHY THE FUCK has it been so quiet?" Grease asked in frustration. "You seen anything?"

"Not a fuckin' thing," I replied, feeling just as frustrated.

After our men had been forced off the road and our truck full of guns stolen, we hadn't heard or seen anything. The night my parents got in, one of the recruits that had been part of that delivery had disappeared. Just vanished, poof, from his post at the gate. Since he was a grown ass adult, there hadn't been much we could do—but it still bothered the hell out of me. Where the fuck had he gone? Was he even still alive? Had he been in on the theft and got out before we could catch him? We had no fucking answers. Thankfully, there hadn't been any more attempts to steal from us, though. I went on every run and we'd had no tails, no eyes on us, no problems at all. If we didn't know better, we'd assume it was a one-off. There hadn't been a single word on the street about whoever took the guns trying to sell them. We had no leads and no idea where to look. It was irritating as all hell.

"They disappeared," Cam said in disgust. "They stole our guns and disappeared."

"They ghosted us," Tommy said with a humorless laugh. "I always knew my history with women would come back to bite me on the ass. This is life going full circle."

A few of the men laughed, but I didn't. Tommy's bullshit comments never helped, and I was sick of listening to him. Yeah, man, we get it. You're the comic fucking relief. Now, sit down and shut up.

"They must be keeping the shit they steal," Casper said. He wasn't laughing, either. "It's the only explanation that makes a damn bit of sense. There hasn't been any word on the shit they've stolen hitting the market."

"You know what their haul has been?" Dragon asked him.

"Not offhand, but I can find out," Casper replied.

"Do that." Dragon leaned back in his seat. "Anything else we need brought to the table?"

I waited for one of Rose's brothers to say something. I'd spent the last couple of weeks waiting on Rose to call me, figuring that once she'd cooled down she'd want to talk shit out, but I hadn't heard from her. I'd been getting a lot of dirty looks from the Hawthorne boys, though. There wasn't anything they could do, no way for them to step in without Rose losing her shit—but I didn't put it past them to say something in church, for no other reason than to call me out in front of the others.

"Alright," Dragon said when no one spoke up. He slammed the gavel down on the table and got to his feet.

"Yo," Casper said as we started dispersing. "Charlie's got a birthday comin' up. Says she wants to do paintball in the back field."

"Daddy's little princess, huh?" Grease joked.

"No shit, man," Casper said with a shake of his head. "Anyway, you're all invited. Next Saturday. We'll barbecue."

"No worries if you and Kara don't have any gear," Cam said to me. "We're bringin' extras, and no way will Trix be a part of any of that."

"You think any of the women will?" I asked as we left the room.

"My mom'll probably get in on it," Cam said with a smile. "Lily and Rose, too. I doubt Aunt Callie will, and who knows with Brenna. She's a dark horse. Molly—maybe. Hawk—definitely."

"It's gonna be a free for all," I said, remembering the water balloon fight at Rebel's birthday.

"No doubt," Cam said, looking at me. "And all of the women know how to shoot, so watch your balls."

"Fuck."

"You knew the score when you went there, man," he said, slapping me on the shoulder. "Take the abuse and say thank you."

"That what you did?" I asked.

"Trix was pregnant," Cam replied with a shake of his head. "I let them do whatever they wanted. Couldn't be worse than what I was doin' myself."

I nodded in understanding.

"'Course, Farrah's my mom, so she was firmly in my camp." His lips turned up in a smile. "But she's definitely not in yours."

Fuck me.

"You'll live," he said easily as he walked away. "But I wasn't joking, man. Wear a cup."

The rest of the day passed by quick. Even though I kept my phone turned all the way up, I still checked it a hundred times. I couldn't believe that Rose was still pissed. She'd completely overreacted to the fact that I didn't want more kids. I'd asked her to move in with me, for Chrissake. It wasn't like I was the villain here.

And sure, if she wanted kids, then things were never going to last long-term. But storming out and going radio silent was immature as hell. I should've known that hooking up with someone so much younger was going to be a fucking headache, but I'd been too caught up to care.

By the time I got off work for the night, I was more pissed than I'd been since Rose walked out. Fuck her. Fuck her dramatics and her immaturity. And fuck me for letting it get so serious that I still couldn't think about anything else weeks after it ended.

I was walking to my bike when my phone rang, and I reached for it so fast that I got irritated all over again.

"Hey, princess," I answered when I saw that it was Kara calling.

"Hey, Dad. Do you care if I stay for dinner? Charlie's mom says she can drive me home."

"You got homework?" I asked, hoping she did. I wasn't real excited about Farrah showing at my house later.

"I finished it right after school," Kara said quickly. "And I did all my morning chores, and I won't be home late."

"Fine with me, I guess."

"Thanks, Dad!"

"Mind your manners," I ordered as I stopped by my bike. "And help with cleanup. You're over there so much, you definitely can't be considered a guest anymore."

"I always help," she replied. "Love you."

"Love you, too."

As soon as she hung up, I stuffed my phone in my pocket, but I didn't climb on my bike. I had nothing to go home to.

Before Rose, I wouldn't have thought twice about going home to enjoy a beer and some TV while the house was quiet. I'd been doing it for years, and I enjoyed the rare time to myself. Now, the house just felt empty as fuck when I was there alone.

"All good?" Grease asked as he came out of the building.

"Yeah, man," I replied. "Fine."

Grease nodded as he stopped next to his bike.

"Your boys have been glarin' at me for weeks, but you haven't," I said, immediately regretting the words.

"My boys are young," Grease said, pausing with his helmet in his hands. "They're just startin' out with their women. Still in the stage where everythin' is either black or white. Haven't had a chance to see all those shades of gray in between."

I nodded, thinking that over.

"She's not sayin' much," Grease said, making my head snap up. "But I know you love my daughter. So whatever's happenin' with you two is none of my business."

"Thanks," I replied.

"Don't thank me," he said flatly. "There comes a time I think it is my business, there's not a place in this world you can hide from me."

I opened my mouth to speak, but he raised his hand to stop me.

"Don't want to know," he said. "I ain't your confessor. Man up and fix shit with my girl, yeah? 'Cause the longer this goes on, the less neutral I'm gonna be."

I laughed to myself as he pulled away and I tugged my helmet on. Wasn't sure how I'd fix shit with Rose when she was the one who'd ended things. I wondered for a second if she was claiming something different, but immediately knew better. Rose wasn't the type to lie about shit just to gain some sympathy. It was more likely that she was saying nothing, so everyone just assumed that I'd fucked up somehow.

I stewed the entire ride home, all the way through my shower, and as I made myself a sandwich for dinner. It wasn't anything new, I'd been doing it for weeks, but for once I didn't try to think about something else. I glared at the table while I ate, letting that last morning play on repeat in my mind.

By the time I was done with my food, I'd looked at the argument from all angles, and I was still pissed as hell at Rose.

I found myself riding to her work a few minutes later. It was earlier than she usually started, but I was on limited time since Kara would be home before too long. I figured if I caught Rose, great. If not? Well, I'd order a beer and enjoy it somewhere other than my couch.

She was behind the bar when I got there, doing her thing like it was any other night, and that made me even angrier. I was sitting at home stewing, and she was moving on with her life like nothing had happened. As I walked up to the bar and she smiled at a customer, I flexed my fists, wanting to break something.

Rose did a double take when she saw me, then, with a resigned expression, walked my way.

"What can I get you?" she asked warily.

"Beer," I replied. "You know what I like."

She swallowed and nodded, reaching for a glass. Silently, she poured me a beer, grabbed a coaster, and set both down in front of me. She turned to walk away and paused when I scoffed.

"Was there something else?" she asked, turning only her head to look at me.

"Shot of whiskey," I replied.

I watched her closely as she grabbed a shot glass and set it next to my beer. Her hands shook as she poured the whiskey, and knowing that she wasn't as unaffected as she seemed tempered my anger a little, but not enough.

"Is that all?" she asked woodenly, her eyes pointed somewhere over my shoulder.

I don't know what made me say it, anger or resentment or some mix of the two, but when she finally looked directly at me, I gave her a nasty smile. "I'd like a shot at the bartender," I said, not bothering to lower my voice. "You on the menu?"

Her head jerked back like I'd slapped her, and all the blood drained from her face.

"No?"

"I don't come into your work and cause problems," she said, her voice so low I could barely hear her. "I expect the same from you. Drink your beer and your whiskey and get the hell out."

"You don't come into my work because you don't want your brothers knowin' that you're the one who left," I shot back. "Easier to play the victim when everybody thinks that I did somethin'."

"I'm not playing anything," she replied, glancing down the bar nervously. "I haven't said anything to anyone, because I prefer my privacy."

"Right," I spat.

"It didn't work out," she said through her teeth. "There's no victim here. But right now, you're being a colossal dick. Go home, Mack."

I laughed, irritated as hell that I couldn't get a rise out of her. I wanted—needed—something. Any sign that she was as fucked up over all this as I was. I'd given her time to think shit over, and I'd kept my distance, but this was complete bullshit.

"You're seriously throwin' it all away," I said flatly. "Because I don't want more kids. Jesus, I know you're young, but figured you were more mature than that."

"From what I can see, the only immature one here is you," she replied. "Finish your drinks. They're on the house. Then get the fuck out."

She walked away before I could say anything else. It was then that I started to feel stupid as fuck. Jesus Christ, what was wrong with me?

I threw a couple of twenties on the bar and left, not bothering to finish anything.

When I got home, Kara, Charlie, and Farrah were sitting on our front porch.

"Shit, sorry," I called as I shut my bike off.

"No problem," Farrah said. "We just got here."

"You got your key?" I asked Kara.

"She already put her stuff inside," Farrah answered. "But she wasn't sure if she was supposed to have company inside."

I looked at Kara in surprise.

"Alright," Farrah said. "I wasn't sure if you wanted us in your house when you weren't there. No big deal."

"For future reference," I said as I reached them, "if I'm not here when you drop her off, you can go inside, or she can stay on her own."

"I can?" Kara asked excitedly.

"When I know you're comin' home and I'm on my way?" I replied. "Sure."

I ignored the way Kara rolled her eyes.

"I'd love a cup of coffee, thanks," Farrah said as she got to her feet.

"I didn't ask," I said as I opened the front door.

"Could've sworn I'd heard you," she said easily, following me inside.

The girls immediately ran upstairs, leaving me with the barracuda. The back of my neck tingled as I made a pot of coffee, and I knew she was staring at me. Farrah was tiny, closer to Kara's size than Rose, but she might've been the most terrifying woman I'd ever met. You just never knew what she was going to do. The only thing that gave me any comfort was that she wasn't carrying the shotgun she liked to pull out when shit got rowdy at the clubhouse.

"What'd you do?" she finally asked as I set a cup of coffee down in front of her.

"Why does everyone think I did somethin'?" I asked in frustration. "Why don't you ask your niece what happened?"

"She's not talking."

"Then why don't you respect that?"

Farrah laughed. "Not the way it works, kid."

"I'm not that much younger than you."

"You'll always be that much younger than me," she replied, taking a sip of her coffee. "Even if we were the same age—which we aren't. Not even close."

"Say what you need to say," I replied.

"This is your show," she announced, waving her hand toward me. "Start talking."

"Nothin' to say."

"Oh, yeah?" she said, tilting her head to the side. "Where were you tonight?"

"None of your fuckin' business."

"Not hasslin' my niece at work, I hope."

"The fuck?"

"Casper's got eyes everywhere, *kid*. Not a damn thing happens that we don't know about."

"Then why the fuck did you let that shit go on with Copper so long?" I shot back.

Her eyes darkened. "Can't see what happens behind closed doors," she said.

"Because you shouldn't. It's none of your goddamn business."

"My kids, my business."

"Last time I checked, Rose was Grease and Callie's."

Farrah chuckled. "If you think that, you haven't been paying attention." She pointed at me. "That girl is as much mine as she is Callie's. Her brothers, too."

We stared at each other for a long time, the girls' laughter in the bedroom the only thing breaking the silence.

"She wants kids," I finally said, irritated that I broke first.

"And you don't?"

"I had a vasectomy years ago."

"Fucking hell," she said as her eyes widened. "I forgot all about that."

"Guess it's a deal-breaker," I said, keeping my expression neutral.

"You didn't tell her?" Farrah asked.

"Thought everyone knew."

"Assuming makes you an ass." Farrah glanced toward the bedroom. "Can't those things be reversed?"

"If I wanted it reversed," I replied.

"Ah," she said in understanding.

"Ah, what?"

"There's a difference between, *sorry, baby, I did this before we met* and *sorry, baby, I don't want any more kids.*" She stood up. "The first one can be fixed—plenty of ways to build your family without sperm. The second one can't."

"That's it?" I asked as she started around the table.

"What?" she laughed. "You want my advice now? Alright, here it is. If you don't want more kids, then stay away from Rose. Even if by some chance you get her back, you're stealing away something precious. Because even if she agrees to go along with it, she'll never be happy. She'll resent the hell out of you."

"I'm not forcing her," I ground out. "If she wants to be with me, she's making that choice."

Farrah looked at me sadly. "If you love her, don't even give her that option."

My stomach sank.

"Charlie-bear," Farrah called. "Let's go."

I stayed there in the kitchen as Charlie ran down the hallway and left with Farrah. I couldn't make my feet move. I'd never had trouble doing the right thing, making a decision and following through with it. My conscience was clear because even if my actions didn't follow with someone else's version of right and wrong, I knew in my gut they were right.

But I didn't think I could do the right thing this time. If I had a chance with Rose, I'd take it and the resentment Farrah was so sure would follow.

CHAPTER 13

ROSE

IT WAS DRIZZLING outside when I got to the clubhouse for Charlie's birthday party, and my hair was wild around my face by the time I walked through the door.

"What in the I-married-my-cousin is *this*?" I asked, pausing with my hands holding my hair back.

"Paintball war," my mom said, coming out from behind the bar. "The boys went a little overboard."

"You think?" The crowd was a sea of camouflage clothing and faces smeared with green and brown paint.

"Are you going to play?" she asked, looking me up and down. I'd worn a pair of jeans and a sweatshirt, nothing out of the ordinary, but I definitely wasn't prepared to be running outside getting hit with paint.

"Why did no one tell me that we were doing paintball?"

"I thought I told you," Hawk said as she walked toward us. She was wearing all black, and had a ski cap pulled over her purple hair.

"Are you planning a little B&E later?" I asked, making my mom snort.

"No way in hell am I putting on camo anything," she replied with a shudder. "This is giving me flashbacks to the douchebags in high school that constantly asked me for blowjobs."

"Gross."

"Mick took care of it," Hawk said with a smile. I felt a little pang, but smiled back. My older brother had been Hawk's best friend in high school before he'd died.

"That's because we raised our boys right," my mom replied.

Just then, Tommy hopped on top of a table and started thrusting his hips.

"Two out of three ain't bad," I told my mom consolingly as she grimaced.

"Are you going to play?" Hawk asked. "You might want to change."

"I didn't bring anything else to wear."

"I can get you something out of your dad's stuff," my mom said. "At least a flannel or something."

"Then, yeah," I replied to Hawk. "I'll play."

"Yes!" She threw up devil horns. "We can work together."

"Don't do it," Molly called from the bar. "She's been asking all of us."

"No, I haven't," Hawk yelled back. She turned to me. "My loyalty is to you, of course."

I laughed, but my skin felt tight as I caught sight of Mack across the room. He hadn't gotten the memo to wear camo, and he was standing with my cousin Cam, wearing a pair of faded, old jeans and a dark green sweatshirt with bleach stains all over it.

"Okay, here's the rules," my Aunt Farrah said, stepping onto a chair.

"There are no rules!" Will yelled jokingly.

"Wrong, Wilfred," she replied, pointing at him. "Number one, inside the club is *off limits*. Under no circumstances will you bring the fight inside. Number two, no face shots. I'm not taking anyone to the hospital today. Number three, one hit is wounded, two hits is down, three hits is out. Once you're out, clear the course."

"There's a course?" I asked quietly to my mom.

"Wait until you see how they set up the back field. It's awesome," she whispered back.

"Number four, if at any time someone wants to quit, all they have to do is put their arms in the air and they're out of the game. Don't be a douchebag about it," Farrah said. Then she climbed off the chair.

I followed my mom into my dad's room and left wearing a pair of her sweatpants and one of my dad's old flannels over my sweatshirt. It wouldn't keep me dry outside, by any means, but it would hopefully keep the paint stains to a minimum.

By the time I got outside, the game had already begun. Everyone was screaming and laughing and racing around the course that my uncle and aunt had set up. There were tractor tires, logs, my dad's beat up old pickup, and even a little shed made out of plywood for cover. They'd also set up a ton of green netting from the army surplus store, making visibility even worse.

"Here," Aunt Farrah said. She pointed out all the elements of the paintball gun and handed me a pair of goggles. "Kick some ass."

"Aren't you playing?" I asked.

"I'll be out there in a bit," she replied. "Working on my strategy."

The rain made it hard to see, and the goggles made it even worse. By the time I'd run and hid behind a lonely tractor tire in the middle of the field, I was drenched and breathing hard. It was like hide and seek on steroids. I peeked over the edge of the tire and watched for my brothers. Out of everyone, they were the ones to beat. They'd played paintball every weekend for years and they knew all the tricks.

I got off a few shots, laughing as I hit my sister-in-law Molly in the ass and completely missed my cousin Cam.

Then, out of nowhere, everything changed.

Someone shot at the tire I was hiding behind, and as I felt the paintball hit with a thump, my ears started ringing. I gasped for air and ripped my goggles off as I stood up. I was disoriented and my heart pounded as I searched the field.

It was so loud. Between the screaming and the laughing and the sound of paintballs hitting people and structures, I could barely think.

"Rose, what are you doing? Put your goggles back on," my brother Tommy yelled at me.

I looked at him in confusion. What?

Then, a few yards away, the plywood shed collapsed with a huge thud, and I found myself on my knees, my hands covering my ears as I made myself as small as humanly possible.

"Rosie," Mack said sweetly, running his hand down my back. "Baby, what's wrong?"

The yard had grown silent.

Embarrassed, I lifted my head and looked around. Everyone was frozen, staring in my direction.

"Where's CeeCee?" I asked instinctively.

"What?" Tommy replied in confusion.

"No." I shook my head. "Nothing. Never mind."

My cousin CeeCee wasn't there. She lived in California and had for years. God, what was I saying?

I pushed myself unsteadily to my feet. "I'm fine," I said, brushing off Mack's hand on my arm.

"I'm fine," I called out, giving everyone a wobbly smile. I raised my hands above my head and shook them jokingly as I walked back toward the building. Mack didn't say a word, but he also didn't leave my side, and I was secretly glad for his presence. I was freezing and my teeth began to chatter.

Every sound still seemed heightened somehow, and when the door shut behind us, I jumped.

"Come on," my mom said worriedly, meeting us in the back hallway. "You can take a shower in Dad's room."

As we passed my uncle's room, I could hear him and my aunt arguing.

"I told you," he said, his voice low and angry.

"Charlie doesn't remember any of it. She wasn't even born yet," Aunt Farrah replied, her voice just as angry. "How was I supposed to tell her no?"

"You see Rose's face?" my uncle snapped. "She obviously hasn't forgotten."

"Don't you think I feel like shit already, Cody?"

"Come on," my mom said, pulling me along.

"I'm fine," I replied. "I can just take a shower at home."

"You're freezing," Mack argued, keeping pace with us. His hand hovered behind my back. "Get in the shower."

My mom walked me into the bathroom and brought me a towel. "I'll find you something to change into," she said as she walked back out.

Glancing down at my hands, I realized they were shaking. Shit. What the hell had happened out there? One minute, I'd been laughing my ass off and the next, it was like I didn't even know where I was. I'd never had something like that happen before.

"Come on, baby," Mack said, pushing open the door. "You need to get in the shower."

"I am," I replied, looking up at him as he stepped into the little room.

"You've been standin' in that same spot for ten minutes."

"No, I haven't," I argued, watching as he turned the shower on.

"Yeah, you have." He turned to me and started unbuttoning the flannel I was wearing.

"I can do it," I muttered, taking over. "I'm fine."

"You're not fine."

"I think I'd be the one who knows if I'm fine or not."

"You didn't see your face out there," Mack said, leaning against the wall as I got undressed. "Where'd you go, baby?"

"Nowhere," I snapped.

"Understandable if it stirred up some old memories," he replied calmly.

"It didn't stir anything up."

"There's a reason your ma and Trix stayed inside," he continued. "And Farrah."

"My aunt was outside," I replied stubbornly.

"No, she wasn't. She outfitted everyone and then came back inside."

"Whatever."

"Lily didn't even come today."

"Gray's too little for paintball," I replied. "And I'm fine. You can go now."

"It's her sister's birthday party," Mack said, his words only hitching a little as I stripped out of my bra and underwear. "But she's not here."

"Drop it," I said, climbing in the shower. I closed the curtain and let the hot water run over me, waiting to hear him leave the room. He didn't. It was quiet for a long time before he spoke.

"Mia slit her wrists in our bathtub," he said, and suddenly, I couldn't breathe. "I didn't find her for hours. Not until I got home from the garage."

I didn't reply when he paused. As my legs began to tremble, I quietly lowered myself to my knees and listened.

"Kara was only five, and she hated taking a shower. Seriously hated it. The water always got in her eyes and it was a bitch to try and rinse out her hair," he said roughly. He cleared his throat and I pressed my fingers against my lips as my eyes began to water. "But I wouldn't let her take a bath. You know what the selling point was when I bought our house? It didn't have a fuckin' tub."

I closed my eyes as his voice grew choked.

"I knew it was bullshit. It was all in my head. But I couldn't put her in a fuckin' bathtub."

Pressing my forehead against my knees, I rocked a little back and forth.

"If I'm bein' honest," he said with an uncomfortable chuckle, "sittin' here with you in there is makin' my skin crawl."

I glanced to the side and traced the tub's edge with my eyes. The other showers in the club were just that, showers with a little drain in the middle. But a few years back when they'd done some renovations, my dad had added a bathtub in his bathroom because my mom loved taking baths. It was silly, and a luxury they didn't need at the club, but she'd looked at him like he'd lassoed the moon, which had been his intention.

"It's not a big deal that playin' paintball freaked you out a little," Mack continued. "Could be worse. Could be afraid of bathtubs."

Without a word, I switched the shower off and let the water run from the faucet as I put the little stopper in the bottom of the tub. As it began to fill, I slid open the curtain and met Mack's eyes.

"That's worse," he told me seriously, gesturing in my direction as he dropped to sit on the closed toilet lid.

"I'm okay," I said over the sound of the water.

Mack swallowed and nodded.

We stared at each other as the bath filled, and as soon as I turned off the water, the silence was almost overpowering.

"Get in with me," I said softly, reaching out my hand.

Mack knelt down by the side of the tub and laced his fingers with mine. "Can't do it, baby."

"Okay." I laid my cheek on my knees and rubbed my thumb over the back of his hand.

My mom chose that moment to stick her head through the bathroom door. "Everything okay?" she asked.

Mack didn't turn his head to look at her, keeping his eyes on me.

"We're fine," I told her.

She glanced between me and Mack and gave me a small smile, then backed out and shut the door firmly behind her.

"Tell me about her," I said, meeting Mack's eyes again.

"Mia?"

"Yeah. What was she like?"

"Beautiful," he said, sitting back so that his ass was on the floor and he could brace his elbows on his knees without ever letting go of my hand. "Total smartass. Sweet. Outgoing. Sad."

"I wasn't around her much," I said, my voice quiet. "But my mom always said that she was a sweetheart."

"Yeah," he said, nodding. "That fits."

"I'm sorry you lost her," I said quietly.

"I'm sorry Kara lost her," he replied, smoothing his hand over his beard. "She was a good mom."

"She's lucky she has you," I said.

"I don't know about that," Mack said with a huff. "But I'm doin' my best."

"You're a fantastic dad."

"Had a good example growin' up," he replied.

I wanted to ask why he didn't want more kids. I wanted to point out that he was already so good at doing it alone, and that it would be so much better if we could do it together. I wanted to tell him that the thought of never having his babies made my chest ache, that I wanted to be able to help with Kara. To take her dress shopping when she started going to school dances and talk to her about boys and explain to her why her attitude wasn't going to help her when she was trying to convince him of something.

I didn't say any of that. When I opened my mouth, something far different came out.

"Me and Cecilia hid behind a tree during the shooting," I told him. I didn't have to clarify which shooting. Everyone knew the story of how a group of men had attacked us at our family barbecue, killing my great gram, our president and his wife, and my older brother Mick.

"Oh, yeah?" he said softly.

"It was barely big enough for both of us," I said, the memory never too far from my mind. "So she stood with her back to it, and held me against the front of her. Every time a shot hit the tree, it made this *thunk* sound, and I swear we could feel it. I don't know how neither of us was hit."

"She protected you," he replied.

"Yep." I nodded. "Too bad she was such a bitch every other moment of her life, or we probably would've been closer."

Mack let out a surprised chuckle.

"I'm thankful," I said with a shrug. "And I'd do the same for her, but it doesn't excuse all the other stuff."

"Can you get outta there now?" Mack asked abruptly. "I'm sorry—it's just really fuckin' with me."

"It's getting cold, anyway," I replied, reaching behind me to pull out the stopper. As we both got to our feet, Mack shuddered.

"That sound," he said, shaking his head. "Jesus."

I stepped over the lip of the tub and wrapped my arms around him, getting water everywhere. I closed my eyes and inhaled the familiar scent of his detergent as he held me against his chest. With heartbreaking certainty, I knew that the moment we left that bathroom, things would go back to exactly as they'd been.

We hadn't fixed anything. I loved Mack and I knew he loved me. I was as sure of that as I'd been of anything in my entire life—but that didn't change the situation we were in. I'd thought it over, sometimes all night long, trying to convince myself that I could give up babies if that meant I had Mack.

The reality was, I couldn't. I wanted to be a mother. And maybe that made me selfish, or shortsighted, but it was the truth. I wanted to raise Kara and give her brothers and sisters, and Mack would never give me that. It was over between us. It had to be. Drawing it out would only make things worse for everyone in the end.

❦ ❦ ❦

A COUPLE MONTHS later, I was still struggling with the decision I'd made.

I knew that I was being a miserable human. No one wanted to be around me. I snapped at my family when they tried to be nice, the way I teased Lily had gone from funny to mean, and I was generally just horrible company. I wanted to change, to go back to my normal self, but I just couldn't seem to do it. I was so angry. Angry with myself for not being able to let go of being a mother. Angry with Mack for not wanting children with me. Angry with fate that I'd fallen in love with a man that wasn't right for me.

There was a part of me, deep down inside, that was also embarrassed. How did I tell people that the man I'd fallen in love with didn't want to have children with me? That he didn't even trust me with the child he already had? When my sister-in-law Hawk cornered me one day, asking what had happened, I'd frozen. When I'd finally gotten my mouth to work, I'd mumbled something about Mack wanting someone else and rushed off before she could ask me questions. I'd felt like shit for lying, but the lie had seemed so much simpler than the truth.

I hadn't seen Mack in almost a month. It had taken some serious dedication and reconnaissance, but I'd been able to successfully avoid him. And I hated it. I hated not seeing his face. I hated that I didn't know if his hair had gotten longer, or if he'd trimmed his beard lately. I hated knowing that he was driving Kara around in the Mustang now that the weather was shitty, but I'd never seen him do it. Mack behind the wheel of a muscle car was a wet dream come to life, and I was missing it.

I hated that I didn't know what was going on with Kara. That I had to accidentally drop by at the same time that she was over at my brother's or aunt's houses, just to be able to see her at all. I hated that we'd just spent Thanksgiving apart, and I'd been weak enough to answer when he'd called to wish me a happy holiday from wherever he was spending the weekend with his parents.

He'd called me at least once a week since the day of Charlie's birthday, just to check in and see how I was. I understood it. I knew that he loved me, and the separation was as hard for him as it was for me, but I'd stopped taking the calls.

I couldn't keep that connection anymore. It was killing me. I barely slept. I'd lost twenty pounds because my appetite was gone. I wasn't moving forward—I was stuck.

"Rose," Lily snapped, making me drop my phone to my lap. "I asked if you could pick up Gray for me tomorrow. With my mom gone, I don't have anyone to grab him from school."

"Sure," I said, shooting her a smile. "Have you heard from your parents yet? What has CeeCee gotten herself into?"

"No, I still don't know anything," she shook her head. "But Trix heard from Cam and said they made it to San Diego."

"Why are they being so mysterious about the whole thing?" I asked. "It seems a bit dramatic, even for CeeCee."

"Who knows," she replied with a sigh. "I've learned to just live my own life and try not to let her stress me out."

"Good call," I replied, glancing at my phone again.

"Stop checking your phone," she ordered quietly. "You don't answer when he calls, anyway."

"I know, it's stupid."

"It's not stupid. It didn't work out, he needs to stop bothering you."

"He's not bothering me," I argued.

"You've lost a ton of weight and your skin looks like crap," she retorted. "You're trying to move on and he's not letting you. It's bullshit."

"He probably thinks I'll change my mind," I mumbled, glancing at my phone again.

"Do you think he'll change his mind?" she asked.

I thought about the absolute finality in his voice when he told me that Kara wasn't mine to raise and that he didn't want any more kids. The frustration in his voice when he'd tried to talk me out of leaving, never once giving an inch. The way his voice had gone rough when he'd talked about Mia.

"No, I don't," I replied.

"Then he should give you the same respect," she said, sitting back in her chair.

"I don't want him to stop calling," I confessed with an uncomfortable laugh. "It means he's still thinking about me."

"Rose," Lily said softly, her eyes sad. "Don't settle. He made it really clear what he was willing to give you and what he wasn't."

"I know," I replied, sitting up straight. "I know that."

"I hate this for you. I know you thought he was the one."

"It's embarrassing," I said with a watery laugh. "Why does this always happen to me? We have this conversation over and over, and I still keep finding these guys who aren't right for me and then completely falling apart."

"You haven't fallen apart," she said firmly. "You're sad. You have the right to be sad."

"This hurts so much worse than it ever has before," I choked out. "Before, it was like I was grieving a dream that I'd lost, you know? I was so intent on finding someone and when it didn't work out, I was so disappointed."

"I know you were."

"But now?" I shook my head. "Lily, it feels like someone died."

"I'm so sorry."

I huffed and scrubbed my hands over my face. "Now, it sounds like I'm trying to convince you that *this* time is different."

"Listen," she said, pulling my hands away from my face. "I hesitate to say this, because I don't want to make things harder for you…"

"Oh, great," I mumbled.

"But, this time *is* different," she said, ignoring my comment. "Mack's a good guy who loves you. He was good to you and he wanted to spend his life with you."

I held back a sob.

"But that's not enough, Rose," she said. "It isn't. Because you want two very different futures."

"I don't understand why he doesn't want to have kids with me," I whispered hoarsely. "Or why he doesn't trust me with Kara."

"I don't, either," Lily replied with a sigh. "But I have a feeling it doesn't actually have anything to do with you."

ALL MY NIGHTS at work had started to blend together, and that night wasn't any different. My customers didn't amuse me anymore, I was dead on my feet most of the time, and it was no longer funny when idiots tried to pick me up. Bottom line, I didn't want to be around people, which made bartending a chore.

I was tired and irritated and watching the clock when Mack strode through the front door, his eyes immediately finding me behind the bar. I should have known that dodging his calls wouldn't last forever, but I'd been under the mistaken impression that he'd eventually give up. Clearly, I was wrong.

I fidgeted with the towel in my hand as he strode toward me, barely noticing the men who followed him inside or the customers standing at the bar waiting for my attention. I couldn't see anything but Mack. His dark flannel fit snug under his cut, and he was wearing a black beanie that I'd never seen before. I wondered if it was new, and my stomach twisted at the thought of not knowing that he'd bought something as insignificant as a hat.

"You got a break comin' up?" he asked as he reached the opposite edge of the bar top.

"I just took one," I replied, glancing over at my boss.

"Take another one," Mack ordered.

I glanced at the crowded bar. "I can't just—"

"Rose," Mack cut me off. "Take another one."

We stared at each other, neither of us willing to concede.

I broke first. Of course I did. I wanted any time I could have with him, even if it was only fifteen minutes in the middle of my shift.

"Matt," I called, setting down the towel that I'd wrung into a wrinkled ball. "I'm taking a break."

"You just—" Matt looked over at Mack. "Uh, okay. I'll hold down the fort."

I walked to the end of the bar and slipped through the opening where the counter was on a hinge, barely making it two steps before Mack was in front of me, his hand held out, palm up. I met his eyes as I laid my hand on his, and my heart beat wildly as he laced his fingers with mine.

"Come on," he said quietly, pulling me out the front door. He didn't slow until we'd rounded the building and stood in the dark alley along the side.

"What are we doing?" I asked, keeping my voice low. The darkness reminded me of that first night he'd kissed me, and even though I'd seen and touched every inch of his body, my stomach still exploded in butterflies when he crowded me up against the wall.

"Can't do this anymore," he said. "I don't wanna live a life without you in it." He dropped his forehead against mine and his hands came up so he could thread his fingers through my hair. My breath caught. "Jesus, Rose, how much weight have you lost? You're so fuckin' skinny, baby. What the fuck?"

His fingers tightened. "We gotta figure this out."

"We already did," I replied sadly. It was hard to remember all of the reasons we didn't work when he was so close I could almost taste him.

"We don't have to decide anythin' now," he said roughly, his thumbs brushing gently over my cheeks. "We got time, baby."

"I'm not going to change my mind," I said, gripping his cut in my fists. "I want a family, Mack. I've always wanted one."

"I get it," he replied. "So lets see where this goes."

"What are you saying?"

Mack let out a huff of breath. "That I'll do whatever it takes," he said with a shrug. "You want 'em, I'll give 'em to you."

"I don't want you to agree with me so that we can get back together," I ground out, my eyes watering. "I want you to *want* to make a family with me. I want you to trust me enough that you don't have any reservations letting me help raise Kara."

"I couldn't keep you from Kara if I tried," he said, his hands tightening in my hair. "You think I don't know you're seein' her still?"

"I wasn't trying to go behind your back—"

Mack let out a deep chuckle. "Baby, you think I care about that? Shit, you know how stupid I felt when I found out you were still goin' to hang with her after all that shit I said when you left?"

"I just wanted her to know that I hadn't abandoned her," I whispered, my throat getting tight. "Our disagreement didn't have anything to do with her."

"Jesus, I love you," he breathed. He tipped his head down to kiss me, but he never made contact.

Everything inside me went still when I looked behind him.

We hadn't noticed the men who'd followed us out of the bar.

Chapter 14

Mack

I STARED INTO Rose's gorgeous brown eyes as my blood turned to ice in my veins.

I'd been distracted. So caught up in getting my woman back that I hadn't paid attention to my surroundings. I hoped she saw the apology in my eyes as I tilted my head slightly to the side, lessening the cold pressure of the gun against the underside of my jaw.

"Don't do anything stupid," the guy behind me ordered.

"Not doin' anythin,' man," I said calmly, tightening my hands on Rose before slowly sliding them away from her. "You want my wallet? Back pocket."

The man laughed. "Nah, I'm good."

Rose parted her lips to speak, but the look on my face had her snapping her mouth closed again. Thank Christ.

"What're you after?" I asked.

My pistol was tucked into the back of my jeans, and as I lowered my hands to my sides, I contemplated how fast I could pull it.

Rose's lips began to tremble.

I wouldn't be fast enough.

Even if by some chance I got my hand on it, the man behind me would blow my head off before I could kill him.

"Let's go," he ordered, grabbing a hold of the back of my cut. I tasted bile as he used it to pull me backward.

"Let her leave," I said as Rose's arms dropped from around my waist. "Whatever problem you got with me ain't got nothin' to do with her."

"Not happening," he man muttered.

That's when a second man stepped out of the darkness and grabbed Rose by the arm. Shit. No way could I take both of them without Rose getting caught in the middle.

"Hey," I snapped, jerking forward.

"No," the man with the gun to my throat said calmly, pressing the barrel harder against the underside of my jaw.

"Don't touch me," Rose snapped, trying to pull her arm from the man's grip.

I swear to Christ, the next few seconds happened in slow motion as her captor pulled a gun and pointed it just inches from her face.

"Stop," I said quickly.

"Bitch," he said quietly, ignoring me. "Gimme a reason."

I was going to kill him.

"Okay," Rose whispered, her eyes black with shock. "I'm going."

I lost sight of Rose as I was pushed toward an older, rusted-out Buick, and my mind raced as I tried to figure out how the fuck I was going to get us out of this. I couldn't believe some motherfuckers got the jump on me. As we reached the edge of the lighted parking lot, I swept my eyes back and forth, looking for anything I could use.

"In," the guy behind me ordered. He reached for the back door of the Buick, and I knew I didn't have a choice. I had to do something, because the minute we got in their car, we were pretty much fucked.

I grabbed the guy's arm as I lurched to the side, and his gun dropped as I jerked him in front of me and slammed his head against the roof of the car. It took less than a second for me to grab the pistol from the back of my jeans and spin, but in that time, the one holding Rose had jammed his gun against her eye and stood there watching me, expressionless.

"Let her leave," I ground out. I knew at this distance that I could blow a hole the size of Rhode Island in his head. He knew it, too. But as Rose quietly cried, her eyes squeezed shut in horror, the man holding her gave me a small smile.

He knew that I was fucked. I could kill him, but before he dropped, he'd take Rose with him.

I slowly lowered my weapon, and as soon as it dangled from my fingertips, the guy I'd fucked up hit me on the back of the head with something hard and heavy. Goddammit. Everything went blurry as I dropped to my knees.

"Check him, you fucking moron," one of the men ordered. "I don't want any more surprises."

I struggled to stay conscious as they loaded me and Rose into the backseat of the car and my stomach churned as Rose's hand found mine.

"You move, I shoot her," the guy who'd held his gun to Rose's head said conversationally.

I squeezed my hand around Rose's and nodded, committing the man's face to memory. He was a dead man, no matter how things played out.

They brought us to a little, run down house that was surrounded by a large field, and I inwardly cursed. There were no neighbors, and even if by some chance I could get Rose to run, there was nowhere for her to hide.

As they shoved us down into the basement, I felt all emotion fade. If I was going to get us out of there, my mind had to be clear.

"On your knees," one of the men ordered.

My gaze found Rose as we lowered ourselves. Her face was as emotionless as mine, but her eyes said everything.

Chapter 15

Trix

I STRODE QUICKLY through the clubhouse and knocked on the door to the war room, or *church* as the boys called it. I'd never been allowed inside and I didn't see that changing anytime soon, but I wasn't going to wait for the men inside to stop scratching their balls and leave. Still, it felt weird interrupting them.

"What?" Tommy barked, throwing open the door. His eyebrows shot up when he saw me standing outside. "Oh, hey, Trix. Everything okay?"

"They're fine," I said, looking around him. "Have you seen Mack?"

Tommy shook his head, leaning a little to the side so I could see the room more clearly. My dad, Grease, and Will sat around, their eyes on me.

"Have any of you seen Mack today?"

"Not answerin' his phone," Will replied.

"Shit," I muttered, pushing at the headache that was starting between my eyes.

"What's goin' on, Little Warrior?" my dad asked, getting to his feet.

"None of you have seen him?" I asked again.

Something wasn't right. My stomach twisted with anxiety.

"Start talkin'," my dad ordered.

"Kara's at our place," I said as the men left their seats and herded me to the main room. "She stayed the night last night."

"Okay?" Grease replied.

"Mack said he'd pick her up around nine," I said, "but he never showed up."

"Slept in, maybe?" Tommy said with a shrug.

"It's noon," I replied, shaking my head. "Mack's never late."

"He isn't," Will said, backing me up. "He's uptight as fuck about it. If he's not sure, he doesn't tell Kara when he'll be there, but if he gives her a time, he doesn't miss it. Maybe he's with Rose?"

Grease's head jerked toward his son. "They back on?"

"Don't know," Will replied. "But I figured it was only a matter of time."

"I've already called her," I cut in. "She didn't answer, either."

"Maybe they're in bed," Tommy said with a disgusted scowl.

"No," Will said, shaking his head. "No way Mack lets the phone ring when Kara's not with him."

"What?" my dad asked when he saw the look on my face.

"Something's not right, Pop," I said quietly. "I can feel it."

"Will," Grease barked. "Head over to Rose's. I'll go to Mack's."

"You keep tryin' to call," my dad ordered, wrapping his hand around the back of my head. He leaned forward and kissed my brow. "Let us know if you get either of them."

"I will."

As the men strode quickly to the front door, I pulled out my phone and dialed Rose again.

※ ※ ※

"WHERE THE FUCK is my daughter?" Grease barked, slamming his hand down on the table.

We'd been searching for hours, but we hadn't found anything good. After the men had no luck at Rose and Mack's houses, they'd met up at Rose's work and found Mack's bike in the parking lot. Rose's boss had met them at the front door, holding her purse and mad as fuck that she'd bailed on him during the middle of her shift.

The couple had vanished and we had no fucking clue where they could've gone.

"She wouldn't just leave her purse," Callie said, her fingers shaking as she picked at her lips nervously.

"Mack wouldn't leave Kara, either," I said, a knot in my throat. God, I wished that Cam was here instead of down in San Diego, bailing his pain in the ass sister out of whatever jam she'd gotten herself in. "Not without asking me at least four times if it was okay and letting his daughter know."

"What do we know?" my dad asked, looking around.

"Mack showed up around ten last night," my little brother Leo said, going over what we already knew. "Rose went on break and they left through the front door. They never came back in. Rose left her shit in the back, and they didn't take the bike. No cameras at the bar because Rose's boss is a cheap piece of shit."

"Poet," Dad said, turning to my gramps. "You got anything?"

"Nothin'," Gramps replied in disgust. "No one knows shit."

"Everyone's reachin' out," Will said, his jaw tight. "We're hittin' dead end after dead end."

"Someone's gotta know somethin'," Grease replied.

"If they do, no one's talkin'," Leo said. His arm was wrapped around Lily, who looked like she was going to lose it at any second.

"Fuck," Tommy yelled, throwing a chair across the room. Hawk didn't even try to calm him down as he paced, his hands gripping his skull.

"Find her, Asa," Callie said quietly, staring at her husband.

Grease's nostrils flared as he looked back at his wife. He swallowed hard and nodded.

My eyes stung as I looked away.

I CREPT INTO my house late that night, tired to my bones. We'd searched all day, and we hadn't found a single thing that pointed us in the direction of Mack and Rose. Tempers were high and nerves were completely frayed.

It didn't help the situation that Casper, Farrah and Cam were all out of town. Casper was the one with all the connections. He had his little spies everywhere.

"Trix?" Kara said quietly from the dark living room, making me jump. "Do you know where my dad is?"

"Hey, kiddo," I whispered back. "What are you doing awake?"

"Something's wrong," she said tightly, stepping over Charlie's sleeping form. "I can tell. My dad's not answering his phone, and he hasn't called me back all day."

"I'm not sure where he is," I replied carefully as she stopped a couple feet from me. "We haven't been able to get ahold of him or Rose all day."

"He's with Rose?" she asked in surprise. Her shoulders slumped in relief. "That's okay, then. They're probably just making up."

"Yeah," I said, giving her a small smile. "I bet that's exactly what they're doing."

I watched her as she rubbed her eyes tiredly, my chest aching. Sometimes when I looked at my boys, or Kara and Charlie, I was surprised at how mature they seemed. Things were so different from when I was a kid. Children grow up faster and know so much more. Then, out of nowhere, I caught a glimpse of the naiveté that they worked so hard to hide.

"Go back to sleep, honey," I said. "Or you're going to be wiped tomorrow."

"Alright."

I waited until she'd climbed into her spot on the floor between Charlie and the couch, then quietly made my way upstairs. The boys were passed out when I checked on them, and I took a minute to throw Draco's blanket back onto his bed, even though I knew he'd kick it off before morning.

"Mom?" Curtis called as I turned to leave the room. "Is everything okay?"

"It's fine, bud," I lied.

"Something happened, didn't it?" he asked, his voice solemn. "That's why Nan stayed with us today."

I crossed the room and sat down on the edge of his bed, ducking a little so I wouldn't hit my head on the top bunk.

"Yeah," I said, brushing his hair back from his face. "But don't worry, the boys'll figure it out."

"Is Dad okay?" he asked, swallowing hard.

"Your dad's fine," I assured him.

His dad was fine, but Kara's might not be. It took everything I had to keep a neutral expression on my face when I wanted to start bawling.

"It's Kara's dad, isn't it?" he said, his voice barely above a whisper. "That's why he didn't pick her up today."

My boy noticed everything.

"We're trying to figure out why he didn't," I replied calmly.

"Oh," he replied, his eyes darkening as he glanced toward his bedroom door. "I won't say anything to Kara."

"Thanks, bud," I choked out, nodding. "I'll talk to her when we have news."

"No need to freak her out," he said wisely, his voice cracking. He bit the inside of his cheek as his chin quivered.

"It's going to be okay, son," I said, leaning forward to kiss his head. "Try and get some sleep."

I left the room and hurried down the hallway, barely getting my bedroom door shut behind me before the first sob left my mouth. Where the fuck were Mack and Rose?

Chapter 16

Will

"Still nothing," Molly told me, dropping her phone onto the table between us. She sighed in frustration. "I've checked every goddamn hospital in a fifty mile radius. No one matching Mack's or Rose's descriptions have been admitted in the past three days."

"This doesn't make any fucking sense," I muttered.

It was like my sister had just disappeared off the face of the planet. We'd contacted every person we knew, brought in support from other chapters and allies along the west coast, called in every favor we had—and we still knew nothing.

The baby sister I'd been protecting our entire lives was going through God knew what, and there was absolutely nothing I could do about it. She'd always counted on me to have her back, and I couldn't even find her. I felt like I was going to come out of my skin.

My mom was barely functioning, her lips and the skin around her fingernails so picked over, they constantly bled. Dad was raging, and Tommy was practically silent. We were barely holding it together.

Nothing had prepared us for something like this. It didn't make a damn bit of sense. We hadn't gotten a ransom call, and no one was claiming responsibility for their disappearance. They were just *gone*.

"Church," Dragon bellowed, striding to the door near the bar.

I kissed Molly and followed him in, my dad and Tommy on my heels.

As soon as the door closed, Dragon started speaking.

"Casper's been in touch," he said, not even bothering to sit down. "Thinks he's figured out where the missin' shipments have been goin'."

I stared at him in disbelief. Honestly, who the fuck cared about the missing guns when my sister was nowhere to be found?

"Bunch of skinheads," Dragon said in disgust. "Not worried about sellin', seein' as how they're busy buildin' their own arsenal."

"Fuck," my dad muttered.

"He wanted to give me a heads-up," Dragon said, meeting my eyes. "Cause he's sure as he can be that they don't give a shit about us. No reason to fuck with a member and his woman when they got what they needed from us already."

"Jesus Christ," Tommy snapped, his hands pressed to the sides of his head. "Where the fuck are they?"

"No luck at the hospitals?" my dad asked me.

"Nothing."

"We're missin' somethin'," Dragon said, shaking his head. He looked at my dad. "But we'll find your girl, Grease."

"Just keep thinkin'," my dad said, his voice hoarse, "that it's a good thing she's with Mack." He covered his mouth with his hand and I had to look away from the helplessness in his eyes. "'Cause he's the only man that'd protect her the way I would."

"Fuck this," Tommy muttered. He stormed toward the door, and just as he swung it open, the rest of the clubhouse went nuts.

"The fuck's happenin'?" Dragon asked as we hurried out of the room.

I caught Molly's wide eyes and shook my head at her as I jogged toward the front door, pulling my pistol out of the holster at my back. Men surrounded me as we poured into the forecourt, and I cursed as a blue car flew up the long, gravel drive, spitting gravel. I raised my arms as it got closer, aiming at the driver as I stared into the front windshield.

Holy fuck.

"Don't shoot," I screamed, dropping my arms as I ran forward. "Don't fucking shoot!"

The second my dad saw Rose, he flew into motion. By the time she'd put the car in park and climbed out of the car, he was there to catch her.

"We have to go back. We have to go *now*," Rose said as I reached them.

"Fuck," my dad choked out, his hands frantically smoothing her hair as he kissed her head over and over.

"Dad," she said, pulling away. "We have to go get Mack."

"Where is he, Rose?" I asked.

"She's bleedin'," Tommy snapped.

"I'm fine," Rose bit out, shaking her head as she took a step back. "Just a scratch."

Tommy made a noise in his throat that I ignored as I watched Rose.

"Where, Rose?" I asked.

"By the old swimming hole," she said urgently. "I'll show you, come on."

"No fuckin' way," my dad said instantly. "You're not goin' anywhere."

"Draw me a map," I said as Rose opened her mouth to argue.

As the boys fired up their bikes around us, Rose knelt in the gravel.

"Through both of these stop signs," she said, using her shaking fingers to draw a map in the rocks. "Keep going, there's a—a turn, no, no, it's just a curve here…"

As soon as she finished describing the house they'd been held in, I helped her to her feet.

"Hurry, brother," she said, her face pale with fear. She let out a quiet sob. "He's in the basement. Someone needs to take a truck."

"A truck?" Tommy said in confusion.

"He's in bad shape," I said, reading between the lines. I held Rose's eyes for a moment more. "I'll get him for you."

As soon as my mom, Molly and Hawk came running out of the clubhouse, I hustled to my bike and Tommy ran to my mom's rig. I didn't even bother with a helmet and the minute after I'd fired up my bike, I led the brothers off the compound.

We hauled ass. I was pretty sure I knew exactly where I was supposed to be going, but I still went over the surprisingly detailed map Rose had drawn in my mind. I had no idea how she'd managed to pay such close attention to where she'd come from, but it made shit a whole lot easier for us.

The shitty old farmhouse was exactly where she'd said it would be, and the place was quiet as a tomb.

"Fuck," my dad said as we jumped off our bikes.

Yeah, that was my thought.

"You and you," Dragon said, pointing, "You take the front door. We'll take the back."

We cautiously moved on the house, even though every single one of us wanted to hurry. Mack was in there somewhere, and from the look on Rose's face, we didn't have time to dick around.

"Rose?" Leo asked as we came up on a body, a pair of gardening scissors imbedded in the man's eye.

"No fuckin' way," Tommy said in disbelief.

"It was her," my dad said, barely glancing at the man on the ground. "I'd bet my bike on it."

We continued forward, ignoring Tommy kicking the body on his way past it.

"Motherfucker," he muttered.

It didn't take much time to clear the house, and it was less than five minutes before we hit the basement stairs.

Bile rose in my mouth and I nearly tripped as I caught sight of the man on the pool table. His face was unrecognizable, and there was so much blood, I was pretty sure his body was completely drained. Jesus, was that Mack?

I jerked my head up as someone groaned from the floor on the far side of the table.

If I'd thought that the man on the pool table was bad, I was wrong.

Mack was worse. His face looked like hamburger.

"You're alright," my dad said, dropping to his knees. "You're gonna be just fine, son."

"Rose," Mack said, his hand barely lifting from the cement floor as he tried to grab my dad's arm.

"We got her," Dad said.

"Rose," Mack said again.

"We got her, son," my dad said again, leaning close to Mack's face. "She's just fine."

"Rose."

"We gotta get him outta here," Dragon said. He knelt beside my dad and ripped the bandana off his head. "Ain't the cleanest, but it'll work," he said as he wrapped it around Mack's thigh.

Fuck. He was bleeding bad.

I glanced around the room, looking for anything we could use as a bandage, and everything in me went still when I spotted a familiar-looking bag sitting at the far end of a couch.

"What're you doin'?" Tommy snapped as I strode toward the couch.

"Jesus fuckin' Christ," I muttered as I gripped the strap and lifted Rose's backpack.

"Need some help over here," Leo called to me.

Loosening the straps, I put the backpack on and strode back to Mack and the boys.

"Nothin' for it," my dad said, using his forearm to wipe at the sweat on his face. His hands were covered in blood to the elbow. "We gotta carry him out."

"Rose," Mack mumbled.

He screamed as we lifted him, then mercifully passed out.

As we carried him carefully up the steps, Dragon spoke.

"This is too much for Molly, we gotta take him to the hospital," he said, looking at each of us. "Someone dropped him at the gates. Didn't see who it was."

"Not a clue who it was," Tommy grunted.

"I'll call a cleaner," Leo said. "Get this place taken care of."

"Me and Tommy'll take Mack," Dad said.

"I'll get Rose," I said as we reached the kitchen.

"You boys head out," Dragon said as we carried Mack to my mom's SUV. "Get the hell out of Eugene."

"You sure?" Old Chase asked.

"Yeah, man," Dragon said. "No need to get all wrapped up in this shit."

"Let us know if you need anythin'."

"Owe ya one," my dad said.

"Hell," Old Chase replied, looking down at Mack as we passed him. "Don't worry about it. We're square."

"Drive like hell," Dragon told my dad as he climbed behind the wheel, Mack laid out in the back seat. "He ain't got much time."

"Yep," my dad replied. Then he was gone, Tommy following on his bike.

"You takin' souvenirs?" Dragon asked, eying the bag on my back.

"It's Rose's," I replied. It didn't take long for him to connect the dots.

"I shoulda let Mack kill him," Dragon replied, his eyes cold. "Fuck."

"He doesn't, I will," I said as I strode toward my bike.

I needed to get back to my sister before she completely lost her mind with worry.

Chapter 17

ROSE

"YOU HAVE TO stay still," Molly ordered, her voice stern. She'd fallen into her nurse role the moment she caught sight of the ugly cut on my arm. "I need to clean this before I stitch it."

"Just bandage it," I said, watching the front room of the club.

My heart stopped as the front door swung open, and I locked eyes with Kara.

"Rose," she whispered. I jumped to my feet as she barreled toward me.

Something inside me settled the minute her arms wrapped around my waist.

"Where's Dad?" she asked, her face pressed against my shoulder.

"The boys went to get him," I said against her hair. I didn't even try to hold back my tears as I held her tight with my good arm.

"I called Nana," she confessed. "I got scared when you didn't come home."

"Good," I said, sniffling. "Are they on their way?"

I made eye contact with Brenna over Kara's shoulder as she mouthed, "I called them, too."

"They'll be here soon," Kara said tearfully.

"I'm so happy to see you," I whispered, kissing her again. Then again. Jesus, I hadn't realized how terrified I'd been of never seeing her again. I'd had to compartmentalize, there'd been no room to worry about anyone but Mack.

"Is Dad okay?" Kara asked, her fingers digging into my back.

Just as I opened my mouth to answer her, the front door opened again, and my brother Will strode in. As our eyes met, my legs lost all feeling. It took everything in me to stay standing as he strode toward me.

"We need to go," he said softly, reaching out to run his hand gently down the back of Kara's head.

"No," Kara said, her arms tightening. "Don't leave me."

"She comes, too," I said, lifting my chin.

"I still need to stitch her arm," Molly interrupted. "She's bleeding all over."

Will glanced at Molly and then down at my arm. "Bandage it," he ordered. "And get her a fresh set of clothes."

"I'll get the clothes," my mom said.

I sat down again, holding Kara's hand as Molly pulled gauze out of her bag.

"Oh, my God," Kara said as she looked at my arm. "What happened?"

"It's just a scratch, princess," I said, squeezing her hand. "It doesn't even hurt."

"You win the scar contest," she said, her voice wobbling as she tried to joke.

"Nailed it," I shot back, giving her a small smile.

Less than five minutes later, I followed Will and Kara to Molly's car, wearing a pair of my mom's yoga pants and flip flops. Molly's sweatshirt hid the bandage on my arm. I climbed into the backseat with Kara as Will got in the driver's seat.

"We'll be right behind you, baby," my mom said as she closed me into the car.

"Where are we going?" Kara asked as Will threw the car into reverse.

"The hospital," Will said, confirming what I already knew. He met my eyes in the rearview mirror. "Mack got dropped off at the gates."

I nodded in understanding.

"He did?" Kara asked, turning to look through the window at the broken gate.

"Kara," I called, waiting for her to look at me before I spoke again. "I've been home."

"What?" she asked in confusion.

"You stayed at Trix's with the kids," I said, tightening my fingers around her hand. "While your dad went out of town."

"I don't—" she shook her head.

"You know you don't talk about the club," I said. I waited for her to understand my meaning.

"Of course not," she said softly, her eyes searching mine. "It's none of my business and it's really not anyone else's business."

I almost laughed, because I knew those words had come directly from Mack.

"This falls under that umbrella," I said. "Can you handle it?"

Kara sniffled.

"No one's going to ask you questions," I murmured, leaning my head against the seat as I watched her. "But you keep your mouth shut if they do."

"I will," she said, her voice trembling as her chin lifted just a fraction.

"It'll be okay," I said as her face fell and she started to cry again.

"You got a black eye wrestling with one of the kids," Will said as he parked at the hospital.

"I have a black eye?" I said as I climbed out of the car.

"Oh, yeah," Kara said as she followed me.

The emergency waiting room was busy, but I saw my dad and Tommy immediately. Trying not to call attention to myself, I hurried toward them, my heart in my throat.

"Took him back to surgery," my dad said as I reached him. He wrapped his arms around me and Kara. "Haven't heard anything yet."

"We should be upstairs, then," Will said.

"Just waitin' on you," Tommy said.

We headed toward the elevator, and Kara let go of me to walk beside my dad. A wave of pain hit me so hard that I nearly stumbled as she put her small hand in his and he looked down at her in surprise.

"He'll be alright," Tommy said, wrapping his arm around my shoulders. "Man's built like a bull."

"Like a Mack truck," Will said as we stepped into the elevator.

"That's why he's called Mack?" I said in surprise. "I thought it was because his last name is MacKenzie."

"Both," my dad said, smiling down at Kara.

"His real name's Jacob," she said. "My Nana and Grandpa call him Cubby."

Tommy snorted. "Oh, hell, yes," he muttered.

"Cubby, huh?" Will said with a chuckle.

"Your dad's gonna kill you," my dad said to Kara.

"My dad's name is Asa," I said, bumping Kara with my shoulder as we got off the elevator. "But you should hear the names my mom calls him."

"Hey, now," my dad said. "Don't be tellin' tales."

I was so thankful that my dad and brothers were keeping things as light as possible for Kara, but as I checked in with the woman working at the desk, my chest felt like it was going to cave in at any second.

Mack had been in really bad shape when I'd left him, and I had no idea how much worse he'd been by the time they found him. Questions were on the tip of my tongue, but it was a while before I had the chance to ask them.

"I'm gonna head downstairs and get Ma," Tommy said, looking up from his phone. "They just pulled in."

"I'll go with you," I said quickly. Everyone looked at me in surprise. "I need to move."

"I'll go, too," Kara said instantly, getting to her feet.

"Nah, baby," my dad said. "You hang with us. They'll be right back."

Kara glanced at him and then back at me. I could see the indecision in her eyes, but her respect for authority had her dropping back in her seat.

"Right back," I said. "Promise."

I kept my mouth shut until the elevator doors closed, blocking the view of my family.

"How bad?" I asked immediately, turning to Tommy.

"Pretty fuckin' bad," he replied, running his hand through his hair as he met my eyes. "Don't know how we got him here in time."

I covered my mouth with my hand, muffling the moan that I couldn't seem to silence.

"He was still breathin'," Tommy said, pulling me against his side. "He was askin' about you when we got there."

"Of course he was," I whispered tearfully. "Did you get the guys who took us?"

Tommy looked at me oddly. "Nah," he said slowly, making my heart stop. "One of 'em was dead in the yard, pair of gardening shears in his face. The other one was mangled on the pool table."

I closed my eyes in relief.

"Gardening shears?" Tommy said as the doors opened. "Seriously?"

"It was the only thing I had," I muttered as we stepped off the elevator.

"Jesus," he said. "I'm never pissin' you off again."

"Give it a couple days," I said dryly as my mom and the rest of the women headed toward us.

"Boys are on the way," my mom said as she hugged me. "They needed to finish some stuff up."

"How's Mack?" Trix asked as we stepped back on the elevator.

"He's in surgery," I told her. "We haven't heard anything."

"How bad is it?" Molly asked nervously.

"It was bad when I left," I choked out, staring at the doors as we moved upward.

"Some stab wounds," Tommy said quietly. "His face was pretty fucked up. Fingers were mangled."

"He's going to be pissed if he wakes up without a beard," Molly said, trying and failing to act nonchalant.

"I think the missing fingernails will probably bother him more," I replied as the doors opened.

Lily's arm wrapped around my waist as I headed for Kara, and I welcomed the support.

"He'll be okay," Lily whispered. "If for no other reason than he wants to make sure you're safe."

I stopped in my tracks and turned my head to look at her.

"Tommy said he asked for me," I said quietly.

"Leo told me that he just kept repeating your name," she confirmed.

My knees buckled.

"Tommy," Lily called, barely getting her arms around me before I hit the floor. "Shit!"

"Come on, little sister," Tommy said, scooping me up. "The floor is filthy."

He carried me to one of the couches, and I wanted to say thank you, but the words felt trapped in the back of my throat. Panic choked me as Kara curled up against my side, her head on my shoulder.

I couldn't lose Mack. We couldn't lose him. God, I was so angry that we'd wasted so much time arguing about hypothetical kids. I'd thought I could walk away because he wouldn't give me what I wanted, and it had seemed so rational at the time that I'd felt proud for standing my ground. How could I have been so stupid?

I'd give up anything to keep Mack.

"Rosie," my dad said, coming to kneel in front of me.

I looked at him, but I couldn't respond.

"I know you're scared," he said gruffly, placing his hands on my knees, his thumbs rubbing in small circles. "I know."

His face grew blurry as my eyes filled with tears.

"I been right where you are," he continued, squeezing my knees. "I couldn't check out and neither can you." He looked pointedly at Kara and I followed his gaze.

Her eyes were closed and her hair was covering most of her face, but what little was showing was blotchy and red from crying. I ran my fingers through her hair, and bit my lip as she shuddered a little, burrowing closer.

"It's going to be okay," I said, resting my cheek on her head. "The waiting is the hardest part."

"That's my girl," my dad said quietly, getting to his feet. "Chin up, eyes forward."

We sat like that for a long time as the waiting room grew crowded with Aces and their old ladies. Coffee was handed out. Quiet voices filled the room. Molly made trips up to the desk to find out if there was any news, shaking her head at me each time she came away with nothing.

We'd been there for two hours when Howie and Louise stepped off the elevator, their faces pale and scared.

"Look who's here," I told Kara.

She lifted her head to look, and I expected her to run to her grandparents, but she didn't move.

Louise's gaze searched the room as they walked forward, and just as her eyes landed on me and Kara, Dragon stopped her. He spoke quietly to Mack's parents for a few moments, and I watched them nod their heads. Then, they came straight for us.

"I'm so glad you're okay," Lou said as she bent to wrap her arms around me and Kara. She pressed her lips against my forehead and held them there for a long moment, then moved to Kara and did the same thing.

"I'm glad you're here," I said as she moved back so Howie could hug us.

"I'm sorry it took so long," she replied, wringing her hands. "We were in Montana, and there were no flights that could get us here faster than driving."

"You shoulda seen your nana cursin' a blue streak," Howie told Kara, giving her a small smile.

"Dad's in surgery," Kara said, swallowing hard. "He's been back there a long time."

"Best place for him," Howie said, crouching down so he was eye level with Kara. "Doctor's know what they're doin.'"

"What if they mess up?" she asked fearfully.

"C'mere," Howie ordered, opening his arms. For the first time in hours, Kara let go of my waist and lurched into her grandpa's arms.

I watched them as he carried her to a chair in the corner of the room. My side felt cold without her pressed against me, and I forced myself not to follow them.

"How're you doing?" Lou asked as she sat down in Kara's spot next to me.

"I'm okay," I replied hoarsely.

"Well, I don't believe that at all," she said with a sigh as she leaned back against the couch. "But I'll let it go for now."

"Thank you," I replied. I meant it. I knew that at some point, I was going to lose it. I could feel the fear and anxiety building with every beat of my heart. But I couldn't let it happen yet. Not in the middle of the waiting room. Not when Kara was only a few feet away.

"Hey, sweetheart," my mom said, walking toward us. "I brought you some coffee. It tastes like shit, but I added a bunch of creamer, so you should be able to choke it down."

"Thanks," I replied, taking it from her hand. I wasn't sure when the last time I'd slept was. Yesterday? The day before? Our time in the basement was already starting to blur together.

"I'm Callie," my mom said, holding her hand out to Louise.

"Rose's mom?" Lou said, getting to her feet. "It's nice to meet you."

Instead of shaking Mom's hand, Lou pulled her in for a hug. I almost smiled as Mom's eyes widened at me over Lou's shoulder.

"Careful, Mom," I said. "She's a kisser."

"I wait until the second date for kissing," Lou said as she let go. She opened her mouth to say something else, but snapped it shut again as two policemen stepped off the elevator.

"Showtime," my mom said under her breath. "You up for it?"

I got to my feet without replying.

"Somethin' I can help you fellas with?" Dragon asked, planting himself between our group and the cops.

"Man, you knew there were gonna be questions," the younger cop said. "Don't give us shit, and we can be out of here quick."

"Ask your questions," my dad said, getting up from his seat.

"For starters," the older cop said, "how'd your man end up here, looking like he'd been tortured and covered in stab wounds?"

Lou inhaled sharply, but kept her shit together.

"Your guess is as good as mine," Dragon said emotionlessly. "He got dropped at the gate in that condition."

"That's the story you're going with?" the younger cop asked, surveying the room.

"Only story there is," Dragon replied.

"What happened to her?" the cop said, gesturing toward me with his chin.

Dragon turned to look at me. "What?" he asked innocently.

"Woman's been beaten," the cop said in disgust. "Miss, can you come over here, please?"

I knew it would happen, but I still felt my heart pound as I made my way toward the officers. Surprisingly, Lou went with me, her shoulder brushing mine.

"Yes?" I asked when I reached them.

"What happened to your face, ma'am?" he asked kindly.

"The eye?" I asked, cocking my head to the side like I couldn't figure out why he was asking.

"Yes."

"I got elbowed in the face," I said with a shrug, "wrestling with my cousin last week."

"Wrestling with your cousin?" he asked dubiously.

"She's thirteen and she tried to steal my remote," I replied.

"You leave any marks on her?" he snapped.

"Over a remote?" I said in disgust. "Of course not."

He stared at me for a long moment. "Ma'am, is there a reason that you haven't seemed to um, bathe—"

"Now, that's just insulting," Louise snapped.

"I apologize," he stuttered.

"We done here?" Dragon asked.

"Not quite," the older cop replied. He looked at me, and I swear he saw right through our story. "You can go back to your seat, miss. I'm sorry my partner bothered you."

I held my shoulders straight as I walked back to my seat, the feel of their eyes on my back burning like a brand.

"You're sticking with your story?" the older cop asked Dragon.

"Got dropped off at the gates," Dragon confirmed. "Brought him straight here."

"We'll be back," the cop replied with a sigh. "Gonna need to talk to Mr. MacKenzie when he wakes up."

"You do that," Dragon said with a nod. Then he turned his back and walked away, showing exactly how much he cared about their presence.

I let out a sigh of relief when the police officers disappeared behind the elevator doors.

A few minutes later, Molly strode toward me, her face emotionless.

"Tell me," I ordered, getting to my feet.

"They're almost done," she said.

"How did it go?" I asked.

"We won't know that until they come out here," she said sympathetically. "The surgery didn't take as long as I thought it would." She looked at Louise then met my eyes again. "That could either mean that it went very well, or that they decided not to put his body through any more trauma."

"Jesus," I muttered, staring blankly at the floor.

"But we'll know soon," she said. "I'm so sorry, Rose."

"Don't be," I said, reaching out to pat her shoulder. "It must suck being the only one who knows what the hell is going on around here."

"How's your arm?" she asked quietly.

"Fine," I replied. "Bandage is still doing its job."

"Let me know if it starts seeping through," she said. "I brought some extra supplies in my purse."

"Thanks, Mol."

I sat back down as she walked away.

"What's wrong with your arm?" Louise asked, her brow furrowed with concern.

"Just a scratch," I said, shaking my head as I watched the doors to the operating rooms.

"It sounds worse than that," she argued.

"One thing at a time," I said tiredly. Thankfully, she dropped it.

I stared at the doors for at least a half hour, silently begging them to open, my knee bouncing up and down. The longer we went without news, the harder it became to keep calm. When they finally opened and two doctors came out, I was almost too afraid to stand up to meet them.

"Family of Jacob MacKenzie?" one of them asked.

"That's us," Will said.

The doctors looked around the room. "Immediate family?"

"Here," I said, striding forward with Louise and Howie on my heels.

"I'm Dr. Halstead and this is Dr. Mark."

"You don't rate a last name?" Howie asked. He wasn't joking.

"My last name is hard to pronounce and Dr. Mark is easier to remember," Dr. Mark said, giving Howie a tired smile.

"How's our boy?" Louise asked, giving Howie a warning glare.

"Ma'am, your son's injuries were extensive and he'd lost a lot of blood," Dr. Halstead said. He crossed his arms over his chest, gripping his biceps. "But we've repaired the worst—the wounds in his chest and thigh. We had to remove part of his lung—" Louise inhaled sharply. "His hands may require another surgery at a later date, but the lacerations on his face have been stitched. He has a concussion and his cheekbone is broken, but those will heal on their own in time."

"Okay," Louise said shakily.

"Our biggest concern now is infection," Dr. Mark said. "So we'll have him on a large dose of antibiotics and we'll monitor him in the ICU for a few days."

"Thank you," Howie said, reaching out to shake hands with both men.

"Absolutely," Dr. Mark said.

"You should be able to go back and see him soon," Dr. Halstead said. "Only a couple people at a time." He looked around the room. "Maybe stick to just a small group."

"Only a few of us will go back," I said, my lips curving into a small smile as I glanced back at the crowded room behind me. "They're all here for us."

Dr. Halstead nodded, then both doctors turned and walked back where they came from.

That's when the crash I'd felt coming on for hours hit me. I looked up and met Lily's eyes as I spoke to Louise. "You'll tell Kara?"

"Sure, honey."

I kept my shit together until Lily led me into the small bathroom down the hall. Then, with a gasp, I let myself fall apart.

"Here," Lily said, pulling off her hoodie. She rolled it into a ball and shoved it in my face.

The scent of her laundry detergent filled my nose as I pressed the sweatshirt hard against my face and screamed. All of the pain and fear and helplessness and *rage* poured out of me as I wailed against that blue sweatshirt, the noise barely muffled in the fabric.

By the time I was finished, I was gasping for air.

"All done?" Lily asked, wetting a paper towel in the sink.

"For now," I rasped tiredly.

"Good," she said, handing me the towel. "Wipe your face and get your shit together, because you need to go see Mack."

"You're such an asshole," I muttered, cleaning off my face.

"If I tried to console you right now, we'd never leave this bathroom," she said, knowingly. "I'll hug you and cry with you later."

I opened the bathroom door just as Louise raised her fist to knock on it.

"They said we can go back to see him," she said. "He's one floor up."

The hallway and waiting room passed by in a blur, and the elevator felt so stifling I wished I'd taken the stairs. I could barely stand still as the nurse signed us into the ICU and gave us little stickers with Mack's room number on them.

"Me and your nana are going to go first," I told Kara, smoothing the sticker onto the chest of her jean jacket. "Then one of us will come out and get you, okay?"

"Maybe I should go with you, and Nana can go with Grandpa," Kara said, her eyes wide and scared.

"We'll be right back," I said softly, cupping her cheek in my hand. "Promise."

I stepped away as Howie wrapped his arm around Kara's shoulders, then me and Lou followed the nurse down the hallway.

"I could've waited," Lou said softly.

"I want to make sure it won't scare her," I replied, my eyes on the nurse in front of us. "And I need to be calm before she gets in there."

I held my breath as the nurse stopped at a sliding glass door and gave us a small smile.

Then all breath left my lungs when I got my first look at Mack.

Louise made a small noise of sorrow, but I couldn't comfort her. I was too busy staying on my feet.

He was gray, his face slack and clean shaven. It was the first time I'd ever seen the shape of his jaw or the small mole low on his cheek. There were tubes and wires everywhere. They hung from beneath his blanket, filled his mouth, and disappeared beneath the skin on his arms. It was terrifying, but as air filled my lungs again, I realized it wasn't half as terrifying as the moment I'd left him tied to that chair.

I moved toward him without conscious thought, and my nose stung with unshed tears as I laced my fingers with his.

"I'm here," I whispered, leaning close to his ear. "I love you. I'm here."

The constant beep of his heart monitor comforted me as I stood straight again.

"Oh, son," Louise said with a sniffle from the other side of the bed. Her hand rested gently on Mack's forearm above the bandages that completely covered his hand. "You're going to be alright, Cubby." She smoothed his hair away from his forehead. "Rest now."

She covered her mouth with her hand and squeezed her eyes shut as a silent sob ripped through her body.

"I'm going to go get Kara," she said softly. "You stay here."

"Okay," I said, nodding. I looked back at Mack as Louise left the room.

"I'm sorry I wasn't there when they came for you," I murmured quietly, running my thumb over his knuckles. "But you knew they wouldn't let me come back, didn't you?" I let out a watery chuckle. "You should have seen me, baby. I plowed right through the front gates."

One of the machines made a weird noise and my head snapped up to look at it, my heart racing, but nothing else happened.

"Everyone was looking for us," I said, tracing the stitches on his face with my gaze. "But they had nothing to go on. I think my dad nearly shit himself when he saw me drive up."

"Rose?" Kara's small voice called from the doorway, making me turn.

"Hey, sweetheart," I said. "Come on in."

"Is he okay?" she asked, her eyes bewildered as she stared at the tube in Mack's mouth.

"They're just helping him breathe right now," I said, letting go of Mack so I could pull her toward me. "But he'll be okay."

"He looks really young," she said.

I glanced back at Mack. She was right. Without the beard, Mack had a baby face. He didn't look much older than me.

"Maybe that's why he wears the beard," I said, smiling.

"Hi, Dad," Kara said, her hands fidgeting at her sides. She looked at me. "Can he hear me?"

"I don't know," I replied honestly. "But I wouldn't spill any secrets, just in case."

Kara scoffed, her eyes brightening a little. "I don't have any secrets."

"Good," I said. "Let's keep it that way."

"What—" she paused, her gaze roaming over the blanket covering Mack. "Where is he hurt?"

"His leg," I said, watching her carefully. "And his chest."

"And his face," she whispered.

"Yeah," I confirmed. "And his hand."

Kara's eyes shot to Mack's bandaged hand on the opposite side of the bed.

"That's the hand he writes with," she said.

"He can still write with it," I said, even though I had no idea if that was true. "Once it heals."

"*What happened?*" she asked, meeting my eyes as hers filled with tears.

"Bad men attacked us," I replied, unsure how much I should tell her.

"But you're okay," she said. There was no accusation in her voice, only confusion.

"That's because your dad protected me," I said, my voice catching. "He made sure I was okay."

"What if they come back?" she asked tightly. "Do they know where we live?"

"No," I said instantly. Jesus, I couldn't imagine what was going through her head. How terrified she must be. "Those men are dead."

Kara jerked, her eyes widening.

Maybe I shouldn't have said it. Maybe I should've sugarcoated it, or gave some bullshit answer to try and placate her. But I remembered being her age. She wasn't stupid, and she saw way more than we gave her credit for. Knowing that, I couldn't let her continue to worry about some faceless man coming after us if I could put her mind at ease.

"Do you think me or your dad would ever let someone hurt you?" I said, leaning close. "Those men will never hurt our family again."

I almost stumbled as Kara suddenly wrapped her arms around my waist, her face hitting my collarbone with a thud. "I'm so glad you're back," she whispered with a shuddery sob. "Don't leave again."

"I'm not going anywhere," I replied, closing my eyes as tears fell down my cheeks. "You're stuck with me, kid."

"Christ almighty," Howie said from the doorway, his steps surprisingly quiet as he came into the room. He stopped next to us, and put his hand on Mack's foot. "You've sure gotten your ass handed to you this time, son."

"Can I go out with Nana?" Kara asked quietly.

"Sure, princess," I said, letting her pull away. "You want me to walk you back?"

She shook her head. "I remember the way." She turned to Mack and lifted her hand, hesitating as she looked at all the wires. Then she laid her hand on his. "I'll be back later, Daddy. Love you."

I walked her to the door and watched her until she rounded the corner to the waiting room.

"They really did a number on him," Howie said to me as I reached Mack's side again. "You were there?"

"Not officially," I said cautiously.

He nodded. "Yeah, talked to the boss man. He let us know what happened."

"He cut me loose," I said, trying to keep my voice steady. "But he wouldn't let me help him."

"Not sure how you could've," Howie said, his eyes on Mack. "You did what you had to."

"I'll never forgive him for making me leave him there." The confession seemed safe, there in the quiet room, the humming and beeping of the machines almost drowning out my voice.

"You don't have to," Howie said simply. "You're alive. He'll gladly deal with anythin' you can throw at him."

"You think so?" I said, exhaustion rolling over me in a wave.

"If I know my son," he replied, "he'd do the exact same thing a thousand times, knowin' you'd be alright. Don't matter how pissed you are."

"We weren't even together," I said, not meeting his eyes. "We broke up months ago."

"Heard somethin' about that," Howie replied, completely unsurprised. "Me and Lou knew it wouldn't last."

"How's that?" I asked dryly.

"You don't look at a woman the way my son looks at you and let her walk away," Howie said with a small smile. "You do what you have to in order to make it right. I'm guessin' it wouldn't have been long before he was offerin' you the moon."

"I didn't want the moon," I said, rolling my eyes. "Just babies."

Howie's eyes widened in surprise. "That's what the fuss was about?"

"I wouldn't call it a fuss, really."

"Girl," he said with a chuckle. "You woulda given him some time to wrap his head around the idea, he woulda came around. Boy played with dolls almost as much as he played with trucks as a kid."

"Really?" I said, tenderness welling up in my chest at the thought of it. God, the guys would never let Mack live that down.

"Oh, yeah," Howie said. "He wanted a whole house full of kids. He'd never say it, but I think he regretted that he and Mia didn't have more."

My stomach twisted with jealousy.

"But she wasn't in no shape to take care of Kara," Howie continued. "Much less any other babies that came along."

"She always seemed like a good mom when I was around her," I said carefully.

"She was," Howie said firmly. "And she loved Kara more than anythin'." He leaned his hip against the foot of the bed, his hand still absently rubbing Mack's foot. "But somethin' broke inside her when she had Kara. Poor thing was afraid of everything by the end, even herself."

"Why didn't she see a doctor?" I asked.

Howie scoffed derisively. "She did. Told him she was havin' some anxiety and he told her, *well, there's nothin' to be anxious about.*"

"What?" I blurted, horrified.

"Old school doctor," Mack said in disgust. "He's lucky my son had his hands full at the time. Course, after that, Mia refused to see anyone else. Thought she needed to just—hell, I don't know—suck it up, I guess."

"That's insane," I whispered.

"Wasn't right," Howie replied. "But they were *so* young. They were wingin' it and Mack didn't want to make it worse for her, so he just tried to keep her happy. Me and Lou were on the road and missed a lot of it." He gave me a sad smile. "Easy to put on a brave face when your man's parents come to town for a week and then leave again."

"That's terrible," I murmured. Poor Mia.

"Can see why he'd be hesitant to go down that road again," Howie said knowingly.

"It wouldn't be the same," I replied.

"No way of knowin' that."

"Yes, there is," I said instantly, surety making my voice firm. "Because Mack would never let it get to that point, even if I couldn't see it happening. And if he somehow dropped the ball, there are about fifteen people in the waiting room right now that wouldn't let it happen, either."

"Well," Howie said looking at Mack. "Thank Christ, you two still have time to make those decisions."

"It doesn't matter anymore," I said, letting out a sigh. "As long as he's okay, I'm happy."

Howie laughed. "I'll ask you if that's still true next year when he's had the chance to piss you off again."

He rounded the bed and leaned down to kiss Mack's forehead gently, avoiding the row of stitches that bisected his eyebrow. "I'll be back later, son. I have a feelin' your mama's dyin' to get back in here and take my place."

"I don't think Kara's eaten," I said as he straightened up again.

"I'll take care of it, darlin'," he replied. He stepped toward me and rested his hand on my shoulder. "You should sit down before you fall down."

"Do I look that bad?" I asked tiredly.

"Worse," he said, giving me a wink.

"Gee, thanks," I called quietly as he left the room.

I couldn't deny the truth in his words, though. I was quickly losing whatever energy I had left. Grabbing the chair in the corner, I dragged it next to the bed and sat down heavily. Relief and gratitude filled me as I lay my head next to Mack's hip, threading my fingers through his. Maybe I'd just close my eyes for a while.

∽∽ ∽∽ ∽∽

I WOKE AT some point later to the most awful choking noise I'd ever heard in my life.

Chapter 18

MACK

MY FIRST THOUGHT was that something was choking me. Second, was Rose.

Hands pinned me down as my eyes flew open.

"Jacob," a woman said. "Jacob, you're okay. You're in a hospital."

I didn't give a fuck where I was. There was something in my goddamn throat. I gagged violently as my eyes searched the faces leaning over me, not recognizing any of them.

I didn't want to hit the pretty woman leaning down in my face, but I would if I had to. I jerked my arms and fire spread through my chest, almost making my eyes roll back in my head.

Then I heard Rose's voice and everything stopped. I searched the room, trying to see past the medical personnel doing their damnedest to keep me still.

"Hey, baby," she said, pushing her way between the man holding my arms and the nurse.

She looked like shit.

Jesus Christ, she was beautiful.

"You had to have surgery," she said, glaring at the nurse who wouldn't move from her spot by my head. Then Rose's eyes met mine, and my shoulders relaxed. "That's why you have a breathing tube." The minute she said something about it, I was hyper aware of the tube in my throat again, and I gagged so hard that it felt like I was going to vomit up my balls.

"Stay still and they'll take it out," Rose said.

I don't know how I differentiated between all the hands gripping me, but I knew the instant Rose wrapped her fingers around my arm. Okay. Yeah, okay. I'd be still. I nodded and forced my body to relax again.

It only took a few minutes to take the tube out, but it was seriously fucking unpleasant. My mouth was dry and my throat burned as the nurse packed up her supplies. She was speaking to me, and I probably should have tried paying attention to what she said, but all I wanted was for her to get the hell out of my face.

I opened my mouth to speak when the nurse moved away, but no sound came out.

"Hey, you," Rose said, smiling wide as tears ran down her cheeks.

I thought everyone had left the room, so when I saw movement out of the corner of my eye, I startled, jerking my head to the side.

"It's just me, Jacob," my mom said soothingly.

I looked at Rose questioningly.

"They called your parents when they couldn't find us," she said. "They got here a couple hours after you were brought into surgery."

Rose lifted a cup of water and swabbed my mouth with a little sponge.

"You okay?" I rasped as she turned to put the cup back down.

"I'm fine," she said.

I didn't believe her. I ignored my mom as she spoke and reached out to catch Rose's wrist as she fidgeted with my blankets. I needed to look at her, really look at her.

I'd never forget the moment I heard shots outside, knowing that I'd sent her out there, defenseless. I'd done the right thing—the only thing I could've done. We hadn't had any other choice—I knew that. But I'd still cursed and yelled and tore at my bindings, crazy with fear and rage. All of the movement and strain had made the bleeding worse and I'd only gotten to the bottom of the stairs by the time asshole number one had come barreling down them.

"I'm okay, Mack," she said softly, bringing me back to the present. "Just tired."

How long had I been in the hospital? What day was it? Had she gotten any rest at all? I knew just looking at her that she hadn't had a chance to shower yet. Her hair was greasy and pulled back in a knot at the back of her head, and I wasn't sure whose clothes she had on, but they weren't hers.

"I'm going to go grab Kara," my mom said. "She'll want to come back to see you."

"Give us a minute, first," I said painfully, clearing my throat when I was done. Damn, my throat was sore.

"Sure, son." She smiled at me and squeezed my arm before walking away.

Then, all my attention was on the woman next to me, staring at me like I was going to disappear at any moment.

"You're okay?" I asked again. I couldn't quite believe that she was there, that I could feel her smooth skin under my fingertips.

I'd thought she was dead. It was the only thing that had kept me on my feet when I'd ambushed the asshole in the basement. I thought he'd killed her.

"I'm okay," she replied, putting her hand over mine on her wrist. "I was able to get to the clubhouse and tell the boys where you were."

I smoothed my fingers over her wrist and paused when I felt the edge of a bandage.

"Just a cut," she said. "Molly cleaned it and bandaged me up."

"Jesus Christ," I murmured, relief and guilt warring inside me. "I'm so sorry, baby."

"For what?" she asked in confusion. "It was an accident. It'll heal in a week."

That's when I remembered the blood that had poured over my fingers when I'd cut the tape binding her wrists. "I did that?" I asked, knowing the answer.

"It's nothing."

"I shoulda seen them comin'," I said, staring at her beautiful brown eyes and the hollows beneath them. "Shoulda never let that happen."

"I didn't see them, either," she said softly.

"Not your job to," I replied in disgust. "I fucked up."

"You saved me," she said, leaning down so our faces were only inches apart.

"Wouldn't have needed savin' if I woulda been watchin' our backs."

"Mack," she breathed, reaching up to trace my jaw with her fingertips. "It's over."

It was then that I realized I could feel her fingers on my bare jaw.

"Shit," I said, raising my hand to my face.

Rose giggled and it was one of the best sounds I'd ever felt in my life.

"They shaved my goddamn face?" I asked incredulously. "All of it?"

Her eyes twinkled as she nodded. "I think they needed to see what they were working with. Your face is a mess, baby."

"Doesn't feel too bad," I replied, moving my jaw around. I tried to give her a reassuring smile, but pain exploded in my cheek.

"The bone's broken," she said, grimacing. "Careful."

"Yep," I replied. "It definitely is."

"Your hand might need surgery," she said quietly. "But they took care of the wound in your thigh and the one in your chest." Her breath hitched. "They had to remove part of your lung."

"Must be why it hurts to breathe," I joked.

Neither of us laughed.

Rose's face crumpled.

"Hey," I said, frustrated that I couldn't pull her against me. "It's alright, baby. I'm fine. We're fine."

"I just kept thinking that we wasted so much time," she said, her words garbled. "And I was so stubborn, and—"

"I'll give you as many kids as you want," I said, cutting her off. "Fuck, Rosie, I'll give you anything."

"We can talk about it later," she said with a watery laugh.

"Kiss me," I rasped, unable to wait any longer to feel her against me, even if it was just her lips.

My mouth tasted like shit and neither of us had brushed our teeth in days, but it was the sweetest kiss we'd ever had by far. I wanted to pull her into bed with me and feel her skin against mine, trace every part of her to make sure she was as okay as she said she was. Hell, I'd be happy to just lay with her in the quiet for a while.

"Child present," Kara announced as she walked into the room.

As Rose stepped back and I got the first glimpse of my daughter, I felt a lump lodge in my throat, making it impossible to speak.

"I couldn't wait any longer," Kara said as she came toward me.

"It's alright," I choked out, lifting my good hand so she could hold it.

"I was really scared," she whispered, staring at me the way she always had, silently asking me to make it better.

"I was too, princess," I confessed. "Did Trix take good care of you?"

"I'm not four," she said, the sarcasm in her voice softened by the smile she shot me. "But, yeah. All the kids camped out at the house while I was there."

"You look tired," I said, soaking in the sight of her face. While we'd been held, I hadn't been able to stop myself from imagining her in my mind, all the expressions she'd made when she was a baby that I still saw on her face now, the way her thumbs were double jointed and how she thought it was hilarious to show people, the way she still spun her way around the house, even though she'd stopped taking dance classes when she was seven. The idea of never seeing her again had damn near killed me.

"I'm okay. But Nana says she's going to take me back to the house so you can get some rest," she complained.

"Probably a good idea," I replied. I sure as hell wasn't going to sleep, but I wasn't too fired up at having her hang around the hospital while I was laid up. Shit had been crazy and she deserved a little normalcy.

Kara wrinkled her nose, but didn't argue.

"Take Rose with you," I said, glancing at my woman. She was swaying a little on her feet, but she still shook her head.

"No way in hell," she said. She looked at Kara. "Sorry, toots."

"I'll come back later, okay?" Kara said, her hand tightening around mine.

"Sounds good, princess."

With a sigh, she let go. "Love you, Dad."

"Love you, too. Be good for Nana."

"Yeah, yeah."

The room was quiet after she left, and I felt my eyes growing heavy, but before I could fall asleep, the sound of heavy footsteps had me looking toward the door.

"Hey, brother," Dragon said as he strode into the room, Will close on his heels. "Rose."

"What, no flowers?" I joked.

Dragon smiled and Will chuckled.

"You up for a chat?" Dragon asked, glancing at Rose. She glared back mutinously.

"Rose," I called, bringing her attention back to me.

"I'll go to the waiting room," she said, leaning down to kiss me. "Even though it's bullshit since I was *there*."

"Go home," I ordered. "Take a shower and a nap."

"Not happening," she shot back.

"Baby, you're about to fall on your face. Go get some rest." Her expression didn't change, so I tried a different approach. "I'm gonna try and sleep for a while as soon as they leave, anyway."

"Will's my ride," she said stubbornly.

"Mom said she can drive you home," Will interrupted helpfully.

Rose stared at me for a long moment. "Fine. I'll be back in a couple hours."

"Four hours," I replied.

"Two."

"Four."

"Three."

"Four," I said firmly.

"Two, it is," she replied. She laid her hand gently against the side of my throat and looked me over as she let out a shuddery breath. "Why are you always making me leave you?"

"It's only for a couple of hours," I said quietly. "Go rest, sweetheart."

She nodded, then kissed me again.

As soon as she was out the door, I looked back at Dragon and Will.

"What's the story?"

I listened while they filled me in on the shit I'd missed while I was out of it, what they'd found at the old farmhouse, and the police coming to question them, warning that they'd be stopping by to see me soon. I wasn't surprised by any of it, and I was glad that they'd figured out a way to keep Rose as far from it as possible.

"That's not all of it," Will said when Dragon finished speaking. "I found Rose's bag at the house."

I stared at him for a minute, wondering what the fuck he was talking about. When realization hit, I damn near jumped out of the bed. Every muscle in my body tightened, and the pain was so fucking intense that I had to hold my breath to keep from screaming.

"Fuckin' Copper?" I asked for clarification. I had to be sure that was what he was trying to tell me. I had to know.

"It's the only thing that makes sense," Will replied. "Don't know cause we couldn't ask them, but workin' theory is that they were only supposed to grab you. Took Rose with 'em to keep you cooperative, but were probably ordered to leave her be."

The fact that they'd left Rose alone had confused the hell out of me, considering they knew I'd do whatever I had to in order to keep her safe. I thought back to the shit they'd asked me about, mostly money and transport routes we used, neither of which I could answer. I didn't deal with club money beyond getting my cut of the profits, and our routes changed constantly because we weren't fucking idiots. Realization hit me like a sledgehammer. They hadn't needed to know anything—they'd just been fucking with me, trying to make me feel even more helpless than I was. That fucking pussy had hired people to do his dirty work because he was too chickenshit to face me himself.

Wait a second…

"Why couldn't you ask?" I said in confusion. "I only took one of them out. Did the other one bail before you got there?"

Dragon and Will shared a look.

"Found the one you took care of on the pool table," Dragon said quietly, watching me. "Other one was dead in the yard."

"Man, I never made it up the stairs," I argued.

Will's lips twitched, irritating the hell out of me. "Rose took care of the other one."

"Say what?" I said in surprise.

"Used a pair of gardening shears," Will replied.

It took everything in me not to let my mouth drop open in surprise.

"Stuck 'em so far into his eye, damn near hit his skull on the opposite side," Dragon said proudly. He looked at me. "If you hadn't noticed, we raise strong women."

I understood the pride because I felt that, too. But I also felt concerned as hell for Rose. Killing a man wasn't something a normal person just brushed off like it was nothing, and Rose was more sensitive than most—even if she tried to hide it.

"Keep an eye on her," I ordered Will.

Jesus, I could feel exhaustion pulling me under, and whatever pain medicine they'd given me was starting to wear off.

"We're already on it," he assured me. "She won't be alone while you're in here."

"She know this was Copper?"

"No," Dragon said firmly. "Only me, you, and Will know. Waited on you, see how you want to proceed."

I looked at him in surprise.

"Brother," Dragon said, "I might be your president, but this was personal as fuck. You tell me how you wanna do this."

"Rose doesn't know," I said, looking at her brother. "She'll blame herself and be all torn up about it."

"Agreed," Will said.

"Round the clock guards on my girls?" I said, finally giving up and laying my head back on the pillow. "I'm awake," I said as I closed my eyes. "Just takin' a break."

"Do whatcha need to," Dragon said in understanding.

"Round him up," I said, curling my good hand into a fist. It was infuriating that I couldn't run the bastard to ground myself, but I wasn't going to be in any shape to do that for a long ass time, and my woman needed to be safe *now*. She'd never be safe while Copper lived. Sick fuck. "Let Grease do it. Then burn the fucker."

"That was oddly nonspecific," Will said in amusement.

I opened my eyes to look at him. "I'm flat on my back, here," I replied flatly. "Your pop'll get the job done the way I would."

"Fair enough," Dragon said, getting to his feet. "We'll let you know when it's finished."

"Appreciate it," I murmured, closing my eyes again. "Tell the nurse to send in some pain meds, yeah?"

"Pussy," Will joked.

I curled my fingers down, but didn't even bother lifting my hand as I flipped him off. Then it was lights out. Even the pain radiating through my body wasn't enough to keep me awake.

∞ ∞ ∞

MY HOSPITAL STAY was a blur of visits from Rose, Kara, my parents, and nearly every brother and old lady in the club. I was rarely alone once I was moved out of ICU, and when I was, it wasn't ever for long. Police came and left when they realized I wasn't going to say anything about how I'd gotten there or who had attacked me. I had so many wounds, there wasn't any way to prove that I remembered a damn thing. Eventually, they gave up.

Rose slowly lost the exhausted, hollow look around her eyes. We didn't talk about our time in the basement, but I knew we'd have to at some point. That shit would fester if we didn't talk it out, and I wasn't going to let that happen.

God, I loved her. Any doubts I'd had disappeared. The knots I used to get in my gut when I saw her mothering Kara were completely gone. She wasn't going anywhere, and I knew with absolute certainty that it didn't matter what happened between us—even if I fucked up big and she left me—she'd never leave my kid.

Rose slept at the hospital most nights, even though I told her over and over to go home and get some sleep in a real bed. It seemed that I wasn't very intimidating when I couldn't even get out of bed to piss without help. I wasn't sure how she did it, but by the time I was cleared to go home, Rose was completely moved into my house. We hadn't discussed it, but I wasn't going to complain. She was exactly where I wanted her.

"What the fuck?" I asked as we stepped through the front door.

"You're not good on stairs yet," she said, following me in. "So I did a little rearranging."

"There are three steps between the upstairs and downstairs," I stated flatly. The house was split-level, it wasn't like I had to crawl up a flight of stairs.

"I had the boys bring the couch to our room," she said, moving around me to put my bag on the edge of the bed. "So Kara can watch TV in there."

"Maybe I want to watch TV in the living room," I said stubbornly.

"Then it's good I brought the smaller TV down here," she replied, unruffled.

"You're forgetting that I have to use the steps to get to the bathroom," I said smugly.

"Bedpan," she said easily.

"Not ever fucking happening," I snapped.

Rose burst out laughing. "You can pee off the back porch," she said with a roll of her eyes. "You only poop once a day, before your shower in the morning, so that's not an issue. I'll just help you up there and leave you to it."

I sputtered.

"What?" she asked innocently. "Was I not supposed to know that you pooped?"

I stood there dumbly, absolutely without words.

"Everybody poops," she whispered, like she was letting me in on a secret.

"This is my life now, isn't it?" I asked as she laughed.

"Yep," she said. "Get used to it."

"How are we supposed to get down when our bed's in the fuckin' livin' room?" I asked, following her into the kitchen. Jesus, I hated the cane I had to use until I was done with physical therapy. Every thump against the floor grated on my nerves and I felt unsteady as hell using my left hand. My right hadn't needed surgery, but I still couldn't use it for much.

"I'll fuck you once you're healed enough to get up the stairs," Rose replied with a shrug.

I automatically turned toward the stairs. I could get up those motherfuckers no problem. I'd crawl if I had to.

"Mack," Rose called in exasperation. "Come sit down while I make dinner."

"I haven't seen you naked or had my mouth on you in too fuckin' long," I argued. "I'm goin' up those stairs."

She jogged around me and planted herself directly in my path, her hands on her hips.

"Jacob MacKenzie," she said, making me stop in my tracks. "I want one night of peace, alright? One night where we have dinner and sleep in our own bed and I don't have to worry." Her eyes filled with tears.

"Aw, baby," I said, instantly feeling like shit. "Come here."

She came to me and wrapped her arms loosely around my waist, careful not to press up against my surgery scars that were already mostly healed. Shit still hurt, and I wasn't going to be one hundred percent for a while, but the hardest parts were behind us, thank Christ.

"I'll come hang out while you make dinner," I said into her hair, enjoying the feel of her against me. It had been too damn long since I'd held her.

"Thank you," she said. "I'll sleep naked tonight."

I grinned. "You're so good to me."

"Say that again tonight when you're hard as a rock and I won't ride you."

I let her lead me into the kitchen again and sat down at the table, propping my leg up on a chair.

"We should have a fire in the pit tonight," I said as she pulled things out of the fridge.

"Getting pretty antsy to be outside, huh?" she asked sympathetically.

"Swear to God, hospitals have recycled air, like airplanes," I grumbled, making her laugh.

"I don't think so."

"Entire place stinks," I said with a sigh. "It's good to be home."

As we ate dinner, we discussed the logistics of our new normal. Kara was staying the night with my parents so they could take her to school the next day, but after that, we'd all be in the same place again. I couldn't fucking wait. It was nice to spend the first night home just me and Rose, though. We needed the time. I was fucking starving for her—not just her body, though that craving was insane—but for her smiles and her looks across the table and the way she moved around the kitchen.

I followed her outside after the dishes were cleared away, and sat on a lawn chair while she lit the fire. Damn, I'd be glad when I was healed up and she didn't have to wait on me. As I watched her, I couldn't help but smile. I knew Rose couldn't wait for me to be back to normal, either, but she seriously got off on helping me. Farrah had been right—Rose loved taking care of the people around her. It was her thing.

"Sit with me," I said as she finished.

"I can't," she said, looking at me in indecision. "I don't want to hurt you."

"You won't hurt me," I assured her, patting my leg. "One of my legs is still good."

"Both of your legs are good," she said as she sat down gingerly on my left thigh.

"Be a while 'til I can ride again," I said, staring at the flames. God, she smelled good.

"But you will," she said sweetly, leaning her head on my shoulder. "Just give it some time."

"Should probably see about gettin' my nuts reconnected," I replied, making her snort incredulously.

"Get your nuts reconnected?" she asked, leaning up to look at me.

"You know, get the vasectomy reversed."

"I knew what you meant," she said with a huff. "*Nuts reconnected.*" She snorted again.

"Just sayin', the time would be now, while I'm not ridin', anyway."

"Is that what you want to do?" she asked tentatively.

"You want more kids, yeah?"

"Yes." The word was so soft I could barely hear it.

"Then I better take care of it."

Rose was silent for a long time.

"It might not even work," she said quietly.

"Then we'll figure something else out," I said, rubbing my hand up and down her back. "Plenty of kids needin' homes out there."

"Maybe we could do both," she said hopefully.

"Well, now you're just pushin' it," I joked.

Rose leaned up again, a small smile playing on her lips. "What made you change your mind?"

"Guess it was probably the same thing that made you change yours," I replied honestly. "Don't wanna be without you."

She opened her mouth to speak and I covered it.

"Don't wanna be the one that takes your dreams away, either, baby." I let my hand drop. "You're not goin' anywhere and neither am I. I'm so tangled up in you, can't even tell where I stop and you start anymore. So if you wanna have some more kids, I'm down. I love bein' a dad, it's no hardship."

"I love you so much," she said, her voice quivering. "I had no idea I could love someone this much."

"Love you, too, Rosie," I murmured as she leaned in to kiss me. I ignored the twinge in my chest as her shoulder pressed against it.

"I want to adopt Kara," she said as she pulled away. There was fear in her eyes, but her chin was tilted in the stubborn way I'd always associate with Rose. "We can wait until we're married, if you want. But I want that piece of paper."

"Okay," I said slowly. "But gettin' married is separate, baby. That's about me and you."

"You don't want to marry me?" she asked, stiffening.

I chuckled. "Could you let your man do the askin'?" I asked in exasperation.

"Oh," she said sheepishly. "Yeah, I can do that."

"Appreciate it."

"I'm happy," she said.

"Me, too."

We sat outside until it got so cold that Rose started shivering.

"Come on," I murmured. "Lets go to bed."

I watched as Rose put out the fire, then followed her inside, losing my balance a little because I was staring at her ass and my cane got caught up on the track of the slider.

"Are you okay?" she asked, looking at me over her shoulder.

When someone knocked on the front door, her face paled. She put on a good show, but I knew it was going to be a while before she felt safe again.

"I'll get it," I said, resting my hand at the base of her spine as I moved around her.

My eyes widened when I opened the door to find Grease standing on the other side.

"Got a few minutes?" he asked.

"Sure, man," I said, swinging the door wide. "Come on in."

"Hey, Dad," Rose said in surprise and she moved to give Grease a hug. "What are you doing out this late?"

"No rest for the wicked," he replied with a smile. He shot me a look over her shoulder.

"Baby," I said as she stepped back from the hug. "Give me and your dad a minute?"

She looked between us, then nodded slowly. "Okay. I'm going to take a quick shower."

It was really fucking inconvenient that I immediately pictured her in the shower, considering her dad was standing less than five feet away.

As soon as Rose was gone and we heard the bathroom door close behind her, Grease spoke.

"Got him," he said.

I nodded as I walked toward the bed. My leg was throbbing like a motherfucker and I needed to get off of it.

"Feel free to sit," I said, waving my hand toward the foot of the bed.

"I'm not sittin' on your fuckin' bed," Grease said, his tone a mixture of amusement and disgust. He walked over to the wall and leaned against it, crossing his arms over his chest.

"Rose didn't want me usin' the stairs," I explained lamely.

He looked toward the tiny flight of stairs and grinned.

"Where'd you find him?" I said, bringing the conversation back around.

"He was holed up in Corvallis," Grease said, the smile disappearing. "Stayin' at a nasty ass motel that rented by the month."

"Fuckin' moron," I huffed. Corvallis was only a couple hours away. Copper hadn't even tried to run.

"Man just about shit his pants when Tommy found him," Grease said, keeping his voice low. "Didn't take much to get him talkin'."

"Ain't surprised."

Grease nodded. "From what I could gather," he said, glancing toward the stairs before continuing, "he set you up so he could save you."

"Come again?" I said, tilting my head to the side. I couldn't have heard him right.

"Yeah," Grease said with a bark of laughter. "Hired a coupla meth heads to take you, figurin' no one would miss 'em when he took 'em out."

"Copper was never there," I said flatly.

"He set up the house, found the men," Grease continued. "Had 'em snatch you. Planned on showin 'up to save the day after they'd worked you over."

I just stared at him.

"Stupid motherfucker got arrested," he said, scoffing. "Drunk and disorderly. By the time he got out and went back to the house, cleaners had already been through—no sign of you."

"Jesus Christ. End game?"

"Thought he'd be forgiven," Grease said flatly. "With a hero's welcome."

"And Rose?" I asked.

"Lost his mind when he found out she was there. Wasn't part of the deal."

"Can't trust a meth head," I said flatly.

"No shit."

"All a'this," I said, thumping my chest lightly, "because he wanted his patch back?"

"Hell of a way to get it," Grease mumbled. "Pay you back for beatin' his ass and come out smellin' like daisies."

I shook my head, staring blankly at the wall. We'd been through hell because some dumb fuck couldn't take his punishment like a man and move the fuck on.

"You took care of it?" I finally asked.

"It's done."

We both looked toward the hall as the shower shut off. A couple minutes later, the bathroom door opened.

"I better get goin'," Grease said.

I got to my feet and accepted the handshake and back thumping hug he offered.

"Almost forgot," he said as he reached into his back pocket and pulled out a small envelope, handing it to me. "Glad you're on the mend."

"Thanks," I said, holding eye contact.

"'Course," he said, moving toward the door. "Wasn't a hardship."

Once he was gone, I opened the envelope. Inside, loose and gruesome, were ten whole fingernails. I glanced at my bandaged fingers, the tips still so fucking sensitive that they ached when the air touched them. Then I hobbled back outside.

I tossed the envelope in the fire pit and pulled out my lighter, smiling as I lit the edge.

"Why are you out here?" Rose asked poking her head out the door. She smiled happily. "And what are you grinning about?"

"Just happy to be home," I replied.

That night, Rose slept naked, as she'd promised, pressed against my side like she couldn't get close enough, even in her sleep. I stared at the ceiling in the living room, enjoying the feeling of her breath tickling my neck. I never could have predicted how our lives would change when I'd tossed her in that pool all those months ago.

I was one lucky motherfucker.

Epilogue
Rose

"I KILLED SOMEONE," my mom said, startling me so bad that I dropped the knife in my hand.

"You what?" I asked, whipping my head up to look at her.

I'd gone to my parents to help my mom with Mack's birthday dinner since our house was too small to hold everyone comfortably, but I suddenly wished that I'd just had it at the clubhouse.

"I did," she said. She glanced up at my face and shrugged as she went back to what she was doing. "It was before you were born."

"Jesus," I muttered. "Who?"

"Your dad's brother," she said, her hands going still as she looked back up.

"You killed Dad's *brother*? I didn't even know he had a brother."

"They weren't raised together," she said. "Not that it mattered, Asa still considered him a brother."

"What happened?" I asked cautiously, unsure whether I even wanted to know.

"He showed up when it was just me and Will," she said. "Strung out on God knows what. Roughed me up a little."

"Roughed you up a little?" I said incredulously, my hand tightening on the knife.

"Beat the shit out of me, would've done worse." She crossed her arms and leaned her elbows on the table. "He was one of the men that killed my parents."

"Holy shit," I breathed. Why hadn't I ever heard this story before?

"It was terrifying," she said. "And I don't like to talk about it."

"Why are you?" I asked.

"Because," she replied, her eyes searching my face, "I wanted you to know."

"I'm okay," I said, holding her gaze.

"When you're protecting someone you love," she continued, "your man or your child, there's nothing you won't do."

"I know," I said.

"There's no shame in that."

"I'm not ashamed, Mom," I said firmly. I set the knife carefully on the table and cleared my throat. "I watched him torture Mack for *days*. I'd do the exact same thing again. I *wish* I could do it again."

Mom gave me a sad smile. "You're going to feel it," she said, raising her hand to stop me when I opened my mouth to speak. "Maybe not now, maybe not for years, but eventually, it'll start wearing at you. Come to me, okay? Or your dad. Or Mack. Just… don't try to keep it to yourself. That never works. It'll only make it worse."

"Okay," I said, a lump in my throat. I knew from the gravity in her voice that she was speaking from experience, and I hated it. My mom was one of the sweetest, most caring people I'd ever met. I couldn't imagine her killing anyone.

We were quiet for a while as I continued cutting potatoes and she diced pickles.

"So," I said finally, trying to keep my voice even. "How'd you do it?"

A startled laugh left her mouth. "You're a terrible daughter," she said, grinning. She paused. "I shot him with your Aunt Farrah's gun."

"Thatta girl," I said. "I mean, I prefer garden tools, but you do you."

My mom's laughter filled the kitchen and I felt my shoulders relax.

An hour later, just as people were supposed to start showing up, we heard my dad's piece of shit pickup pull into the front yard.

"Dad's home," I said, just as he walked in the front door.

"Sugar?" my dad called.

"I'm right here," Mom replied, coming out of the pantry.

"My leathers in the closet upstairs?"

"No, I hung them in the downstairs closet," she replied, following him as he spun on his heel. "What's going on, Asa?"

"Gotta meet your brother," he said as he reached into the closet.

"They're on the way home?" mom asked.

"Yeah," dad said, pausing. "Boys are ridin' down to meet 'em."

"Meet them where?"

"As far south as we can," he said darkly. "Escortin' 'em home."

"Oh, shit," my mom murmured.

"Should be fine," dad assured her. "Just a precaution."

"Are they bringing CeeCee?"

"Yep."

"What aren't you telling me?" she asked, crossing her arms over her chest.

"Tellin' you what I can, Calliope," he replied, reaching out to brush her cheek with his thumb. Then he went back to pulling his leathers out of the closet. "Can you get me some coffee for the road?"

"Yes," she said, turning back toward the kitchen.

"In that thermos that keeps shit hot for a long ass time," he called out.

"I know how to pack you coffee for the road, Asa," Mom shot back.

As my dad rushed through the house getting his crap together, people started arriving. Molly looked at me worriedly as Reb brought her tablet into the living room and plopped down on the couch.

"Do you know what's happening?" she asked. "The weather is complete shit. They're going into snow, for God's sake."

"They know what they're doing," I replied, watching the door. I understood her fear. I was so thankful that Mack wasn't riding yet, though I'd never tell him that. He was going to be pissed that he couldn't go with them.

"We're here," Lily said, ushering Gray in from the rain. "Leo and Dragon are going to meet you guys at the restaurant right off the highway."

"Smart fuckers," Tommy said, coming inside behind her with Hawk on his heels. "I shoulda thought of that."

"Grab some dinner," my mom said. "You, too, Will. Eat before you go."

"Doubt we have time, Ma," Will said as my dad jogged down the stairs. "Just waiting on the old man."

"Let's go," my dad said, confirming Will's words. He strode toward my mom and kissed her long and hard, his hands on her ass. I wrinkled my nose in disgust. So gross.

Just as he pulled away, Mack strode in the front door, his parents and Kara right behind him.

"You got this?" my dad asked.

"Yup," Mack replied. They did a weird man-handshake. "Go take care of shit. Happy trails."

"Where are you going?" Kara asked my dad.

"Just takin' care of some business, sweetheart," he replied. "Keep an eye on Callie 'til I get back?"

"Sure." Kara smiled over at my mom.

"We'll keep her company," Lou said, wrapping her arm around Kara's shoulders.

"Appreciate it," my dad said with a nod.

My brothers kissed their women before following my dad out of the house, and those of us left behind just sort of stared at each other.

"Leave it to my sister to ruin Mack's birthday party," Lily said dryly.

"Fucking figures."

I couldn't stop the laugh that fell out of my mouth.

"Come on," my mom said, still staring at the door my dad had gone through. She shook her head and smiled at me, but it didn't reach her eyes. "Let's eat."

"They'll be alright," Mack said in my ear as he walked me back into the kitchen. "Don't worry."

I *hadn't* been worried, but I sure as hell was now.

ACKNOWLEDGEMENTS

To my girls and my boy – you three are the reason I exist. I'm so freaking proud of you guys, I could burst. I love you.

Mom and Dad – Thanks for letting me crash at your place. I promise to return the favor when you guys need someone to organize your medicine and make sure your favorite shows are recorded on the television. I love you guys.

Nikki – we did it again. Thanks for always having my back and always being ready to help me buff these books until they shine.

Letitia – you knocked it out of the park with this cover. Thank you so much!

Donna – I'll thank you for every single book, because without you, there would be no Aces series… at least not that anyone had actually read.

Marisa – thank you for everything you do.

Readers and Bloggers – Thank you for all of your support and patience. I know you've been waiting a long time for this book. I'm so excited that I finally get to share it with you.

Printed in Great Britain
by Amazon